Sherlock Holmes, The Missing Years: Japan

ON LINE

Sherlock Holmes, The Missing Years: Japan

Vasudev Murthy

Poisoned Pen Press

First U.S. Edition 2015

10 9 8 7 6 5 4 3 2 1

Library of Congress Catalog Card Number: 2014951273

ISBN: 9781464203633   Hardcover
       9781464203657   Trade Paperback

Poisoned Pen Press
6962 E. First Ave., Ste. 103
Scottsdale, AZ 85251
www.poisonedpenpress.com
info@poisonedpenpress.com

Printed in the United States of America

In memory of my mother

Acknowledgments

There are many who made this book possible:

My wife Vidya, for innumerable suggestions along the way and for being a focused and very fussy reviewer. We thought of this book while on a brief visit to Cambodia many years ago. She believed in the idea and believed in me. The rest was mere detail.

My son Sarang, for his inspired suggestions on Sherlock Holmes' journey through India.

Many friends around the world who encouraged me at every turn. In particular, Herma Caelen and Frauke Hertel from Brussels.

Barbara Peters, the astonishingly professional Editor-in-Chief of Poisoned Pen Press, who held my hand from distant Arizona and made me understand the importance of striving for perfection (though I am still quite some distance away from it!).

Karthika V K and Ajitha G S of Harper Collins India for helping me balance the content. Karthika's objectivity helped me in so many ways. I realized that writing is easy, while editing is the more difficult skill. Thank you.

Sudarshana Ghosh for constantly encouraging me and for being my unpaid publicist!

Japan, a country I admire, that provided so many motifs that helped develop the theme.

And finally, to Arthur Conan Doyle, for creating a character who will live through the ages and provide endless inspiration to so many.

Vasudev Murthy
Bangalore, India

Preface

I first encountered the Sherlock Holmes Society of London in 2001 when I was invited by a friend to accompany the Society on a Baltic cruise to celebrate its fiftieth anniversary. My wife and I were given plenty of notice for the trip, but a few weeks beforehand we learned that a number of the visits en route would need to be conducted in the contemporary costume of 1895—when Holmes was thriving. Several hasty visits to costumiers ensued.

As we visited various countries on that trip, we were struck by the international popularity of Sherlock Holmes. In Copenhagen we were taken on a trip around the canals by the local Sherlock Holmes Society to do 'canonical boat spotting.' Owners of boats on the canals had been encouraged to rename their vessels after characters and places in the Sherlock Holmes stories and we had to identify them. In Stockholm, the local society presented us with the skeleton keys to the city. And in St. Petersburg, we met a Russian fan who had travelled for two days from Siberia to join our celebrations.

Sherlock Holmes is clearly a character who has captured the imagination of people all around the world. And of course the stories have been replayed endlessly on stage, TV, and film, almost from the time that the stories first appeared in print. Beyond this, however, the characters of Holmes and Watson have been used in countless pastiches—new stories and films that have portrayed them in new situations.

Some commentators have wondered about the attitude of the Sherlock Holmes Society of London to these newcomers, expecting us to be guardians of the purity of the original stories and characters, resisting the possibility of any transgression. The reality is the reverse: We welcome these new explorations of Holmes—some of which continue to be set in Victorian London, but others that bring him into the current day.

Jazz fans will be familiar with this attitude. Great musicians take classic ballads and perform them with a new twist, giving a fresh interpretation of how the tune might sound. So it is with the characters of Holmes and Watson when authors write them into new milieux and situations.

Of course, Sherlock Holmes was not concerned only with crime, although his description of himself as a 'consulting detective' would perhaps lead to that conclusion. 'Private investigator' is a more accurate description of his profession, and many of the stories involve no crime at all; they are about resolving mysterious circumstances. No surprise then that many of the stories are titled 'The Adventure of...'. There is plenty of scope for authors to place Holmes in situations that are far removed from the classical detective genre.

Vasudev Murthy and I met in the course of our work some years ago but it was only on a train ride out of London that we discussed our shared interest in Sherlock Holmes. Vasu confided in me that he was hoping to write a novel about Holmes' adventures during what fans call the 'great hiatus.' This is the period from May 1891 to April 1894, between the supposed death of Holmes at the hands of Professor Moriarty at the Reichenbach Falls and his reappearance in 'The Adventure of the Empty House.' It is not at all clear what Holmes was up to at that time; he was less than open with Watson, or it may well be that Watson himself was being discreet or indeed deliberately not revealing all the details that he knew. Holmes does admit, though, to having travelled to Tibet, Mecca, and Khartoum; who knows where else he may have been during that period.

Well, India is a distinct possibility. In 2012, the Sherlock Holmes Society of London began planning a trip to India for early 2014. Although none of the adventures are set in India, Dr. Watson would almost certainly have passed through during the time of his military service in Afghanistan, and there are other references to events and characters associated with India, notably in 'The Sign of Four.' Moreover, there is a sense of India being part of that essential pulse of the Victorian times: a presence affecting almost every family in some way.

But I remembered that Vasu conjectured that Holmes would have spent some of his absence in Japan. This would have been at a particularly turbulent time in the country's history. Until the mid-nineteenth century, Japan was all but closed to foreign influences. Changes introduced during the Meiji Restoration accelerated the opening of the country to the world and entailed a rapid industrialization that bridged feudalism to the modern age in just a few years. Even at the end of the century, Japan would have been an exotic destination for most Victorians. It would certainly have appealed to Sherlock Holmes.

So we now have a new adventure set in new locations. In the Sherlock Holmes stories, Dr. Watson is the primary narrator; there are a few, however, in which Holmes himself tells the story. In Vasu's story, there are a number of voices—admittedly reported by Dr. Watson—but each contributing to the tale in a unique way.

One of the joys of the Sherlock Holmes stories is the incidental detail—of weather (notably fogs, which were exacerbated by the coal-burning homes and factories in London in those days, often creating a thick smog), of travel by road, sea, and train, and the manners and entertainments that Holmes and Watson enjoy. It is giving nothing away about this book to say that it involves travel halfway around the world to Japan. Of course this was a much more challenging endeavour at the close of the nineteenth century than it is today. Trips that today take a day or two would then have taken several weeks and had a far greater sense of the exotic than the commoditized experience air travel provides now.

This story has great richness of voice and will take you on a fascinating journey. It is both an adventure and a colourful experience.

Enjoy it!

London, December 2012
CALVERT MARKHAM
Treasurer of the Sherlock Holmes Society of London

The Rt. Hon. Walter Campbell Esq.
Secretary
The Publishers' Guild
Wimpole Street
Cavendish Square
London

June 25, 1909

Dear Sir,

I may be excused for presuming that my name is already known to you, given the not-inconsiderable publicity that my chronicles of the adventures of my distinguished friend Sherlock Holmes have attracted over the past several years through the good offices of members of your own Guild. I humbly accept the fact that my own modest fame, if any, is a direct consequence of a fortuitous association with a very eminent man, who will always be remembered as someone of exceptional intellect.

I write this formal letter of complaint with considerable reluctance. However, given the gravity of the matter, I have decided, after consulting my solicitors, that candid communication is best. You—and indeed the public, for I have chosen to make this letter public—have a right to understand my anguish.

At the outset, I would like to express my admiration and regard for the high degree of professionalism that members of your Guild have exhibited during the years that I have known them. At no stage or time has an editor found it necessary to advance more than a few constructive suggestions on my writing; these have mostly pertained to the need to expand on a particular point to assist the reader in understanding a possibly arcane reference. I have always respected the judgment of the editor, and our association has been noted for its harmony. Perhaps I am fortunate that my writing has always met the rather stringent and exacting standards you have set; nothing has been altered between the time I wrote something and the time it reached the public.

However, without wishing to sound pompous and needlessly sensitive, I am compelled, Sir, to formally register my unease, irritation and, frankly, outrage, about a development in your professional community that promises to have serious detrimental repercussions for all involved.

I refer here to the introduction of a new kind of bold and overly assertive editor, most often a young, educated girl, usually pretty and invariably well-read (perhaps excessively so, at a time when breadth is valued more than depth), with an entirely new lexicon. My publisher, Messrs Poisoned Pen Press, in distant Arizona, a member of your Guild, has, most regrettably, succumbed to this trend and foisted on me one such young lady who insists on providing an endless stream of outrageous, unsolicited, unwanted, unwarranted, and presumptuous suggestions, by Royal Mail, telegram, telephone, and in person.

I am a chronicler, Sir, and am unused to young women offering unnecessary suggestions on how I should be writing for the so-called 'modern audience.' She suggests, repeatedly, that I look into aspects of pace, weaknesses in the plot, apparent contradictions, and so on. She would have me believe, Sir, that I am a novice and that I lack the ability to hold the audience's attention. Indeed her whole manner could be easily construed as pitying and tolerant, as perhaps a missionary might view a heathen in some corner of our overseas territories.

My contention, Sir, is that I do *not* write for salacious readers and do not believe that I am obliged to 'hold' my audience's attention. I do not invent or make special efforts to appeal to the morbid and celebrate the sensational. I report facts and do not pander to the 'modern readership,' which, I am told by this young lady is restless, impatient, and suspicious, constantly seeking gratification on every page, in the absence of which a work of rigour is dismissed cursorily. I am not obliged, Sir, to create a racy piece of fiction to solicit cries of delight from an immature readership that relishes murder and mayhem. I report true facts faithfully. To expect that every second of Sherlock Holmes' life was filled with tension, shocking events, evil men and women, and sinister plots is a grave affront to the sensibilities of anyone associated even remotely with him.

I could certainly point out a few specifics in a recent communication from this young lady.

The pace slackened at—
I don't think this is necessary—
Holmes is unlikely to say—

The temerity of this pretty, energetic, bright-eyed junior editor to suppose that she should hold my pen and write on my behalf—this is a matter of the deepest concern. Why then am I necessary, Sir? How dare she say to me, with a touch of patronizing sarcasm, that *'Holmes is unlikely to have said...'*? She never met him and never will. I spent many years with him and my faithful notes have stood the test of time and scrutiny. Why should there be an expectation that Holmes speak in precisely one way and not another? He was a linguist, a violinist, a scientist, a great scholar, and certainly someone with a gift for disguise. Nothing can be asserted with absolute certainty about him, except that he was a man of the utmost integrity.

My mind is now filled with grave doubts, Sir, as to whether my work will ever reach the public eye without meddling by this overly educated editor. We see now the deleterious effect of Universal Suffrage in the most sacred space—the editorial desk of respected publishers. I have demanded that this letter of protest be included in the final manuscript since I no longer believe that my work will emerge unscathed.

The modern woman is devious, my dear Sir, and counts on the need of a gentleman to always be a gentleman under all circumstances. However, it is the possible besmirching of the reputation of my distinguished friend Sherlock Holmes that most exercises my mind. Needless to say, I am in discussion with my solicitors Llewellyn, Harwood and Fox, 15, Lincoln's Inn Fields, London, W.C. for appropriate legal recourse and recovery of damages, should the machinations of this attractive young woman succeed.

I trust I have succeeded in drawing your attention to this matter and I am confident that your respected organization will institute suitable enquiries and provide correction to Messrs Poisoned Pen Press and similar others on their misguided attempts to suffocate writers with unacceptable attentions.

I remain, Sir,

Yours truly,
John H. Watson, M.D.
221B Baker Street
London, W.C.

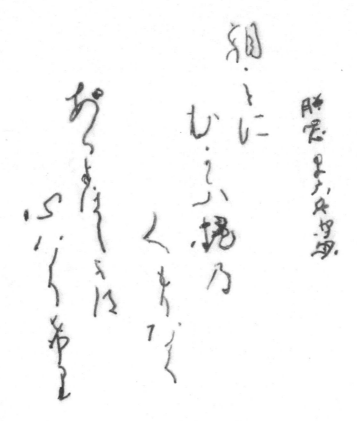

Every morning
We gaze into our mirrors
Which are unblemished;
Oh, that we could attain
Such a purity of soul.

A Waka poem by Empress Shoken
9 May 1849–9 April 1914

A Letter from Yokohama

 My friend, you may have lived in Osaka and I in Nagoya for the past thirty years. And yet the bonds of our silent friendship are stronger than the steel of a Samurai's sword.

When I wrote *The Final Problem*, advising the public on the circumstances leading to the death of Sherlock Holmes and his arch-enemy Professor Moriarty at Reichenbach Falls near the village of Meiringen in Switzerland, I had not bargained for the reaction. To say that the man on the street felt no embarrassment in joining a collective cry of anguish would be an understatement; his rooms at 221B Baker Street became a veritable shrine for the devout. The costermonger, the clerk in the shipping office, the constable, Holmes' friends in the criminal class—all stood shoulder to shoulder outside in silence, mourning his passing. My eyes misted when I saw how much love my strange and solitary friend had commanded from the citizenry of the city; of course, he himself would have dismissed such speculation contemptuously, for, in his rational mind, love of any kind had no place except as a lens into the behaviour of the human mind, a tool he frequently used in his investigations.

Thereafter, a number of unscrupulous individuals attempted to profit from such sentiments by reporting the alleged spotting of Holmes in many places—he was in Bombay trading in Indian antiquities, said one dispatch. A confirmed sighting in Durban, swore an Army colonel. In Santiago as a respected violinist, calmly asserted a returning ship's captain. An innkeeper in Vaasa, Finland, said the excited wife of the second secretary of our Embassy in that country.

I, however, reconciled to his death and went back quietly to my country home with my wife. I swore to keep his memory alive and began the onerous task of collecting and organizing his papers, personal effects, and correspondence; I was keenly aware of how history would view and idolize the memory of this great man and was not unaware that my association with him would be remarked upon favourably. Holmes' brother Mycroft most generously handed over whatever he had of his brother's effects, including his beloved Stradivarius violin, saying, 'The bonds of blood do not always take precedence over the bonds of loyal friendship, Watson.' I was deeply touched.

The letter from Japan, a little over two years after the affair at Reichenbach Falls, came as a complete surprise. The handwriting was vaguely familiar. I dismissed the surge in my heart and speculated on the contents inside the yellow envelope with the unfamiliar stamps and markings. I saw that it had taken more than three months for the letter to reach me from the city of Yokohama. I opened the envelope and was mystified to see a single first-class ticket for carriage from Liverpool to Yokohama on the merchant ship *North Star* for the 13th of June 1893.

I glanced at my calendar; the date was barely a week away. As I examined the ticket again, a single scrap of paper fell out of the envelope on to my desk. It was a terse note in Sherlock Holmes' hand.

Watson, I need you. My violin, please. S.H.

I stared at the paper, stupefied. It seemed impossible, and yet, there was no mistake. It was Holmes' handwriting. And the slight whiff of a familiar tobacco confirmed it. Sherlock Holmes was alive and he had sent the note!

I threw logic aside at once. Holmes had often rather cruelly remarked that my mediocre medical qualifications came in the way of alert thinking and that I was a creature of conditioning who would follow the mob if I could at all help it. 'I am sorry if my remarks pain you, Watson, but mere action in Afghanistan does not imply the highest in mental faculties,' he had once said with a mocking laugh. But here I was, joyfully accepting an invitation to Japan from a friend who I believed had died so tragically two years ago!

I made preparations, post-haste, for the journey. I took my wife into confidence and was surprised to see her ready approval. She saw no foolishness in the proposition that Holmes might still be alive and that he might be in Japan; she felt a certain pride that I had been called to his side in such strange circumstances. With her usual efficiency, she ensured that I was well equipped for an unusual journey. And in a few days, we departed for Liverpool.

'Look after yourself, my dear,' I said, pressing her hand. We stood at the Langton Dock, while I prepared to board the *North Star*, a small ship that carried only a few passengers in first-class while ferrying goods between several ports.

'Don't worry about me,' she responded with a smile, her eyes unusually bright. 'Your place is by Mr. Holmes' side. I always believed he was alive. He needs you now more than I do.'

I was greatly touched and recalled Holmes' understated appreciation for her. 'A fine lady there, Watson. Perhaps she deserves better,' he had said, filling my heart with both pride and resentful anger at his jibe. I turned, unable to speak, and soon boarded the *North Star* with my friend's beloved Stradivarius in a special rectangular case that could also pass off as hand luggage. As the ship sailed out of Liverpool and the raucous crowd on the dock faded away, I wondered what new adventure awaited me in a strange land, in the company of Sherlock Holmes.

The Voyage Begins

My friend, do not stop me. I must begin without knowing that I shall end. I have heard that the seas will never reveal their secrets but shall bless the brave who set forth to do their duty.

The long journey to Yokohama was to take me through the Strait of Gibraltar, halting at Marseilles, Alexandria, Aden, Bombay, Singapore, and Shanghai. I had hoped that the sea breeze and the solitude would allow me to consider various possibilities and scenarios, undisturbed, pertaining to the pleasant but baffling re-emergence of Sherlock Holmes.

I shared my cabin with a tall, quiet, and distinguished Japanese gentleman, Kazushi Hashimoto, who indicated that he was returning to Japan after a sojourn of some six months in Scotland looking after certain business matters. He kept himself absorbed in a Japanese board game of some kind, which suited me perfectly. He had with him an interesting musical instrument he called a *koto,* which he strummed gently in the evenings after asking my permission and apologizing profusely for the inconvenience. The sounds were not unpleasant, though unusual, and I was able to block them out of my consciousness after a short while. Indeed, they almost helped my meditative reflections in the evening. I found myself quite comfortable in his presence and in a couple of days moved into a routine of sorts.

The captain of the *North Star* was Samuel Groves, a curious individual of middle height, aged about fifty, who conveyed a mix of competence with a mild dissolution in manner that I found unsettling.

He spoke in restless disconnected phrases. 'Good weather! Good people! Never liked Gibraltar! Can't stand the place!'

On the first night, he joined us in the first-class dining room. I looked around the table. On my right was Mrs. Edith Andrews, a lady aged about thirty with an aristocratic demeanour, who said she was joining her husband at the governor's residence in Aden after a brief holiday at her country home near Bury St. Edmunds. To her right was Colonel James Burrowe, who said he was with the Royal Horse artillery regiment. I was sure we would have acquaintances in common. He said he was travelling to Penang. However, since Mrs. Andrews separated us, I could not speak much with him without seeming impolite. I decided to have a word with him as soon as possible.

To my left was a Sikh gentleman, Mr. Shamsher Singh, who introduced himself as an aide to the maharajah of the Princely State of Patiala in the Panjab. He was a striking turbaned man with piercing eyes and indisputable charisma. He spoke English extremely well, though with a pronounced Indian accent.

He expressed interest in Shakespeare and impressed me with his knowledge of the activities of the British Museum. I found him slightly disconcerting, though I could not say why; perhaps it was his overwhelmingly strong personality.

To his left sat Mr. Hashimoto and beyond was Miss Clara Bryant, a small fading lady in her late forties with intelligent blue eyes and a quiet, though sprightly, manner. She said she was travelling to Shanghai, where she was the tutor to the Japanese consul-general's children. I made a mental note to speak to her later; after all, here was my first tangible English link to Japan. Seated next to her was Mr. Simon Fletcher, who introduced himself as a banker travelling to Singapore. He was very correct in his manner and quite polished, though bland. He must have been about fifty-five and was on the heavier side.

The captain breezed in and wished us all a good evening.

'We have the most excellent wines,' he said heartily. 'Good winds this evening! Thirty voyages captaining this ship! Aden, an excellent place to rest for a day and see the sights! Decent library on the ship, plenty of books on crime!'

'You will be leaving us at Aden, Madam,' he said, turning to Mrs. Andrews.

She coloured unexpectedly. 'I don't much care for the place, honestly.'

'Ah? Why so?' asked the captain, interested.

'It's very hot and I don't care for the natives,' Mrs. Andrews said with a shudder.

Miss Bryant suddenly interjected from across the table, 'You *can* make yourself like any place, you know. I love Shanghai now, though I once thought I never would—the beastly weather, the Chinese. But now I rather like them. I'm glad to be going back. There's something eternal about the culture.'

I liked her attitude and saw Mr. Hashimoto look at her sideways with approval. Mrs. Andrews turned to me, a silent plea in her eyes. I took the hint and changed the topic.

'I have never been to the Far East. I wonder if any of you could give me some suggestions on what I might expect,' I said, looking around the table.

'Be careful,' chortled the captain.

Shamsher Singh agreed. 'Yes,' he nodded. 'Be careful. Do not believe anyone, including me.'

'Avoid exploring the ports of call, if you can. They attract the scum of the earth,' said Simon Fletcher with a vehemence that seemed out of character. 'Just get to where you want to go and damn the local culture!'

I saw Mr. Hashimoto look at Simon Fletcher thoughtfully.

'I do intend to visit Alexandria, if we can be allowed,' said Mr. Singh in a deep and deliberate voice. 'I find the Egyptian culture interesting, though somewhat barbaric.'

'Oh yes, you'll have a couple of days to look around, if you like. Good people. Fruits. Water—be careful! Very careful! Mosquitoes! Plenty of little crooks!' said the captain.

'Perhaps you will join me,' said Mr. Singh, turning toward me. It was a command and I found myself agreeing without hesitation.

From across the table, Miss Bryant spoke up. 'I shall join you too, if I may?'

'So shall I,' said Mr. Hashimoto. Something in his voice made me look at him quickly, but his face was inscrutable.

'Not I,' chuckled Colonel Burrowe. 'I'll spend some quiet time in the ship's library and have a few drinks. Alexandria is fine and I've been around a few times, but nothing like Bombay, my friends, nothing like Bombay!'

One evening, just prior to reaching Marseilles, we were back in our cabin after supper and I had settled down to a cigar and a book when Mr. Hashimoto suddenly looked up from his game.

'Dr. Watson, it is not in my nature to be inquisitive, but may I ask you the purpose of your proposed visit to my country?' he asked in unaccented, precise English.

I hesitated for the briefest fraction of a second.

'I have a weak constitution and have been advised a bracing sea voyage,' I said.

'I see,' he responded thoughtfully. 'It is rare, of course, to travel to Japan for constitutional improvement,' he said with a friendly smile.

I smiled, but did not respond, seeking the safety of my book.

'I do sense the presence of evil on this ship,' he said quite suddenly.

I put down my book. 'Really, my dear sir…'

'I am sorry to alarm you. Nevertheless, I must share with you the fact that I am uneasy.'

'On what do you base your remark?'

In answer, he pulled out from under his pillow, very carefully, a piece of paper.

'I found this placed under our door when I came in after breakfast.'

The paper had this written on it:

ヤクザ

'But what does it mean?' I asked, surprised.

Mr. Hashimoto looked at me quietly for a few seconds.

'Dr. Watson, all that I can share with you is that there is grave danger about us. Let us exercise caution and not take needless risks or strike up unnecessary friendships. For some reason that I do not know, we have been warned by someone.'

A chill crept down my spine. Accompanying it was a feeling of *déjà vu*. I almost felt as though I was speaking to my old friend Holmes! But that was impossible. Holmes was dead. No, he was in Japan. And Mr. Hashimoto was an old and distinguished-looking Japanese gentleman. I looked across the room and saw him observing me impassively. He had taken out his *koto* and had started strumming it very softly.

The unfamiliar sounds of Japan filled the room.

Murder on the North Star

 Be wary of strangers, my friend. Who knows what darkness lies in them? They shall spill blood and go on their way. Only a frail, old wife in Hiroshima may grieve and that is of no concern to them.

At Marseilles, the captain took on some cargo and three more passengers. Two were Japanese gentlemen who indicated they could not speak English at all, and after much bowing and smiling, retreated to their assigned cabin and indicated that they preferred to have their supper and breakfast there, served by the steward. The third was an Irishman, David Joyce, who seemed a surly and uncommunicative individual. He too retired to his single cabin, which happened to be next to the one assigned to Colonel Burrowe.

We began our journey to Alexandria on placid seas. The spare sounds of Mr. Hashimoto's *koto* danced on the little waves of the Mediterranean. And Mr. Shamsher Singh leaned on the railings watching the approaching darkness, lost in thought, his eyebrows knit.

I mentioned to Mr. Hashimoto that we had new companions; he had skipped dinner, as had Miss Bryant. This was while we were getting ready for breakfast.

'There were two Japanese gentlemen, by the way, and one Irishman.'

'Indeed?' said Mr. Hashimoto, adjusting the sleeves of his jacket. 'What did the Irishman look like?' I found the question quite strange, but I described Mr. Joyce as best as I could and he nodded in a curious, satisfied manner.

The rooms were designed in the following manner: a cabin, such as ours, was large, with considerable privacy afforded by separate bedrooms and a shared room in the middle. On one side was a similar cabin that Mrs. Andrews and Miss Bryant shared. On the other side was the library, which was locked by the steward precisely at eleven o'clock. There were no rooms above us. There were single cabins as well, such as the ones to which Mr. Joyce and Colonel Burrowe had been assigned.

My bedroom had a porthole at a height of about ten feet above sea level. As we moved east, my porthole opened to the south, as did Mr. Hashimoto's. There was one more porthole in the common area of the cabin. They were too narrow for an average person to squeeze through, but a child or a slim individual could, perhaps, pull through with some difficulty. At any rate, we had plenty of light and the Mediterranean was mild, as expected.

The journey from Marseilles to Alexandria took about five days. They were uneventful, though I must describe a couple of apparently innocuous events that were to have great significance later.

Miss Bryant and Mrs. Andrews were thrown together, as they were the only ladies on board. They made for an unlikely pair—a young lady who did not seem very enthusiastic about the trip and an older and wiser lady who seemed to relish life and looked forward to reaching her destination. They would walk together on the deck in silence in the mornings to get some exercise and sea breeze. I could hear them shut and open their door and would greet them as they passed by if I happened to be in the common area of my cabin. Occasionally, I would accompany them on their little walk.

The first morning after departing from Marseilles, as we walked along together, we passed by the two Japanese gentlemen who had recently joined us. I was a couple of feet ahead of the ladies, as the passageway narrowed somewhat at places. The men were at the railing, engaged in conversation. They had, quite indecorously, removed their shirts and were enjoying a smoke and the pleasant sun. I noticed that their bare arms and chests had several complicated colourful tattoos with motifs that were entirely foreign to me. They turned when they heard us approaching.

Their smiles vanished just as they were forming. I saw a flash of recognition in their eyes. There was a gasp behind me; the sounds of conversation suddenly stopped. I turned back and was astonished to see the two ladies walking rapidly away from the Japanese gentlemen, who were watching them with what appeared to be consternation. I assumed they had forgotten something or felt embarrassed in the company of bare-chested gentlemen and continued with my walk.

When I described this incident to Mr. Hashimoto later in the afternoon, I saw him stiffen.

'Could you describe their hands to me?'

'Their hands?'

'Yes, the men—did you notice anything unusual about their fingers?'

'I'm afraid not,' I responded, frankly puzzled and irritated. 'Why would I do that?'

'It is a trifling matter; please disregard my question,' Mr. Hashimoto said in an apologetic tone, sensing that I had not liked the question.

One night, it happened that I was awake a little later than usual. As I dimmed the cabin lights and prepared to retire for the night, I heard the patter of feet above and then a faint banging on the side of the ship in the direction of the adjacent library, the sound becoming indistinct in a few seconds. I walked across and put my head out through the porthole to look. There was nothing. I was baffled. I asked the captain about it the next day, but he expressed his ignorance of the matter.

The night before we were to dock at Alexandria, I found myself seated next to Mr. Singh at dinner. I noticed a certain reserve and preoccupation; he was constantly stroking his beard and looking elsewhere. Miss Bryant was missing as usual, complaining of a light headache. The two Japanese gentlemen had not appeared, as was their practice. Colonel Burrowe and Simon Fletcher were seated together in conversation.

Mr. Hashimoto had managed to strike up an acquaintance with David Joyce at the far end of the table. I remarked to Mr. Singh on the freshness of the bread. It somehow reminded me of something I had once tasted in Afghanistan.

'I particularly enjoyed the unusual fragrance of Afghan bread; it had a uniqueness that can best be described as burnt gold,' I said, reminiscing pleasantly.

Mr. Singh turned toward me and spoke in a low, urgent voice. 'I was unaware that Miss Bryant and the Japanese gentlemen knew each other.'

'I beg your pardon?'

'Yes, I saw them conversing in the billiards room just before dinner.'

'Doubtless she was brushing up on her Japanese. As you know, she is a tutor to the children of the Japanese consul in Shanghai.'

He stared at me.

'Dr. Watson, do not believe anyone,' he snapped and turned back to his dinner. He did not speak again.

After dinner, we moved to the lounge where I struck up a conversation with Miss Bryant, who said she was much better and had come down from her room to pick up a magazine. She told me quite a bit about China. We spoke about the Great Wall, Chinese ceramics, the invention of paper and gunpowder, Inner Mongolia, and so on. She was very knowledgeable and loquacious that evening and her enthusiasm for the country was evident. She insisted that we have a cup of tea before retiring to our respective rooms; in fact, she served me herself. I sincerely admired her feminine grace and clear evidence of good breeding.

I walked back to my cabin with Mr. Hashimoto, thinking about Mr. Singh's strange comment. I was tired and drowsy and went straight to bed, hoping to wake up early and see the ancient city of Alexandria at dawn.

I slept extremely well. I dreamt about Holmes and what he might be busy with in Japan. In the rather vivid dream, I saw Holmes smash open a window in a bid to rescue someone and distinctly heard the sound of breaking glass. As the night wore on, it got quite cold. I wrapped my blanket tightly about me, regretting that I had not heeded my wife's advice to carry warmer pyjamas.

I woke with a start. The rays of the rising sun had managed to creep into our room.

I jumped up and went into the common room, with the intent of waking Mr. Hashimoto as planned. He was already seated on the sofa near the door. The porthole was open and swinging on its hinges and the room was damp.

'Oh, what a pity the porthole was open last night!' I exclaimed, moving across the room.

Mr. Hashimoto did not respond. I saw shards of glass on the floor just below the porthole.

'Why, it's broken! How did that happen, Mr. Hashimoto?' I cried out. I was quite alarmed now, and some long-dormant sixth sense stirred.

I looked around the room in the dim light. Mr. Hashimoto was dressed as he had been the previous night and was asleep with his head on the backrest of the sofa. I saw large puddles at his feet.

'Mr. Hashimoto! This is most irregular! What happened last night?'

He did not reply.

Somehow, I did not expect him to.

I rushed toward him and saw that his eyes were open and staring at the ceiling. A dagger stuck out grotesquely from under his ribs near the sternum. I felt his pulse. There was no doubt about it.

Mr. Hashimoto had been murdered.

I pulled the bell to summon the steward. When he arrived, I asked him to summon the captain, the doctor, and any other able-bodied man he might meet. Meanwhile, I examined the body. There was only that one stab, with the dagger still embedded. Blood loss and shock must have been the reason for death. In minutes, the captain rushed in with the ship's physician, Dr. James Israel. Mr. Singh and Mr. Fletcher followed.

'Passenger murdered! First time in twenty-five years…the scandal! Arrangements! Doctor's opinion…inquest!' babbled the captain, quite agitated and incoherent.

Mr. Singh was more collected. I saw his keen and intelligent eyes quickly survey the room, stopping momentarily at the open window and noting the cold draught coming through in gusts. He studied the puddles of blood—which I had originally mistaken for water—at Mr. Hashimoto's feet. I also saw a trail of blood from the porthole to the sofa. Mr. Hashimoto had seemingly dragged himself to the sofa and bled to death.

'How long has he been dead, Dr. Israel?' he asked with a natural authority.

'Judging by the state of rigor mortis, I would say about six hours. That means he was, most likely, murdered at about half past one this morning.'

Simon Fletcher was examining the broken porthole. He commented quietly, 'Hmm...very singular. A piece of fibre in the glass. I wonder how it got there.'

The captain gave us permission to move Mr. Hashimoto's body to his room. Mr. Singh and Mr. Fletcher transported the body with great care.

Presently, Dr. Israel and I examined the body. 'Do you notice something peculiar about the wound, Dr. Watson?' Dr. Israel asked after a few minutes.

'A deep wound and a peculiar angle of entry,' I said after a careful examination.

'Quite so. The inquest will have more to say.'

We removed the long, slim, curved dagger, which had oriental inscriptions on it, and kept it aside. Then we cleaned the wound and tidied him up as best we could. We came outside to find the captain, Mr. Singh, and Mr. Fletcher looking at something just behind the sofa.

'You might like to look at this,' said the captain.

Lying on the floor was another sheet of paper with this written on it:

ヤクザ

The characters had faded to a dull brown, presumably having been written by Mr. Hashimoto himself in his own blood.

'Of course!' I thought I heard someone mutter in an undertone, 'Of course!'

Alexandria

Have you not seen a Kabuki performance, my friend?
How strange that the man who you know to be
quiet and gentle becomes so violent and expressive
once he wears a mask on stage!

The public assumes, quite reasonably, that frequent encounters with crimes of the most shocking variety would have caused members of the constabulary—and certainly Holmes and me—to become hardened. To some extent, this is true. Yes, we recovered our presence of mind faster and tended not to descend into hysterics. But to say that murder did not affect us at all would be grossly untrue.

I had developed a liking for the suave Mr. Hashimoto and had found him an ideal companion, with restrained habits and consideration for his fellow travellers. In itself, to have been so close to extreme violence and not to have known about it was certainly disconcerting. But to have seen a man I was getting to know suddenly become the victim of a heinous crime was a severe shock.

I wished for Holmes' presence. I knew that he would have seen possibilities and shadows where I could only see tangibles.

The captain insisted on moving me to another large and well-appointed cabin and I gratefully agreed. Then he had the porthole and the cabin sealed. We docked soon in Alexandria. The local police were waiting, having been sent a message earlier. A representative of the British consul and a British police inspector came on board, accompanied by four Egyptian constables and a physician, and set to work. They removed Mr. Hashimoto's body respectfully.

They then took our passports, quite rightly, and formally told us that we were all under suspicion, but that we would not be detained unless there was some circumstantial evidence pointing at any person or persons. They took our statements separately and then conducted a search of our quarters, which turned up nothing. After being given guarantees by the British consul's representative, the police allowed us to leave the ship for a short while, if we wished. The captain suggested that we visit the city and take in the sights but return soon, as he felt it was possible the police would have additional questions for us.

Mr. Singh and I set out, accompanied by the efficient Miss Bryant, who seemed a trifle subdued, a perfectly understandable state considering the circumstances.

'Be careful!' shouted Simon Fletcher, standing at the railings with Mrs. Andrews by his side. We waved at them and carried on. Someone pointed us toward the famous Jewish Quarter and we decided to go there and soak in the atmosphere. The streets were crowded and full of antique sellers, fruit vendors, men selling dates swarming with flies, and all manner of beggars, foreigners, and natives. Camels, cattle, and dogs roamed unhindered. Swarthy Arab men with *keffiyehs* on their heads and veiled women walked about. It was noisy, dirty, and exotic—and extremely hot and humid. But the three of us were used to it from our past experiences. I could imagine Mrs. Andrews finding it overwhelming and thought it quite appropriate that she had chosen to stay behind.

'How horrible, Dr. Watson! A beastly, beastly affair! And such a nice man too! I was hoping to learn so much more from him about Japan! Oh, I wonder about his family!' exclaimed Miss Bryant suddenly.

'A tragedy indeed, Miss Bryant. We must, of course, help the police in any way possible.'

'Did you hear anything at all, Madam?' asked Mr. Singh, walking onwards purposefully.

I noticed Miss Bryant casting a quick glance at him. 'No, I'm afraid not.'

'Ah. A pity.'

We carried on. We turned a corner into another noisy, colourful alley filled with hundreds of people. I found myself enjoying the confusion and entirely alien atmosphere.

'*Effendi!* You come here, *Effendi*! Buy! Very cheap! Very cheap, *Effendi*!' shouted the vendors. It was all very energetic and stimulating.

Mr. Singh suddenly stumbled against me and I tripped and fell on the road. I heard something whistle past just above. Someone groaned loudly behind us and I turned. An elderly Egyptian was clutching his neck and buckling, blood spurting out, his face contorted in horror. A knife had gone clean through. Mr. Singh pulled Miss Bryant and me to the side as a huge commotion began with screams and shouts, people gesticulating and running. Dozens of agitated Egyptians milled about the dying man.

'Do not get involved,' said Mr. Singh in a firm voice. He moved us along as though nothing had happened. I was shaken.

'How fortuitous, Mr. Singh, that you stumbled. Otherwise, one of us would have been killed. I wonder what happened!'

'Very lucky, indeed!' exclaimed Miss Bryant, catching her breath. 'Now that's the second murder we've seen today and it's not even noon! Ought we to return to the ship, do you think?'

'No, I think that would be cowardly. Ah, I see our Japanese friends there, far ahead,' he pointed. 'Let us join them.'

I had a glimpse of the two Japanese gentlemen in a crowded narrow lane. They seemed too distant for us to catch up and were moving rapidly away, almost running. 'Never mind,' I said. But Mr. Singh had already left us and was weaving his way through the crowd. In no time at all, we lost him.

I was perplexed by what appeared to be an unexpected streak of irresponsibility in the man. Here we were, in the middle of an unfamiliar crowded market in the Jewish Quarter of Alexandria, having just been witness to the murder of a man in broad daylight and Mr. Singh was apparently intent on giving us further cause for anxiety.

'Look, a *souk*, a market! We really must go there and buy a few things!' cried Miss Bryant, excited by the prospect. Her enthusiasm was both charming and refreshing.

'I shall stay here, if you please, and wait for Mr. Singh. I expect he will be by presently,' I said, pausing under the awning of a shop. 'But please do return soon.'

Assuring me she would be back in an hour, Miss Bryant disappeared inside and I waited at the entrance of the *souk*, looking anxiously for the tall Sikh. But there was no sign of him. Almost three-quarters of an hour later, when I was becoming increasingly restless, a little boy rushed up to me and started jabbering in Arabic. I assumed he was a beggar and ignored him. He persisted. I tried to wave him off. He grabbed my hand and thrust a scrap of paper in my palm and ran away.

'I'm back, Dr. Watson! Look what I found! Scarabs and interesting odds and ends!' Miss Bryant held up some bags triumphantly, as she emerged from the *souk*.

'Let me help you with those,' I put the paper in the pocket of my trousers and extended a hand.

Miss Bryant gave me a few bags, gratefully. 'Thank you,' she beamed. 'I shall hold on to the rest! Has Mr. Singh returned?'

'No,' I said, feeling very anxious now. 'But I think it would be wise for us to return and wait for him on board.'

Miss Bryant agreed and we walked back to the dock. Simon Fletcher was waiting for us at the railings of the *North Star*. He waved cheerfully.

'Welcome back! How was your day? Soaked in the local atmosphere?'

'Well, a mixed morning, Fletcher,' I responded.

I briefly described our singular experience.

'Well, these ports are not civilized, Dr. Watson. I did warn you. Wasn't Mr. Singh with you? I don't see the gentleman.'

'We lost each other an hour ago, but I imagine he should be back soon. He is a most resourceful man.'

We repaired to our rooms and agreed to meet for lunch in an hour.

I felt hot and sweaty and loosened my collar, sitting on the bed in my new room. I decided a short nap would be in order. Presently, I woke up with a mild headache and stretched my limbs. Something crinkled in my trouser pocket. It was the paper I had slipped in earlier.

On it, in Holmes' unmistakable handwriting, were the words *'Be careful, Watson'.*

I stared at the slip for a long time. I did not know what to think.

Presently, there was a knock on the door and, on my invitation, the captain entered.

'Mr. Singh has not returned and the police would like to speak with him.' He sounded very worried.

'Extraordinary! Has everyone else reported?'

The captain was overwrought. All this had been very trying for him. He was sweating profusely and was intensely agitated.

'Yes. And I'm afraid we will have to leave for Port Suez this evening with or without him. If he does not return, the police will certainly issue a warrant for his arrest on suspicion of having murdered Mr. Hashimoto. When will this nightmare end?'

We walked to the deck and scanned the dock anxiously. All were accounted for except Mr. Singh. Simon Fletcher was silent and smoking, lost in thought. The captain grew more anxious by the minute.

But his dread was shortly put to rest when we saw Mr. Singh walk up to the *North Star*, striding quickly up the gangplank.

'I apologize for the delay, Captain,' he said with sincerity, nodding at Miss Bryant and at me. 'I thought I saw our Japanese friends at a distance and went looking for them. I soon lost my way and by the time I returned to the last point where we were together, you had left too.'

'All accounted for, Captain?' enquired Fletcher. 'The ladies are in their cabin, are they not? The Japanese gentlemen returned quite some time ago, if I recall.'

'Yes, thank heavens!' said the captain, relief evident in his voice. 'Let me go and retrieve our passports!'

He walked down to the port office and returned presently with the British police inspector, Baynes, and his Egyptian staff. Baynes was a taciturn individual and after conferring with the captain in his room, returned our passports to us and bade us good-bye. We were soon on our way to Port Said, at the mouth of the Suez Canal.

In Paris, Professor Moriarty studied the wire that had just been brought to him.

'Incompetence! Sheer incompetence!' he hissed.

He opened a map and studied a certain section with considerable attention.

Presently, he closed his eyes and sat back in his chair. He was not asleep.

Alexandria to Bombay

Who dwells in the mighty Sea, my friend?
The fish and the spirits observe silently as we
move onwards, spurred on by reluctant winds,
knowing exactly whether it is doom or glory that awaits us.

The *North Star* moved on from Alexandria toward Port Said from whence we were to pass through the Suez Canal and then into the Red Sea and onward to Aden. It would be an uncomfortable few days; all of us were considering theories in our heads about the death of Mr. Hashimoto and the incident at Alexandria. The tension was palpable, with the heat and humidity adding to our discomfort. We grew irritable and suspicious and tried to avoid each other's company as far as possible. This was not very practical, because the necessities of social intercourse over breakfast, lunch, and dinner forced us into contact. The captain continued his attempts at humour, but his jokes fell flat and he eventually gave up.

Mrs. Andrews could see her journey coming to a close soon and brightened visibly. It was now just a small matter of going down through the Red Sea and Aden would be right around the corner. She seemed the only member of the group who was cheerful.

'Dr. Watson, do come and visit us in Aden on your way back. We would be so delighted!'

'It would be my pleasure.'

'I feel so nervous around those Japanese men. That's the whole thing about foreigners—their language, their customs! I am not really one for travel, Dr. Watson.'

'Ah, one must have a broad outlook, Mrs. Andrews. Perhaps they view us in a like manner. Who can say?'

'Well, I don't know, but I shall be glad when we reach Aden. All this has been very wearing.'

Meanwhile I, too, was in a ferment trying to guess who on the ship Sherlock Holmes was. He was here, of that there was no doubt. He had warned me in writing—in the midst of a shopping expedition. There was no one who seemed a match and yet, knowing Holmes' methods, I imagined that it could be any one of them. Colonel Burrowe? No, his military manner was too authentic. Simon Fletcher? No, too bland and parochial. Was it Mr. Shamsher Singh, perhaps? Yes, it seemed likely—he had a natural authority and seemed about the right height and build. His alertness and decisiveness at the Jewish Quarter at Alexandria seemed another strong hint; they seemed so characteristic of Holmes. Yes, I concluded, it was probably him. But how was I to unmask him?

Shamsher Singh accosted me one morning in the lounge as we moved past Port Said and into the Canal. I was reading a book on Egyptian antiquities and was lost in a section on the god *Ra*.

'Dr. Watson, do you have any theory on how someone entered the porthole and killed Mr. Hashimoto?' he asked in his deep voice.

'Not really. I thought for a moment that it could have been the Japanese, especially since Mr. Hashimoto left behind those Japanese symbols. But they seem too bulky to have forced themselves through a porthole, killed Mr. Hashimoto, and left the same way.'

'Hmm. Well, do you know what the Japanese inscriptions meant?'

'No. I am not familiar with the script.'

'Mr. Fletcher told me they stand for the numbers 8-9-3, which is the signature of an organization in Japanese society.'

'Unusual! I did not know that Mr. Fletcher knew how to read the Japanese script.'

'No one is who he appears to be, Dr. Watson,' said Mr. Singh, looking at me very keenly. 'Mr. Simon Fletcher is an intelligent man.'

'Oh?' I had formed no opinion of Fletcher, though he had been helpful in assisting us when we had to move Mr. Hashimoto's body. 'And what do you infer from all this?'

'We—Mr. Fletcher and I—infer that Mr. Hashimoto was assassinated by someone from the organization, whatever it is, and for reasons we do not know.'

'Quite plausible. As I mentioned earlier, someone had slipped a note with a similar inscription under the door soon after we began our voyage and Mr. Hashimoto was subdued after that.'

Simon Fletcher joined us at that moment.

'Dr. Watson, I happened to hear you as I came up. So someone slipped in a note with those numerals—'

'Yes. How does it happen that you are familiar with Japanese numerals, Mr. Fletcher?'

'A banker who deals in foreign currencies, as I do, must know of other numeral systems. That should not be a surprise.'

'True,' I admitted.

'Now please recall—was the note slipped under your door before Marseilles or after Marseilles?'

'Before.'

'Now that is very interesting, very interesting indeed. The Japanese joined us at Marseilles. It may mean that they are not involved or that there is another angle of inquiry that must be investigated.'

'Did you tell Dr. Watson of your discovery?' Mr. Singh asked Simon Fletcher.

Fletcher shook his head. 'No, we did not get a chance. Well, let me tell you, Dr. Watson, that I have a theory which I explored and validated. I found a small piece of fibre, most probably part of a hemp rope caught in the shards of glass.'

'Yes, I recall you mentioning that.'

'I wondered how it got there. The porthole is a good fifteen feet below the level of the deck. On Mr. Singh's suggestion, I went up to check and examined the railings just above. I happened to have a magnifying glass—I am a philatelist and always carry one—and I saw clear evidence that someone had tied some strong rope to the railings, clambered down the side of the ship, broken the porthole, and committed the crime. A piece of fibre was left behind in the glass as the murderer entered or exited the porthole. I leaned down the side as far as I could and searched for further evidence. The paint on the metal had been scratched—clearly by someone who scrambled up after the attack, and who had pieces of glass embedded in the soles of his shoes. In addition, there were a few very small pieces of glass on the deck, which I then matched with the glass of the broken window. There was no doubt at all.'

'Astonishing!' I cried. 'Your methods are admirable!'

'Thank you. I am a mere amateur. Now, what I conclude is that someone of light build and weight—and considerable daring and courage—tied this rope to the railing and executed this audacious plan.'

'The Japanese?'

Shamsher Singh shook his head. 'No, they are not slim and the hemp rope would not have supported their weight. They could not have entered the porthole.'

'Have you reported this to the captain?'

'Not yet,' said Mr. Singh. 'The fewer who know, the better. We thought of confiding in you. I suppose it is for the police to investigate and ask us. If they do not do so at Aden, I shall inform the captain.'

The information was unsettling.

Mrs. Andrews and Colonel Burrowe came in for some tea and we stopped our conversation.

We walked onto the deck and watched the western side of the canal—at a distance, in the haze, our fertile and agitated minds persuaded us briefly that we could actually see some of the famed pyramids of Giza, resting places for the royal dead. There was something eerie about the mirage, given our recent experience.

Soon we slipped into the Red Sea and the *North Star* made rapid progress in the deep waters as it headed toward the historic port of Jeddah. The bright sun lifted our spirits a little. We saw dolphins jumping in the sea at one point; it was a most pleasant sight. Slowly the feeling of darkness was lifting.

As we drew closer to Jeddah, I visited the library. I wanted to find a map of the area just to get my bearings right. As I searched in a quiet area, tucked away from sight, I heard a woman whispering in a strange language. Peeping through the books, I saw Miss Bryant having an animated discussion with the two Japanese men. I managed to prevent myself from exclaiming out loud.

Due to the unfamiliarity of the language, I could not catch most of what was said. But I heard words like 'Shanghai,' 'Yakuza,' 'Paris,' 'Nippon,' 'Sumiyoshi-kai,' and 'Joyce-san.' It seemed clear from the strong and sure way in which she was expressing herself that Miss Bryant was in command of the conversation. The Japanese did not speak as much and generally responded with '*Hai*' and nodded vigorously. They left shortly, leaving me quite intrigued.

The halt at Jeddah was brief and without incident. The ship loaded a few supplies and was soon on its way to Aden. I decided to confront Mr. Shamsher Singh.

I sought him out shortly after breakfast. He was sitting by himself on the deck.

'Ah, Dr. Watson,' he nodded affably.

'Holmes, there is no need to carry this charade any further.'

'I beg your pardon?'

I smiled. This time I was a step ahead.

'Holmes, you do me an injustice. An old friendship such as ours—is it necessary to deceive me day after day in this manner? Especially given the circumstances?'

'I am afraid I don't understand you, Dr. Watson. Are you all right?'

'You, Sir, are a fraud!' I declared with vehemence, smiling, feeling extremely smug.

Mr. Singh started violently. 'A fraud? A fraud! What do you mean by this conduct, Sir? You are certainly either mistaking me for someone else or are deliberately insulting me! How dare you call me a fraud? I demand an apology, Sir!'

'Tut, Holmes! My dear fellow, the game is up! "Mr. Shamsher Singh" indeed! Quite clever! Quite clever! But you have forgotten that I have seen you as an old woman, a beggar, a horseman—this disguise has worn thin now, Holmes. The turban, the beard, the swarthy complexion and the complex Indian accent—well, well, keep it if it makes you happy and if there is a need for it. You will no doubt tell me, by and by, why you are doing what you are doing. But know, my dear fellow, that I have seen through your little game! A most remarkable disguise indeed! But enough! Please accept that John Watson MD recognizes the great Sherlock Holmes conclusively!' I laughed loudly, attracting the attention of a couple of passengers nearby, who turned for a moment and then resumed their business.

Shamsher Singh's face had become a deep red and the veins on his forehead were throbbing. He clenched his fists and stood up, then controlled himself with an effort.

'Dr. Watson. Listen to me very carefully. I would like you to know that I am a man easily provoked to violence. You have been a gentleman thus far and I shall hold back one more time. I do not know who Mr. Sherlock Holmes is and I do not care. I am Shamsher Singh, an aide to the maharajah of Patiala. I am not in any kind of disguise and have no need to be. I strongly suggest you seek medical attention—Englishmen are not used to the heat and humidity of this part of the world and have been known to suffer nervous breakdowns. I can call the physician, if you like. Otherwise this interview is at an end and I must demand that you leave or I shall report this outrage to the captain!'

Simon Fletcher came by just then. 'Gentlemen, is everything all right?'

I realized that I had made an unfortunate mistake and that it would be better to make amends and close the matter quickly.

'I apologize, Mr. Singh! It certainly was a most unforgivable lapse in judgment. I was quite sure you were a close and dear friend in disguise. Your reaction is conclusive. Do excuse me.' I bowed, quite red-faced with embarrassment.

'Your apology is accepted, Dr. Watson,' said Mr. Singh, suddenly gentle and most solicitous. 'These things happen to all of us. Whoever Mr. Sherlock Holmes is, well, he should be honoured to have such a fine friend as yourself. Think no more of it, Sir. If you will sit here—no, no, I insist!—I shall be back in a moment with a whisky and soda. No doubt the voyage and the recent events have had a regrettable effect. You are a doctor and undoubtedly know about such conditions and how they may be addressed medically. I shall be back, Sir.' His magnanimity left me even more embarrassed at my conduct.

'Did you mistake him for the late Sherlock Holmes, the famous detective?' asked Fletcher, quite amused at my discomfiture.

'Yes. I do not know what came over me,' I said, mortified. 'Have you heard of Sherlock Holmes, Mr. Fletcher?'

'Of course! Who hasn't? He is quite well known in banking circles as the one who solved the cheque forgery case at the Standard Norwich Bank. The reputation of the bank would have suffered irreparably if not for his intervention. Yes, we— and I—know the name.'

Shamsher Singh came back with drinks and the three of us sat together to review matters.

'We have a murderer on board, gentlemen,' said Simon Fletcher, gravely. 'All of us are suspects. Let us take the time to look at all the names and their antecedents.'

He wrote on a sheet of paper.

1. Hashimoto—dead
2. Samuel Groves—Captain
3. Col. James Burrowe—Royal Horse—Penang
4. Simon Fletcher—banker—Bombay
5. Mr. Shamsher Singh—Aide to the maharajah of
    Patiala—Bombay
6. David Joyce—who is he?
7. Dr. James Israel—Physician on board
8. Dr. John Watson—Yokohama
9. Japanese Gentleman 1—who is he?
10. Japanese Gentleman 2—who is he?
11. Miss Clara Bryant—Shanghai
12. Mrs. Edith Andrews—Aden

He crossed out Mr. Hashimoto's name.

'We do not know anything about anyone. If I say I am a banker, can you prove or disprove it? If you say you are an aide to a maharajah, can we prove or disprove it? The answer is no and further, you are not obliged to respond to the question.'

'I believe, gentlemen, that it is quite possible that another incident may occur and therefore we should be careful.'

'Why do you feel so?' asked Mr. Singh.

'Well, I do not know why Mr. Fletcher feels that way, but I certainly feel it is possible. This is why.' I told them about the conversation I had overheard in the library.

'Most unusual,' murmured Mr. Singh, stroking his beard. 'Certainly suspicious.'

Fletcher shrugged. 'It is difficult to say. There is some reason why they choose not to be seen in each other's company. The only name that we recognize from that conversation is Joyce. That could mean he is a fellow conspirator or a victim or someone of interest.'

'The reserved Irish gentleman who joined us at Marseilles?'

'Yes, not very communicative. Keeps his distance.'

'Assuming the reference was to him, what does it mean?'

'I think he is a plainclothesman,' remarked Shamsher Singh.

'Is that so? And do I recall seeing you speak with him at the dining table a few days ago?'

Shamsher Singh nodded. 'Yes. I did speak to him quite casually. Mostly about the voyage and the weather along the way. I did most of the talking, though I have to admit he was pleasant enough with me. These men have certain characteristics. I am familiar with them because I have handled the security of the maharajah of Patiala in the past and have used such individuals. A certain confidence, a taciturn manner, their alert eyes, the manner in which they walk, their efforts to be inconspicuous, their nondescript attire—if you consider the matter, you will see that it is quite easy to detect them, defeating the very purpose they are intended for! But of course, there are exceptions and you have to know what you are looking for.'

'I see your point.'

Simon Fletcher turned toward me suddenly and spoke aggressively. 'And you, Dr, Watson? Why should we not suspect you?'

I was taken aback. 'I—'

Shamsher Singh interjected 'Quite fair, since we are all suspects. You shared the room with the victim. You claim that you slept soundly and never heard the window being shattered and the agony of a man being done to death violently not thirty feet away! Why should we believe you?'

I was silent for a moment. 'Yes, that certainly is something to think about. All I can say is that it is the truth. I slept very soundly that night.'

Shamsher Singh turned toward Simon Fletcher. 'A banker en route to Singapore? Very interesting. What is your alibi?'

'None, except that I had never met Mr. Hashimoto before—and I cannot prove that either. I am heavy. I could not possibly have come down the side of the ship and entered the cabin that way.'

'But you could have entered the cabin the regular way by picking the lock and staged everything while I was sound asleep,' I pointed out.

'Possible, but not probable. The porthole, the Japanese numerals scrawled on the paper by Mr. Hashimoto—no, a good try, but I think I pass.'

'I have nothing specific in my defence,' said Shamsher Singh, pre-empting us. 'I spoke to Mr. Hashimoto only a couple of times, introducing myself once and asking about the weather the next time. I do not know how to swim and would not have rappelled down the side of ship. My size again rules out entry.'

'So, do we, three intelligent men, assert that only a very light and lithe person is likely to have entered the porthole by rappelling down the side of the ship, killed a person twice his size, and disappeared quietly without alarming Dr. Watson? Barely credible,' said Simon Fletcher, a trifle cynically.

We halted our conjectures at this point as Mrs. Andrews came up excitedly.

'Another day! Just another day and I can stretch my legs at

Aden! I am so happy! The end of this horrible voyage! Won't the three of you come up to the governor's residence to see us?'

'Perhaps on our return, Mrs. Andrews,' I said, politely.

We had a rather quiet and solemn dinner and retired to our cabins quickly, locking our doors securely.

We reached Aden at dawn. The British outpost would have been an opportunity to step outside and refresh ourselves in relatively familiar conditions. But we were all still a little apprehensive, unsure about what to expect and so chose to stay on board. Mrs. Andrews disembarked after saying good-bye. It was a pleasure to see her joy on sighting her husband, a man of some forty summers and an excellent specimen of the kind of expatriate Englishman that is spoken of so admiringly at the highest levels.

And so we moved on quickly. Our next stop was to be Bombay, which I had visited once many years ago while a young doctor in the British Army.

There was now, on the *North Star*, one less passenger.

Three days after sailing from Aden, several nautical miles from the shores of Yemen and in the heart of the Arabian Sea, David Joyce vanished.

At breakfast, we did not remark upon his absence because we knew he was a man of irregular habits, usually given to eating in his cabin. At lunch, Simon Fletcher remarked upon his absence as did Colonel Burrowe. The captain promised to inquire if Mr. Joyce's health was a concern.

Shamsher Singh, Simon Fletcher, and I were in the lounge reading old editions of *The Times* when the captain rushed in, very upset.

'Missing! He is missing!'

'Who is?' enquired Simon Fletcher, his manner alert, limbs quivering with nervous tension.

'David Joyce! The gentleman we picked up at Marseilles! I went to his cabin to check on him, but he was not there. I alerted the crew and everyone has looked for him, but he has vanished. Gone!' The captain's face was red with agitation.

'He can't just vanish!' I said, trying to calm him. 'Let us see! Perhaps the library? The lounge? Maybe the deck?'

The captain was once again a nervous wreck. 'Thorough search! Looked everywhere! Missing! Nothing but trouble!'

The four of us rushed to David Joyce's cabin. The bed looked as though it had been slept in, with the blankets half on the floor. We looked around for a clue to his whereabouts.

'Here!' exclaimed Shamsher Singh, pointing under a mat on the wooden floor. 'Look! Those stains—blood?'

There were several irregular patches on the floor. Fletcher and I bent down to look closely.

'Yes,' I said slowly. 'This is blood and it has not dried yet. You can see stains on the mat too. It was placed there to cover them up.'

The four of us looked at each other. A cold chill had crept into the room.

Dr. James Israel rushed in, summoned by the captain. With a practiced eye, he took in the scene and raised his eyebrow. 'Man missing?'

'Yes,' said the captain, his voice trembling.

Simon Fletcher spoke with great deliberation. 'I think he was woken up in the morning and killed when he opened the door. No sign yet of a struggle. The cabin is only ten feet from the railings. I suspect he was stabbed and thrown overboard. I do not think we will find him.'

The captain sat down heavily on the nearest chair, his face ashen. He said nothing, too overwhelmed to express himself. The nightmare simply refused to end.

The rest of us examined the room for any other indication of what might have happened.

'Not a clue, but I think you are right, Mr. Singh. He was from the police. Take a look.'

On a little table were some of David Joyce's effects: a pen, some money, a Scotland Yard badge, and a blank sheet of paper showing clear impressions of writing on a separate sheet.

'Interesting...interesting,' muttered Simon Fletcher, holding the paper up against the light from the cabin's porthole and squinting.

'Ah! It seems that David Joyce was drafting a telegram to one Mr. Lestrade of Scotland Yard. Let me read whatever I can.

YAKUZA MEMBERS CLEARLY UNDER THE CONTROL OF...it's indistinct...can't tell what it is...

HASHIMOTO KILLED IN THE MANNER SUSPECTED AND DESCRIBED TO YOU EARLIER. INFORM CONSUL. H. IS SAFE.

'I think we have to conclude that David Joyce's body will not be recovered from the sea. It may have been several hours ago that he was killed by a person or persons unknown. But we have a clue—something—possibly a group—called Yakuza.'

'How many days to Bombay, Captain?' I asked.

'Three,' he whispered, pale as a sheet.

'Then we can do nothing but wait. Let us take precautions and not let each other out of sight for even a moment.'

There was no response, nor was one needed.

'Can we hold the Japanese on suspicion?'

'Why the Japanese? Why do you suspect them?' enquired Captain Graves.

I again mentioned the conversation I had overheard in the library.

'Significant, very significant...,' muttered Simon Fletcher.

'Baffling indeed,' remarked Shamsher Singh. He continued with some heat. 'But I find it strange that you do not equally suspect Miss Bryant. She is the one who spoke while the Japanese listened. Yet you ask for the Japanese to be held. If they are to be held, then so must the Englishwoman!'

'A fair point,' I admitted, a little contrite, displeased with myself for having possibly come across as prejudiced.

The captain shook his head. 'No one can be held without proof. Nonetheless, I can attempt to question them as the ship's authority. No, even that seems unlawful. A mere conversation in the library overheard by one person cannot implicate anyone. There is no proof that they were here in this room, is there? This has to be investigated by the police in Bombay. If they wish to question the passengers, they can.'

'I agree,' said Mr. Singh. 'However, it may be wise to keep them under watch.'

We sealed the room and continued our grim journey. Ill winds, miasma, call it what you will—the mood was tense and oppressive, with everyone on edge. This was by no means a pleasant journey and all we longed for was closure. I could hardly believe that I was to continue onward to Yokohama, far beyond Bombay. Would I ever reach it?

The captain opined that there was strength in numbers and requested me to share my commodious quarters with Simon Fletcher. While I was uncomfortable with the anticipated lack of privacy, I saw the practical necessity and the three of us moved Fletcher's effects to my cabin. Shamsher Singh moved in with the captain.

I walked to the railing on the deck. I needed fresh air and wished to be alone.

I heard Simon Fletcher walk up behind me, but was in no mood for company. Turning my back to him, I pulled my overcoat firmly about myself, hoping to be ignored. But he refused to take the hint and came up and stood by my side.

'Watson, do not be alarmed and do not respond,' said the low, steely voice of Sherlock Holmes.

I did not react. I was paralysed with shock.

'I shall explain everything soon, Watson. At this time, continue the charade. I am Simon Fletcher. You and I will travel together to the hotel in Bombay. Mr. Singh may join us, perhaps. I would like to avoid Colonel Burrowe and the rest if possible. Be very, very careful, Watson. Unfortunate accidents are quite possible and very likely. There is a larger canvas available in a city, lacking the constraints of a ship. At the same time, there is a different kind of danger lurking on board as we have just seen. Let us stick close together. There is no other way. Do not ask any questions now.'

I leaned on the railing to support myself. The familiar firm grip of Holmes on my left arm steadied me. We spent twenty minutes in silence and then returned to our cabin.

I shut the door. I turned and stared at a smiling Sherlock Holmes.

He stood there, completely transformed from the ordinary and slightly stout English banker Simon Fletcher to the tall, lean, confident, and charismatic friend I knew so well.

'Holmes! Can it be you?' I finally said, overcome by some emotion, finding it difficult to stand, my head swimming. I held onto a chair for support.

Holmes rushed forward and helped me onto a sofa. 'Watson, my sincerest apologies! Had I known you would have been affected in this manner, I would have exercised greater care! Sit down, my dear fellow, and let me get you a drink.'

A few sips of a brandy that Holmes produced and I was soon sitting up, staring open-mouthed at the man I had thought swept away at Reichenbach Falls and presumed dead, but now, to my utter shock and amazement, had actually travelled with me as 'Simon Fletcher' all the way from Liverpool.

'So you are alive!' I finally whispered.

'Yes,' said Holmes, 'and I owe you an explanation. I will tell you all, by and by. But only once we reach Bombay. Till then, we continue our charade.'

And somehow, with the ship shuddering along, pushed by malevolent winds, three tense days passed on the secretive Arabian Sea and we closed in on Bombay, the Gateway to India.

Meiringen—Vladivostok—Yokohama

 My friend, you and I are but helpless straw in the mighty currents of the Universe. Accept the inevitable, for it was decided even before you were born in a village in Chiba prefecture. I am sorry. I cannot help you.

Putting together as complex a story as this involves the independent confirmation of many events that purportedly happened, and for which I was not personally present. Indeed, no event occurs in isolation. People recall the same incident in different ways and it is a matter of personal integrity for a chronicler to cross-check and present other perspectives as best as possible. One is also faced with the need to occasionally obfuscate events and mask names to protect the privacy of individuals. I have applied my judgment in this case, but a gifted few may still be able to draw precise conclusions.

What does a reader expect from one of my narratives? I shall guess that he seeks to escape briefly from the wearying torment of daily events that erodes his spirit. He desires to remain in a state of suspense and excited anticipation, looking forward to hearing how Sherlock Holmes solved a particularly heinous or baffling crime with exemplary mental dexterity and pure genius, noting minutiae and deducing the astonishing. But is that necessarily fair? Is it right for me, Holmes' chronicler, to focus only on such cases?

The answer is, no. There are possibly three hundred extremely sensitive cases that detail how Holmes prevented a catastrophe from occurring in the first place. The tales may not thrill or satisfy the morbid because of the lack of blood or because the majesty of the law was not allowed to be flagrantly violated. However, as anyone from Scotland Yard will tell you, it is the prevention or derailing of a crime that is more satisfying than coming in after the fact and struggling to trace the offender and create a

legally sound case for prosecution. It may not make for delight-
ful reading or appeal to the regrettable bloodthirsty tastes of the
general public at a time of questionable social decadence, but
the discerning scholar will find satisfaction in the clever control
of reckless ambition, the prevention of grief, and the thwarting
of murderous intent. Sherlock Holmes was himself one such
scholar, fairly scornful of 'solving' a crime, which, in his view,
was merely an application of logical thinking.

But when he was involved in a battle of wits, where the
hunted and the hunter were known to each other and the end
object was in itself no secret—that was when he found true satisfaction. Many crimes take time to commit. Similarly, the process
of counterintelligence is extremely subtle, requiring extraordinary patience and creativity, with issues like the psychology of
the individual, cultural peculiarities, and national sensitivities
playing an important role. Whether in the world of crime or that
of diplomacy, the most influential remain practically anonymous.
For every crime with international dimensions you read about,
there are a dozen that were not allowed to happen.

After the entire episode involving Japan came to a satisfactory
conclusion, I researched key events in order to ensure that my
chronicles were purely objective and not coloured by my own
limited perspective. I was fortunate that Holmes shared his notes.
It was a little more difficult getting the notes of Ambassador
Sugiyama and Professor Moriarty, but I finally did so using the
good offices of many friends. I thought it prudent and ethical
that parts of the narrative be in their own voice.

The reader must remember that he has been a helpless
onlooker—if that—to events that could have completely altered
the global balance of power and influence. Many individuals pos-
sessing significant intelligence and determined motives competed
to change the flow of history and commerce. The average citizen
either had no idea of the currents or, if he was fortunate enough
to read the limited commentary available in the newspapers of the
time, could have done nothing since the reports were infrequent,
cloaked in hints and of no clear relevance to his everyday life.

I present to you the notes of Sherlock Holmes, the Honourable Ambassador Sugiyama and Professor Moriarty, with only minimal editing, principally to gently camouflage names. I have not included my own notes of that period, simply because I was under the impression that Holmes was dead (and I was therefore in the grip of severe distress) and I was not, in any case, present. However, I present first the letter that Holmes wrote to me just before his presumed accident on May 4th, 1891.

MY DEAR WATSON,

I write these few lines through the courtesy of Professor Moriarty, who awaits my convenience for the final discussion of those questions which lie between us. He has been giving me a sketch of the methods by which he avoided the English police and kept himself informed of our movements. They certainly confirm the very high opinion I have formed of his abilities.

I am pleased to think that I shall be able to free society from any further effects of his presence, though I fear that it is at a cost which will give pain to my friends and especially, my dear Watson, to you. I have already explained to you, however, that my career had in any case reached its crisis and that no possible conclusion to it could be more congenial to me than this. Indeed, if I may make a full confession to you, I was quite convinced that the letter from Meiringen was a hoax and I allowed you to depart on that errand under the persuasion that some development of this sort would follow.

Tell Inspector Patterson that the papers he needs in order to convict the gang are in pigeonhole M., done up in a blue envelope and inscribed 'Professor Moriarty.' I made every disposition of my property before leaving England and handed it to my brother Mycroft. Pray give my greetings to Mrs. Watson and believe me to be, my dear fellow

Very sincerely yours,
Sherlock Holmes[1]

---

[1] The reader may refer to *The Final Problem* for the immediate context in which Holmes composed this message.

The Account of Sherlock Holmes *(from his personal papers)*

I lost my balance and fell off the ledge at Reichenbach Falls and plunged into the icy cold water below. And thus began a journey that I never thought I would undertake in my lifetime. A journey so strange, so full of unusual events that, as I write this, I wonder if it all really happened.

I knew through reading the newspapers that many were very anxious to know my whereabouts and many grieved for me. It caused me embarrassment to know that I was thus missed. I could have done something—but no, I could NOT have done anything; shadows, dangers, the relentless battle between good and evil—I had to do what I had to do and that meant absolute silence. I hope I will be forgiven, as my deliberate silence helped me in the subsequent events that unfolded, which were full of the gravest import to modern civilization. How close were the mighty empires England and France to cultural annihilation, in a manner almost impossible to comprehend. And Japan! Without exaggeration, I believe that the rest of the world would have attacked Japan and destroyed it had I not intervened. Thankfully, the entire sordid matter never became public. Circumspection. It is the first word in the dictionary of diplomats and detectives and is a trait absolutely necessary for keeping the honour and integrity of nations and individuals intact.

But let me start from that infamous fall.

After Professor Moriarty allowed me time to write a final letter, which I addressed to Watson, I also readied myself to fight him physically. I am no coward and found an opportune moment to pounce on Professor Moriarty. We fought on that narrow ledge high above the Falls. We had to reach a conclusion and while it appeared that both of us lost our balance and fell, it would now appear that Professor Moriarty managed to cling on to a protruding shrub and survived.

The fall was from quite a height, but I was not alarmed. In fact, I felt a strange sense of anticipation. I remember wondering how the experience of death was likely to be; death is, after all, a natural and logical conclusion to one's life force and I did not feel any fear. I tried to calculate the rate of descent and the force of compression on my flesh and bones. I would not survive. The surface tension of the water would shatter me completely, I remember thinking with equanimity. Much has been said about the velocity of thoughts as one approaches the point of death and I can say that in my case my mind moved with remarkable speed in a million directions.

When I hit the water, it was certainly with greater force than I had calculated. While the cold was intense, the force of the impact was even more so. I lost consciousness, though I have a vague recollection of boulders splashing into the water as well. I probably sank to the bottom and was taken away quickly by the raging current. Had there been onlookers, they would have concluded, quite logically, that I had been killed on impact or by drowning. I was carried away in a state of unconsciousness over a considerable distance very swiftly. I marvel that I did not hit a rock when I fell.

When I regained my senses, it was night and I was stuck between the large roots of a tree on the banks of the swiftly flowing stream. It was bitterly cold even in May. I knew that I would suffer from hypothermia if I did not do something quickly. Slowly and deliberately, I got up and examined myself for injuries. Other than a mild headache, a bruised shoulder, and a throbbing sensation in my right calf, I was surprisingly unharmed.

I made a rude staff from a tree branch and collected my thoughts. What should I do? Where could I go? Danger was still in the air and the safest strategy was to avoid drawing attention to myself. My mind moved swiftly and I decided that Professor Moriarty and his men would be better served if they believed I was dead and unaccounted for. And at that time, it may be recalled, I had no idea what had happened to him and thought it better to assume that he too had survived and might well be close at hand, determined to conclude matters. He would not rest till he was sure of my destruction.

At a distance of perhaps half a mile, I saw the weak flicker of a light. I began walking toward it, knowing that I needed warmth and rest. I needed to recuperate in order to think clearly and plan a course of action. Death could not be cheated twice.

The light came from a small hut set in the middle of a pasture, the kind that some Swiss farms keep for visitors and tourists. I concluded that it was as safe an option as any. I hobbled toward the hut—for the pain was now acute—and looked around to see if there was anyone outside. There was nobody that I could see. I moved closer and peeped in cautiously. I could see someone reading in the dim light. A middle-aged man, perhaps, resting in front of a warm and inviting fire.

I did not hesitate. I knocked firmly and heard the gentleman push back his chair and walk toward the door.

'Who is there?' enquired a confident voice in an unusual accent.

'A traveler in need. I seek your help, sir, and shall trouble you no more than necessary.'

The bolt was withdrawn and the door opened.

Instead of the clean, ruddy face of a Swiss farmer, I saw an oriental visage peer out. I did not allow my surprise to manifest; it would have been poor manners.

'I have had a minor accident and request your assistance,' I said, surprised to hear my voice quaver just a little. The incident had obviously weakened me more than I had realized.

'Please come in, please come in!' The gentleman gestured hospitably and soon enough I was in the warm hut.

He examined me in the light and exclaimed, 'Ah, you are wet and hurt! I must insist that you change—here, I have an extra set of clothes, though I am sorry that they may be of an inadequate size, since you are tall and I am not! And I see a wound on your head. That will not do, that will not do at all!'

With considerable fussing, this courteous gentleman quickly ensured that I was dry and warm and that my head was bandaged. I was taken by his efficiency and attention to detail, traits that I was to find useful in subsequent days.

He busied himself and served me an excellent hot dinner in short order. Within an hour of my arrival in that remote hut, I was feeling better. He was also silent and far from inquisitive.

But he smiled often and kept the fire going. The warmth of this memory remains today, starting with the warm hut in which he ministered to me.

I felt I owed my unusual host an explanation.

'I sincerely regret the intrusion,' I said. 'I have taken undue advantage of your hospitality, Sir. I would like to explain my situation.'

'Please do not mention it,' said my host, with a warm smile. 'All that can wait till you are rested. Please sleep and we shall talk tomorrow.'

I continued, nevertheless. 'My name is Sherlock Holmes, and I am a consulting detective. I was in the vicinity, conducting an investigation, and regrettably suffered a minor setback and fell at the Reichenbach Falls. I was washed ashore quite close by. It is important that my presence remain undetected, though I can hardly insist on it, given that it is I who have walked in unannounced. I regret to say that my life is in considerable danger.'

'I am Hiroshi Sugiyama, ambassador of Japan to Switzerland,' said my host, with the most elegant bow. 'And of course, Mr. Holmes, while I was not expecting you, I am delighted to make your acquaintance. I am already aware of your reputation through my friend Masataka Kawase, who was our ambassador plenipotentiary in London, and consider it a remarkable honour to meet you at all. As for my presence here, I was merely taking a brief holiday, indulging in a private passion, writing *haikus*. The Swiss farms provide great inspiration for poetry, with their bracing climate. I shall leave for Berne shortly and resume my duties.'

I had already realized that this was no ordinary person. I had observed his deliberate choice of words, his careful enunciation, the porcelain hands that conveyed an interest in the arts, the extreme tidiness of his hut and his tact. I felt he would have to be taken into confidence. There was no time to lose.

'Mr. Sugiyama, I am being pursued by certain criminal elements. I am presently at a disadvantage and need to be invisible, in a manner of speaking. Certain nations and men of integrity would be better placed if I conduct additional investigations under cover. May I stay here for a few days? I would, of course, recompense you for your inconvenience.'

'I see,' responded Mr. Sugiyama, thoughtfully. 'A most unfortunate circumstance, Mr. Holmes, most unfortunate. I am happy that you are presently safe and shall endeavour to be of assistance.'

After a moment's silence, he said, 'We must plan the next course of action soon. You must first sleep. That will allow facts to be weighed dispassionately in the morning.'

'Evil, Mr. Sugiyama, is everywhere. There is a web around us. I need time to recoup and think of a new plan. Professor Moriarty does not give up. Till he sees actual proof of my demise, he will assume I am alive and will work accordingly. I must not be seen. I must be believed dead and not traceable. I must not stay anywhere a second more than necessary.'

I heard Mr. Sugiyama take a sudden sharp intake of breath. Something had registered.

'Professor Moriarty, did you say, Mr. Holmes? You may be surprised to know that I know that name,' he said, after a few moments. There was a clear note of urgency in his voice. 'Interesting, very interesting. And perhaps, fortuitous—yes, few know of him and we know he prefers it that way. The Japanese government is also aware of him and his influence. It is automatically my duty to find a way to help you. Not another word, Sir. I order you to close your eyes and rest. I will find a solution overnight.'

Mr. Sugiyama returned to his table, thinking and reading and writing *haikus*. Outside, an owl flitted by in the moonless night.

Thus assured, I fell asleep.

The next morning, Mr. Sugiyama showed me the English translation of a *haiku* he had written.

The moon is silent
A cold wind murmurs, afraid
The brave gather strength

Professor Moriarty's Note *(Acquired through the good offices of the French Sûreté many years after the event, at my request. Certain observations at the end of a few chapters are also reflective of my attempts at reconstructing the acts of Professor Moriarty and how he responded to them.)*

At every turn, Sherlock Holmes and I have stepped away from each other at the very last moment. My prior attempts to have him eliminated had not been successful, largely because of the incompetence and limited intelligence of those who were assigned the task. When the reports of these failed attempts reached me, I could see with absolute clarity that it was not the stratagem itself that was at fault, but the failure of the man of the moment to react in the right manner. And it is a fact that Sherlock Holmes was close to me in intelligence and did have an instinct and an ability to think that was superior to the police force, whom I hold in absolute contempt.

On the ledge at Reichenbach Falls, I was surprised by Holmes' gall—I was his physical and intellectual superior and there was really no possible way he could have prevailed. He was simply wasting my time. A man of his logical temperament should have seen the futility of fighting against a greater power.

Nevertheless, we struggled for several minutes. He thrust his right hand into my face, managing to scratch me and draw blood, and also attempted to throw me off balance. I held him close and landed a few punches in his midriff and shoulders. We staggered; it was a fight to the death. The slippery mud complicated matters but we fought on, neither a clear victor, landing blows on each other. I was still collected and asked Holmes to stop and not waste his energy and my time. But he seemed deaf to me and carried on. And then, as we tottered at the edge, he gripped my waistcoat to regain his balance. He tripped again, falling backwards, and my waistcoat suddenly tore off. Both of us lost our balance and tipped over the edge.

While Holmes was thrown clean off into space, I managed to catch the ledge as I fell and, as I slid down for another ten feet or so, I was able to break the fall. Finally I came to rest against a large shrub that was protruding from the side of the cliff. There I caught my breath and collected my thoughts.

I looked down. I had seen Holmes as he began his downward journey. As I looked at the raging torrents of the pool below, I could see no sign of him. He was probably dead. But I would need to verify that thoroughly and quickly.

I first looked for a way back and found it quite easily. The natural protrusions of rock and small shrubs needed to get a grip were more than enough for me to quickly climb to the top. I was dirty and tired, but absolutely infuriated by Holmes' behaviour. I am always appalled by stupidity and this was another ridiculous instance of that quality.

I quickly walked up to Meiringen to my hotel, changed my attire and destroyed all evidence of my most recent experience, which included muddy shoes, a torn waistcoat, and dirty clothes. There was also the little matter of masking the visible injuries on my face. That was easy as I am a master of disguise and hiding a facial injury is child's play. I was sure I had won the battle for now, but till I received irrefutable proof of his death, I was not prepared to believe I had won the war. I set LeFevre on the task.

I left the hotel the next morning. It was imperative that I reach Paris, where I had some unfinished business involving my counterfeit operations.

I took the eleven o'clock train to Berne and Lausanne. My first-class cabin had only a few co-passengers: an old lady with a Bernese dog, two young boys, a middle-aged French couple, an elderly Japanese tourist, and a portly gentleman wearing a typical Swiss hat. I reached Lausanne and left instructions with Babineaux there to forward all reports on Sherlock Holmes to me without delay.

Holmes had caused deep but not absolute damage to my ambitions, but he knew little about the real extent of my network and activities. His schoolboyish attempts at detection only found superficial examples of inefficiency and inferior intelligence within my organization, which are in themselves useful to know, for a vibrant organization must always be in a state of flux and regeneration. Of course, the recent arrest of so many of my aides was exasperating, but I had always known the value of redundancy and the need for constant obfuscation. This was merely a small setback. In a month, all would be well.

I pity Holmes and his small set of mediocre associates. His right hand man, Dr. Watson, is extremely limited in his intelligence. I believe Holmes managed to expose his own lack of judgment by having such an inferior associate. Men of intelligence need extremely thorough and discerning assistants in their professional quests. We must ruthlessly replace these assistants on a regular basis to prevent stagnation. That is why Holmes has always failed, while I have always succeeded and will continue to do so.

Our new activities promise untold power. Money is merely a means; the ability to alter history as one wills is the true test of success. The world is becoming smaller and smaller and to be overly focused on Europe and dismissive of distant countries like Japan and China is a mistake. Absurd notions like democracy and public order are a distraction, but perhaps, on reflection, convenient devices to keep lesser men busy. It is amusing that peoples and nations believe they possess the ability to craft their own destinies. Let the fools continue to think so. They are pawns in a chess game. I am the Grandmaster and shall do with them what I please.

Well, Holmes, here's to your memory!

The Diplomatic Artefacts of Hiroshi Sugiyama, Ambassador of Japan to Switzerland *(Note from Dr. Watson: Holmes was referred to as PNY32 and Professor Moriarty as TWJ22 in the official encrypted wires or secret paper correspondence.)*

TOP SECRET

May 5 1891
CH-AHS-876
The Foreign Desk
Tokyo

Attn: KX-56

1. This is with reference to your Memos 67, 68, and 69 apropos of the expansion plans of _____ which necessitates immediate and decisive action through Operation Kobe55.
2. Acted on your suggestion regarding our guest PYN32.
3. PYN32 was in a shaken physical condition and I was able to bring him back to his normal self quickly and easily. His fortuitous arrival can be of great assistance to us at this sensitive time.
4. I told him that I wished to take him to our Embassy in Berne and then on to Japan where he would be safe. He agreed readily but emphasized the need for disguise. I went up to the farmer's residence to close accounts and

procured the clothes needed for PYN32 to pass off as a
stout farmer, saying that I would like a sample of Swiss
clothing as a souvenir.

5. After a light breakfast, we both prepared for the journey.
Our guest is very competent in the matter of disguise. He
transformed into a Swiss farmer, complete with a ruddy
complexion, a hearty manner, and a certain typical gait
that Swiss men have. His powers of observation are acute.

6. We walked to Meiringen railway station. I took a couple
of first-class tickets to Berne and stepped into the waiting
room. We sat in silence. Other travellers came and went
but none took notice of PYN32, with most directing a brief
glance at me for obvious reasons. We took the eleven o'clock
train in the company of an old lady with a large Bernese
dog, a French couple, perhaps in their forties, a couple of
talkative teenage boys, and a taciturn gentleman with pen-
etrating dark eyes and a hostile air, who seemed absorbed in
thought and stared outside unblinking. The journey passed.

7. We walked to the Embassy, which is barely a mile away
on Engestrasse. Along the way, PYN32 made the surprising claim that TWJ22 was on the train and was the single
grim gentleman staring out of the window. He felt he was
likely to be on his way to Lausanne or Paris. Please assign
someone to watch the stations.

8. PNY32 is safe in his guest quarters. However, speed is of
the essence.

                                                        HS

                            TOP SECRET

May 6 1891
CH-AHS-877
The Foreign Desk
Tokyo

Attn: KX-56

1. Have worked on the suggested plan overnight. We shall
avoid the sea route via Marseilles because we need to keep
a distance between us and TWJ22. We shall take the route
to Japan via Moscow.

2. We must reach Japan as early as possible, so I need your

assistance in getting tickets and papers arranged; please have them ready with our Ambassador there. We are departing this evening and should be in Moscow in two days.

3. I have not yet told PNY32 that I have a mission for him. It is best that he be told about Operation Kobe55 when we reach Tokyo. His own intention is to disappear for as long as possible and I have no doubt that he will cooperate fully when we seek his assistance.

4. Additionally, please ensure that reports regarding the movements of TWJ22 reach Moscow in anticipation of our arrival.

HS

TOP SECRET

May 7 1891
The Foreign Desk—KX-56

Attn: CH-HS from Berne

1. Arrangements have been made. Ambassador Toyoda will hand over the documents to you personally.
2. We hope your journey from Berne to Moscow was uneventful.
3. TWJ22 reached Lausanne and then travelled to Paris. He was seen at Gare du Nord and then lost. But thus far we have no reason to believe he is aware of your movements.
4. News of events continues to be prominent in papers, as you would have noticed.
5. Operation Kobe55 must move quickly. At Vladivostok, WRT77 will be at hand and will escort you to Tokyo.

KX-56

TOP SECRET

May 9 1891
CH-AHS-877 camp Moscow
The Foreign Desk
Tokyo

Attn: KX-56

1. Our journey from Berne to Moscow was not entirely without incident. We took the overland coach to Vienna

and then upwards through Warsaw, Minsk, and then into Moscow, changing coaches as often as possible. While we took every possible precaution, PNY32 and I felt we were being watched or followed.

2. At a station near Warsaw, we rested and partook of refreshments. One of our fellow passengers, a loquacious Englishman, perhaps a travelling salesman, was unusually inquisitive and insisted on imposing his company on us and asked us many questions in a very loud voice.

3. We managed to shrug him off, but it appeared that the unnecessarily loud conversation had attracted the attention of shrewder individuals.

4. A rough-looking passenger accosted PNY32 when he stepped out for a cigarette and asked him for his papers. PNY32 refused and demanded identification and the man went away. We feared that word would get around about two unusual travellers.

5. Ambassador Toyoda met us in Moscow and handed over the relevant documents. We are setting off on the experimental Trans-Siberian this evening. Many parts of this new Railroad are not completely ready yet so there will be some hardship. But this is the safest way.

6. PNY32 is in a reflective mood and has sensed that we have something to request of him. His powers of observation are acute. He continues to be in disguise and is very comfortable.

7. While generally being knowledgeable about smuggling, he does not, as far as I can tell, have much knowledge about the context of Operation Kobe55. I believe he will see the strategic urgency of Operation Kobe55 and his pivotal role.

HS

Ambassador Sugiyama's Aide Memoir *(Note from Dr. Watson: In the following rather long, somewhat informal, Aide Memoir, I have replaced PNY32, the code name for Holmes, with his name to avoid any confusion and made the tone conversational. In addition, I have used Professor Moriarty's name as well, instead of his code name, TWJ22.)*

TOP SECRET

24 May 1891
CH-AHS-877—Aide Memoir
The Foreign Desk
Tokyo

Attn: KX-56

We thank you for the impeccable arrangements made in the safe transfer of [Holmes] to our Tokyo safe house.

We stayed at our Embassy in Moscow for barely a day. The journey from Moscow to Vladivostok, while long and frequently disturbed due to the construction of the railway line, was not without incident. We felt we were being followed right from the time we left the Embassy premises. I obviously stood out because of my features, but my sixth sense told me that I was being looked at with more than idle curiosity.

[Holmes] refused to travel without a disguise and so took on the persona of a French businessman and was given a fake passport by our Embassy. He had picked up a smattering of Russian and, having the powers of gentle persuasion, managed to get us a very private first-class coupé for the first leg, instead of a cabin that would have had two additional passengers. The coupé was warm and comfortable and had been designed with many conveniences, except that the common toilet was at the other end of the carriage. The staff would visit often, serving tea or taking any orders for refreshments. In the evening they brought in fresh, warm blankets and took them away the next morning. We avoided unnecessary contact and [Holmes] spent time smoking and thinking. Occasionally, we would test each other's observation skills or play chess.

'You are a widower, Mr. Sugiyama. Also a painter. You have spent some time in Germany and are an accountant by training.'

'Correct on all counts, [Mr. Holmes]! Please explain how you deduced this.'

'We have spent several days with each other, Mr. Sugiyama. I have observed your habits and seen that you are quite self-reliant though not entirely so. Not once have you mentioned a wife but I noticed that you have difficulty in arranging your personal effects, showing that you were quite used to someone else doing it for you until recently.'

'Quite so. My wife passed away after an illness, about a year ago. And about being a painter?'

'Whoever has a passion finds ways to keep the embers glowing and alive. Along the way, you were observing the landscape. A painter uses his thumb to gauge depth and perspective. You did that several times and were satisfied and perhaps made a mental note for a future project. And later, you spent several minutes observing the paintings in the waiting room at Moscow. You nodded in appreciation at a couple and I saw you attempt to trace the hand of the painter over some complex lines.'

'True enough!'

'Your suitcase is marked with baggage tags from Berlin and Munich and your German is unusually fluent. This suggests you spent time in Germany, obviously as part of your diplomatic duties.'

'That is indeed the case!'

'Only an accountant would hold on to a copy of Harper's *Accountants' Directory* with such care and, judging from the condition of its pages, I see that you refer to it often. You are in all probability a member of the Institute of Chartered Accountants in England and Wales—did they not turn down the application of Mary Smith some years ago? And in addition, though in a minor way, the meticulous and confident way you wrote down the accounts for our journey from Vienna.'

'Absurdly simple! I thought you had done something clever, but I now see it was child's play.'

'Indeed, Mr. Sugiyama,' responded [Holmes] with some asperity.

'Would you care to make any calculated observation about me, Mr. Sugiyama? You are a diplomat and perhaps have acuity in your perception in these matters significantly greater than most individuals.'

'I am flattered, [Mr. Holmes]. I am not a detective. But let me try.'

'Hmm. I believe you have an older sibling who you admire greatly and your energy springs from a desire to keep pace with him. You have an interest in chess or games of a similar nature. You are not enamoured of women. You have an unfortunate belief in the curative and stimulating powers of cocaine and possibly make use of it frequently.'

[Holmes] stared at me for an extended period, his face expressionless.

'Please explain your method of deduction, Mr. Sugiyama. I am intrigued.'

'In my experience as a diplomat, most action-oriented individuals—exceptions abound, of course—are younger siblings
who try to catch up with the accomplishments of an older one.
A professional will always ensure his skills are kept finely honed.
A renowned detective such as you is likely to exercise his brain
constantly through some means and not take his skills for granted.
I see only chess and *baduk* as games that you may like. The fact
that you are indifferent to women I infer indirectly from the fact
that you have not referred to any family all these days and yet
are extremely organized, suggesting that you have managed
very well without a wife. As to cocaine, I guessed that when I
was attending to you when we met, but I did not comment on the
puncture marks I saw on the veins of your arms.

'Of course Mr. [Holmes], my observations are unlikely to have
a scientific basis, but at best can be ascribed to experience. I defer
to you in this matter.'

[Holmes] did not say a word for several moments. Then he
grasped my hand firmly and with feeling.

'My dear fellow, I am delighted! Simply delighted! You are
quite right, quite right indeed!'

On one occasion, a day after we started our journey, he asked
me whether I had an opinion about a particular waiter who
served us.

'Not really,' I answered.

'He is a plainclothesman, with orders to protect you, I would
imagine, perhaps because you are an ambassador and therefore an
important person. And, completely irrelevantly, he is also a pianist.'

'How do you know this? The ambassador did not tell me that
he had sought any assistance from the Russian police.'

'Nevertheless, it is so. His eyes are alert and he walks about with
a firm purpose without a wasted movement. He takes orders, does
not offer suggestions and is not knowledgeable about the menu.
Before he enters our coupé, he knocks sharply, like someone who
would not take "no" for an answer. When I open the door, he looks
up and down the corridor to see if anyone is around, with his hand
ready in his pocket. I conjecture he has a revolver that he keeps
handy there. He enters and stands sideways and is always in a state
of extreme alertness. His fingers are very long and elegant and
I have observed him moving them about in a deliberate impatient
way while he awaits our order. It was as though he were playing
a concerto. If there had been a piano here, judging by the way his

fingers were moving, I am almost sure we would have heard Liszt's dazzling *étude Feux Follet*. Ah, the brilliance!'

'I must compliment your astuteness!'

On the morning of the second day into the journey, the waiter appeared again shortly after breakfast. After looking up and down the corridor in his usual style, he moved in quickly and handed over a revolver to [Holmes] who, with a similar fluid movement, pocketed it without looking surprised in the slightest. The waiter turned to me and said in Japanese, 'WRT77 asked me to keep an eye on you. I can see that you would not know how to handle a firearm and that your friend is in better physical condition. Please be alert.' He turned and vanished as abruptly as he had appeared. [Holmes] had been right.

[Holmes] patted the revolver in his pocket. 'This is obviously a more sensitive mission than you have disclosed thus far. It is improbable that someone wants to guard you and hands over a revolver to an unknown person. Are you in danger or am I? Or perhaps the both of us? And why?'

'You are correct, [Mr. Holmes]. It is known at the highest levels that I am travelling to Japan with a very important unidentified person. The waiter referred to someone in our Intelligence Service. It would be safe to say we should both be on our guard. Your presumption about the waiter seems accurate. I am surprised at myself for not noticing.'

On the third morning, I took a walk along the carriages to stretch my limbs and get some exercise. I then returned and looked over some papers I had brought with me. [Holmes] was busy reading a newspaper he had picked up at the Moscow railway station.

The train suddenly stopped at about eleven o'clock at the Gostovskaya station. We could see no obvious reason for the halt. [Holmes] looked out of the window cautiously and reported a commotion two carriages away. He went outside to investigate, after ensuring the revolver was in his pocket. He was back in ten minutes.

'The waiter has been found dead,' he reported grimly. 'Shot through the heart. It is no ordinary crime. Someone is following us and is on this train. The police from the nearby town have been summoned. We shall be delayed for a few hours, I presume.'

I was too shocked to respond.

'Mr. Sugiyama, please stay alert. We cannot both be asleep at the same time. Do not step outside for any reason without informing me. I am the stronger of the two and will have to protect you, should the need arise. For now, till the train starts again, we must both sit here and not venture out.'

We watched the chaos outside as an ambulance arrived and almost a dozen noisy policemen took charge of the dead waiter's body. Within minutes, we heard the hobnailed boots of the police as they entered our compartment, knocked harshly on each closed door, asked questions in Russian and then moved on.

As expected, they knocked on ours as well, shouting *Atkriytiy, Politsiya, Politsiya! Atkriytiy!*

I opened the door. Three large agitated policemen stood outside and one of them launched into an incomprehensible tirade in Russian. I invited them in and proffered my diplomatic passport, which immediately lowered tensions. They looked suspiciously at [Holmes] and examined his passport, which claimed he was a French national. They asked me if they could search the coupé. I had no choice but to agree.

I remembered that the waiter had given [Holmes] a revolver and thought that all was lost. Luckily, their perfunctory search revealed nothing and they bid us good-bye and moved to the next cabin.

After an hour or so, the train moved on, with no satisfactory conclusion to the search for a suspect. I was both relieved and anxious.

I asked [Holmes] about the revolver.

'I placed the revolver on a ledge near the ceiling in the common toilet once I heard that there had been a murder. I shall go now and retrieve it.'

He returned quickly with the revolver and we considered the situation.

'I believe there are a number of possibilities. Let us look at each one of them carefully. One is that someone in your diplomatic communications wing has possibly tipped off [Professor Moriarty's] network—the Japanese ambassador to Switzerland suddenly vanishes from Berne with another unidentified person—yes, he would have considered the possibility that I survived and am travelling with you. Perhaps the minor incidents that exasperated us on our journey from Berne to Moscow reached [Moriarty's] network and they are now on this train trying to find us. Perhaps your man in Vladivostok has betrayed us too or has himself been compromised. All roads lead to the same conclusion. Or perhaps this is a purely accidental murder; perhaps our waiter found something he should not have. Quite the opposite of serendipity. An unusual coincidence, but a coincidence nevertheless.'

'And what do you feel is most likely?'

'The first. The persons we met on our journey lacked the circumspection needed to be effective criminals—they were simply a nuisance and would not have had the skills needed to observe unusual behaviour and report the matter. I conjecture that someone in your Embassy in Moscow made arrangements to eliminate us on this journey. They are possibly aware that we are armed and are waiting for an opportunity to strike.'

'If true, that would be most disturbing. It may mean we have traitors in our Embassies!'

'Nothing is impossible, Sir! But for now, let us preserve our energies in trying to stay alive.'

The train staff continued serving the first-class passengers in their coupés. We ate little, fearing poison. Luckily, [Holmes] had insisted on taking along food supplies for the journey, though I had then felt it to be unnecessary since the train was committed to first-rate service.

The long journey passed slowly with many changes due to ongoing construction, adding to my apprehension every moment. Neither of us slept well. It took me two days to regain my equanimity. [Sherlock Holmes], though, was quite unperturbed.

'Thank you for helping me. I hope to be of similar assistance to you one day.'

'You will be safe in Tokyo, [Mr. Holmes]. We do indeed need your assistance for a matter of great international import.'

'I am, of course, at a disadvantage as far as language is concerned. But other than that, I am ready to help. What I personally need is time—to recoup and gain the resources I need in order to apprehend [Professor Moriarty].'

On the tenth day, another waiter appeared. 'We arrive at Vladivostok in an hour, Sirs,' he announced in accented English and moved on.

[Holmes] smiled grimly on his departure.

'He is not a waiter. He is someone hired to keep an eye on us. Perhaps another attempt was considered imprudent. Perhaps we are being lured into a trap.'

At Vladivostok station, I found DRT33 waiting for us instead of WRT77. DRT33 had worked with me in Singapore in a different capacity, many years ago. He gave us the troubling news that

WRT77 had been found brutally murdered at the Vladivostok docks the previous day. There were no clues, said DRT33. WRT77 had not been a conspicuous person and was a mere facilitator of events. There was nothing to be gained from his death, we thought, except perhaps the news that we were expected from Moscow. Vladivostok was already a place we needed to leave without delay.

DRT33 had arranged for our passage on a small passenger ship headed straight for Yokohama. This time, our journey was completed without any difficulty, though [Holmes] was mildly seasick on a couple of occasions. He told me that he believed the ship was being monitored and we were not necessarily safe.

We arrived in Yokohama and went through Customs very quickly, as WRT77 had made relevant arrangements ahead of time.

I welcomed [Holmes] to our country and took him to the transit facility in Tokyo, where he could rest for a day. Jiro Hamada was assigned to be his cook, valet, and bodyguard. Hamada is a former sumo wrestler with a very alert and fearless temperament.

By the time I met [Holmes] again, he was in perfect health, despite the long and tiring journey. He had also become familiar with a few Japanese words, courtesy of Hamada-san. He had expressed interest in learning judo and asked Hamada-san for a *koto* to play. He has certainly been a most perfect guest with a very flattering interest in our country and its culture.

[Holmes], Hamada-san, and I went to meet the director of Intelligence Research, Shigeo Oshima, as planned. In response to his questions, I had told [Holmes] that Oshima-san was a quiet, intense man with extraordinary intelligence who had a reputation for directness in thought and action. He is liberal in attitude and has an admirable ability to size up a person within a minute, following world events and the underworld with great interest. He has not stepped outside Japan for many years and is no longer permitted to do so due to his sensitive position, but he speaks many languages fluently and is a voracious reader.

[Holmes] enquired after Oshima-san's work habits. I informed him that each day, he reads the dispatches of his agents from all the major capitals of the world and spends an hour in quiet thought during which he is not to be disturbed. At the end of that period, he dictates memorandums nonstop for three hours using the information he has assimilated in his precise memory. Naturally, he is well connected in the underworld and knows the value of liaising with criminal elements. He has an uncanny ability to connect two apparently disconnected events in two parts of the world at two different times and arrive at a conclusion. His judgment is considered to be exceptional; he is even summoned by the Imperial Court of Emperor Meiji to help decipher baffling situations. He is also an avid student of world history.

Given what I had learned about our guest, the two were likely to understand each other immediately.

We reached Adachi-ku in Tokyo and walked to a bland building from where Oshima-san operated. There was an immediate feeling of tension that we experienced as we entered the doors and passed by multiple physical security layers. Oshima-san knew too much and his life was possibly even more valuable than the emperor's.

Hamada-san remained outside while [Holmes] and I went into Oshima-san's private office with his secretary, Suzuki-san, who had worked with Oshima-san for over twenty years.

The office was full of things that were important to Oshima-san. On the walls were beautiful paintings from the Edo era. At various corners there were delicate Ikebana arrangements and even a very small statue of the Buddha. At one corner was—quite incongruously—a *koto*, implying that Oshima-san is a musician (indeed he is; his father was quite a well-known artiste in his time). I observed [Holmes] take in the scene, quietly and methodically.

He also took in the small slight man, about fifty-five years old, with a pencil moustache and wearing a business suit, who stood up from his chair, walked around his neat and precise desk, and bowed first to [Holmes] and then to me.

'Welcome to Japan, [Mr. Holmes]. This is a great honour for me. I have looked forward to the day when I would meet you. I never imagined you would one day be in my office under such circumstances. Alas, due to my responsibilities, I am not permitted to leave Japan, else I would have certainly visited you in London to pay my respects.'

'You are too kind,' murmured [Holmes] and bowed in return. '*Ohayo Gozaimasu*, Oshima-san,' he said, in unaccented Japanese, establishing an immediate rapport.

'Sugiyama-san, we meet again and I am, as usual, delighted. I envy your posting. Switzerland!'

We bowed formally to each other and seated ourselves around Oshima-san's desk.

An attendant entered deferentially and poured out some Japanese tea (referred to as '*O-Cha*') and served all of us. He left discreetly.

'[Mr. Holmes], I understand from Sugiyama-san's reports that you have had an eventful past few weeks. We are pleased that you are safe and in our care. Hamada-san is my best agent and will look after your every need.'

'I thank you for the courtesies extended to me. Your distinguished ambassador has taken considerable trouble in personally escorting me all the way from Berne. I am anxious to be of assistance to you while working out the next steps for the detention or containment of [Professor Moriarty] and his syndicate.'

'There is a possibility that both objectives can be met at the same time.'

'That would be ideal, of course,' said [Holmes], accepting the offer of a cigarette from Oshima-san, as did I. 'Please tell me what you wish to and how you believe I can be of assistance.' He settled back in the high chair to listen.

We have now begun the execution of Operation Kobe55.

HS

Shigeo Oshima

It may be that you do not notice the first snowflakes on the trees of your village in Hokkaido. You kicked a stone as you walked on that familiar path. The winds whisper about you to him. Your secrets are already his. He listens. And waits.

A note: *I have assembled the following narrative based on interviews with a number of individuals, including Sherlock Holmes and some Japanese government officials, whose names must be kept confidential. This pertains to the commencement of Operation Kobe55, by far one of the most sensitive and secret overseas counter-intelligence operations ever undertaken by the Secret Service of the Imperial Kingdom of Japan. I confess to have rarely been confronted with a more complex assembly of players. I hope my narrative is found to be accurate; any errors can be ascribed to faulty memories or even the incorrect interpretation of notes.*

The reader can be forgiven if he has not heard of the Yakuza. In London, we are truly not as well informed as we would like to believe we are and do not fully appreciate the menace of global crime. Scotland Yard excels in crime detection, but in the matter of close liaison with and prevention of illegality elsewhere in the world—with the exception of certain European police forces and, of course, the colonies—not a great deal can be confidently asserted.

Yet, as Holmes often remarked, crime thrives where man exists, and the methods and motives of the criminal class across the world are not altogether different. It is axiomatic that the same contrivances that afford conveniences to us are likely to be used by the criminal class to further their nefarious ends. Whether the telegraph, the principles of the locomotive or the use of chemicals—the master criminal is as likely to find a powerful destructive use where the benign social scientist sees benefits. We have not yet reached a stage in the advancement of mankind where information is quickly available and an international police organization of some kind could maintain records of the activities of individuals of the criminal class around the world in a systematic, orderly manner, much as you might find in Holmes' index cards.

Even Holmes had no real idea about the Yakuza before he was spirited away to Japan. Apart from the fact that he was aware of the Japanese martial art of judo, he had limited knowledge of the country and therefore, by extension, of the nature of local crime. In simple terms, the Yakuza of Japan are roughly the equivalent of the American Mafia.

Going back to the seventeenth century, a certain group of the ceremonial warrior clans, the Samurai, previously entrusted with the job of public security, moved into crime and banditry. The group evolved with the passage of time and developed their own nuances and peculiarities. Now the group takes pride in being at the fringes of society. There are three groups within the Yakuza: the *tekiya* (dubious street merchants), *bakuto* (gamblers), and *gurentai* (violent criminals). As part of a vast world-spanning web, the financial management and operational agility of the Yakuza are like any other large business conglomerate. It has its own code of conduct and system of justice, as it were. The head of the syndicate is called *kumicho;* at the time of our adventures, Shinobu Tsukasa from the island of Kyushu had just become the *kumicho* of a large clan, the Sumiyoshi-kai. Two very large Yakuza clans—the Sumiyoshi-kai and the Inagawa-kai—were in a state of uneasy equilibrium. Territorial claims to various kinds of illegal activities were usually the cause for tension.

The very word 'Yakuza' reflects rejection or loss. Holmes told me that *ya* means eight, *ku* means nine, and *sa* means three. The numbers add up to twenty, which is a losing hand in the Japanese card game *hana-fuda*. There is probably a fair amount of dramatic myth-making and exaggeration, but presumably those striving for a career in crime found it advantageous to be affiliated with the Yakuza as it afforded them visible symbols of power and influence.

Like any other brotherhood—the Freemasons, the Skoptsi, the Illuminati, and the Rosicrucians, for example—it is the sense of belonging that is vitally important, a feeling that the group is somehow privy to something unique and different and has some kind of advantage that others do not possess, perhaps an insight into the future that they have been chosen to receive. This leads to a single-minded fanaticism, which others find impossible to understand.

Loyalty to the Yakuza is a cornerstone of membership. Indeed, the most visible physical sign of affiliation to the Yakuza is the missing digit, which is seen as a sign of atonement. The digit is severed at a ceremony called the *ubitsume*. It renders, so the notion goes, the individual weaker and creates an even more fanatical loyalty to the clan. And complex body tattoos are also common, though I do recall Holmes finding it strange that a member would advertise his antecedents so openly. 'A kind of *braggadocio*,' he once remarked. Nevertheless, such is the case.

Indeed, Holmes found it quite curious that the Yakuza operated openly in Japan and even had some amount of formal recognition. This dissonance was perplexing, but again, it was a matter peculiar to the culture that had to be accepted.

This digression is pertinent to subsequent events. In perusing my notes, I see that Oshima-san patiently created the context for Holmes. 'No detail,' remarked Holmes, 'is too small. As I have often commented, we see but we do not observe. The superficialities of the routine dull the untrained mind even more and leave it unable to comprehend or detect anything out of the ordinary. But first, Watson, one has to collect and organize data. Then must begin the process of creating a plan of action. I appreciate the thorough mind of Mr. Oshima.[2] There is an unstated understanding between us; he resembles my brother Mycroft in certain aspects, though not physically, obviously. The

---

[2] Holmes never referred to the director as 'Oshima-san'

same high intelligence marked by a large cranium, the ability to merely sit and think and process information, the ability to ask the right questions and come to conclusions that are invariably right. Mr. Oshima is also not a man of action, but that is not necessary at all, as other organizations exist to enquire and act on his behalf. His office and desk told me a lot about the man. We differ only in the appreciation for nature, but we both have an affinity for music.'

Oshima-san summarized the situation in a few telling words after he gave Holmes a brief understanding of the Yakuza.

'Mr. Holmes,' he said, leaning forward in his chair, 'there is a very real possibility of a disturbance in the world order. In our country there exists a rather complex organization called the Yakuza. They are criminal elements and are not above anything in regard to criminal activities. Gambling, prostitution, extortion, kidnapping—these are their chosen fields of interest.'

Oshima-san then spoke about the history of the Yakuza and elaborated upon some interesting aspects, in the manner described earlier.

'Mr. Holmes, every country and civilization possesses a certain class of people who prefer to operate at the fringes and have a different view on economic ethics. Even in your remarkable country, the tales of Robin Hood have come down the ages, I am told. Who was he? If you asked a policeman, he would vigorously say, "Why, nothing but an ordinary bandit!" Yet he is deified for somehow challenging the established order and acting in the interests of the poor and deprived.

'There are such stories in Japan too—we have a legendary figure called Ishikawa Goemon, going back some four hundred years, who was supposed to have been a bandit who stole from the rich and gave to the poor and achieved fame and notoriety. For his troubles, he was boiled alive—some say with his infant son. Yes, very disturbing. But his legend lives on and can never be erased. Naturally, with time, facts get distorted and embellished. You find such tales in all countries. This is fascinating and quite thrilling to the common man, who possibly lives in a state of perpetual resentment that his lot never really improves because his destiny is controlled by those in power, creating a sullen dislike for the visible instruments of authority—in our case, the police. Therefore, anyone seen as scoffing impudently at them or fooling them in some manner is likely to be applauded, sometimes silently, at other times openly.

'The Yakuza thrive in such situations. The common citizen empathizes with their activities or is, at best, indifferent. For us, given how large and socially influential the Yakuza clans are, it is important to continuously monitor and observe them. It is futile for us to dream of destroying this organization and it is not often practical to wish to do so. Some extremely secret missions of the Japanese government have even used the Yakuza to obtain documents, to assassinate undesirables, or attain certain advantages in foreign policy.'

Holmes remarked, 'Unusual, but I can see the practical use of liaising with the criminal class. I do it myself, though not for violent objectives. But pray continue.' He closed his eyes again and placed the tips of his fingers together as he resumed listening.

'Of late, we have been concerned that two Yakuza clans have become extremely ambitious. You may not be aware, Mr. Holmes, that the Yakuza also have a connection to Korea, a country with which we have ancient cultural and social ties. Many Yakuza heads and their operatives have Korean blood and are referred to as *burakamin*. To that extent, it is understandable that their operations extend into the Korean peninsula.

'Now, however, we have reason to believe that the Yakuza have become active in China and have significant plans to expand into British India, the Arab world, and Europe. This is not mere petty crime, Mr. Holmes. The implications are so extraordinary that they can disrupt world commerce and the overall balance of power and make a mockery of concepts like "rule of law" and "nation states." They are not instruments of state power—we are talking about the Yakuza wishing to control the economy of the world. Have I made myself clear?'

'Yes. Do continue.'

'Our informants say that the Yakuza—both the Sumiyoshi-kai and the Inagawa-kai, but not, interestingly, the largest, the Yumiguchi-gumi, perhaps because it was considered simply too big—have been hired by a Chinese drug syndicate based in Shanghai to set up their operations in Europe. The syndicate, called the Green Gang Triad, deals in opium.

'You have, I imagine, some awareness of the two Opium Wars fought between your country and China. The creation of Hong Kong was the result of the first war. Now, in 1891, the British continue to trade in opium through the East India Company. The consumption of opium in China resulted in the deaths of many Chinese and an overall weakening of the authority of the Chinese emperor. The fact is that the Chinese now control the opium trade from Shanghai, even though opium is actually pro-duced in India. There is no possible way to stop the movement of raw opium from India to China because of the numerous land routes. The sea routes are a different matter, though even there, we face limitations.

'But as far as the syndicate is concerned, the real market is Europe. There is even a theory that the Chinese hope to inflict the same body blows to Europe as they were dealt in China by the British. By this I mean that Chinese nationalists hold the Europeans responsible for the weakening of the Chinese state by the introduction of opium as first a means of payment for tea imports and then to harm the citizens through the escalating consumption of an addictive narcotic. There was a time, not too long ago, when there was one opium den for about seventy citizens; China was devastated and this has not been forgotten. With the Qing Emperor presently worried about the Russian war threats in the region of Shenyang, the time is perfect for the Shanghai syndicates to make their moves.

'By exporting opium into Europe, the Shanghai syndicate controlled by Tsong Wang, called the king of opium, believes that a peculiar form of revenge can be extracted. There will be economic dominance and the final seal of cultural superiority will be stamped, so they believe.'

'I am not sure I understand.'

'Have you been to an opium house, Mr. Holmes? It is a grim sight. The dregs of humanity spend hours together in a daze, smoking opium and creating a make-believe perfect world into which they escape. There is an awareness of its medicinal use, but as a narcotic that puts you into a poisonous daze for hours and days together—well, you may have to see it to believe it. Addiction happens quickly and then life becomes quite pointless without it. Addicts no longer work, and to keep their habit going, resort to crime.

'Imagine then, that opium usage spreads in Europe. Imagine opium dens in Berne, Prague, Lyons, Warsaw—slowly but surely, the economy would be crippled, as daring and reckless young people start consuming something novel, supposedly innocuous and interesting. Crime would escalate, too. All of this is fertile ground for both the syndicates and our own Yakuza. Outlandish? Fanciful to the extreme? I would neither agree nor disagree with you whatever your response might be, but let it be said that in my analysis of various kinds of crime and underground mass movements over the past decades, I have noticed that people are motivated by bizarre ideologies and visions and will make complex plans to achieve them.'

'I occasionally consume a drug called cocaine,' observed Holmes thoughtfully. 'It helps me think very clearly. I do not know very much about the effects of opium, but doubtless you are right.'

'I know nothing about cocaine, Mr. Holmes, but in my limited wisdom, I would say that the consumption of anything unnatural would produce short-term gains but long-term detriment. No doubt you have thought of that aspect. Users of opium are known to say the same thing—that they feel happy and think clearly, but over a period of time, the situation becomes irretrievable for an average person. We are both presumably of a scientific temperament and know that a man under the influence of a drug for prolonged periods is no longer a productive member of society.

'To some extent, this is conjecture and will have to be verified. But my sources are fairly certain that this is the direction the syndicate wishes to take. For this, they need two essential ingredients.

'First, contacts with extensive networks in Europe. A criminal syndicate that moves men and material silently without calling attention to itself is a must. The syndicate in Shanghai does not possess either the expertise or the ability to develop such contacts. Obviously, the matter must be absolutely secret and driven through a channel that no one will ever be suspicious of.

'Second, a certain ruthlessness is needed to actually run the business. A local network with a reputation for enforcing a code of conduct, to create accounting processes and move money efficiently between countries and then continents.'

Oshima-san looked steadily at Sugiyama-san.

'Mr. Holmes, your benefactor here, Sugiyama-san, was once head of Japanese counterintelligence. He was made ambassador to Switzerland for many reasons. He speaks German, French, and English fluently and has spent many years in Europe. Switzerland is, of course, quite famous for its unique banks and we know that the Yakuza maintains accounts there to fund its growing operations in Europe. So his presence there is useful.

'But most importantly, the fact is that we believe the Yakuza has infiltrated the Japanese Diplomatic Service and influenced the same of other countries. Sugiyama-san is presently our most important and trusted representative there. But in a general sense, we do not have a security clearance anymore for any of our diplomats and related staff. Are they who they say they are? Do they work for us or the Yakuza?'

'Yes,' replied Holmes. 'I have no doubt that someone from the Japanese Embassy in Moscow tried to assassinate us on the train. Your theory is eminently tenable.'

'I did see a note from Sugiyama-san on that matter. I believe you are right. However, we cannot react spontaneously and in any obvious way, or these operatives will know they are under suspicion. My belief is that Japanese diplomatic pouches are being used for communication between Yakuza members here—possibly even in the Foreign Ministry—and their operatives at our Embassies. You know that diplomatic packages are considered inviolable by general reciprocal agreement between nations. They are the property of particular countries and may not be examined by the Customs at ports of entry. Clearly, they are intended for legitimate diplomatic materials and not for smuggling opium, or anything else, for that matter.

'In addition, we think it is possible that some of our Embassies provide documentation and various kinds of support for illegal activities, including the import of drugs from Japan under the guise of innocuous merchandise. If this is proved true, it would be, of course, a matter of great shame and the national humiliation would be intolerable.'

'I can certainly imagine the consequences. But what of your second point?'

'Ah, yes. I spoke of the obvious need to have an alliance with an invisible criminal network in Europe. The Yakuza stand out in many ways in Europe, where tattoos are uncommon. The language is alien, as are the physical features of the members. A typical Yakuza member would be unable to operate effectively and will need a local alliance. So a European network is a must. And—'

'Professor Moriarty!'

'Precisely, Mr. Holmes, precisely! There is only one man with the extreme intelligence, resources, ruthlessness, courage, and direct control of multiple networks whom the Yakuza can work with. You will recall the case of the Japanese tourist found dead in the Paris catacombs that your colleague Monsieur Dubugue[3] of the Sûreté was unable to solve. The murder was reported as if it were the result of a random attack by ruffians. The victim was, in fact, a policeman deputed by us at a very early stage when we started becoming suspicious several months ago. We believe he was assassinated before he could close in on the name of the Japanese diplomat who was in touch with Professor Moriarty.'

---

[3] Readers may refer to *The Naval Treaty* for an introduction to Monsieur Dubugue.

'Dubugue did mention this peculiar case to me, and I, in turn, discussed this with my brother Mycroft,' observed Holmes. 'He too concluded that there was an aspect of the diplomatic world at play here. But we did not take the matter forward as we did not have enough facts and Dubugue was unable to meet us in person.'

'Imagine now, Mr. Holmes, the repercussions of such a situation unfolding. Our problems with the Americans and the British will go out of control if it were discovered that the Japanese Diplomatic Service was working with the Japanese Yakuza, the Shanghai Green Gang Triad opium syndicate and the most feared criminal gang in Europe. If we do not act, and if the strategy of the syndicate works, the control of a weakened Europe's economy could pass into the hands of Professor Moriarty. The Yakuza could quite easily take over Japan, additionally taking advantage of the current restless political climate in the country, about which you will be briefed very soon.

'There are other scenarios that can be imagined, such as a World War involving several countries across continents if cultural or economic sensibilities are affected beyond tolerance. Such eventualities are unacceptable. But nothing is specious or far-fetched. In our office, we rule out nothing. Every possible scenario and possibility is given respect and considered. It is a never-ending exercise. That is my job.'

'Your description is thorough. Certainly, an eviscerated Europe with its productive workforce in opium dens is an unthinkable eventuality. Indeed, I now recall reading an article recently about a Dutch movement to legalize the consumption of drugs in small amounts.'

'Yes, Mr. Holmes. I am aware of that. It is almost certainly a trial balloon from Professor Moriarty's organization on behalf of the Yakuza to gauge public opinion and perhaps gradually and subtly influence it in a suitable way. What is the harm, some reason, in consuming a drug that has been extant for thousands of years and is used in laudanum to control excited individuals or in morphine to relieve pain? Such a drug, they argue, should be legalized and taxed, failing which, a disreputable underground may address the same needs. The argument is cloaked in excellent logic, but does not reveal the serious economic and public health issues that may develop. If Holland is won, then this distorted way of thinking will definitely spread.'

There was silence as an attendant came in and served more *O-cha* and departed again.

'This is the time for action, Mr. Holmes. I myself can only strategize and pave the way for action. But it is rare individuals like you who have the ability to execute utterly audacious and dangerous counterintelligence plans.

'We conceived Operation Kobe55 about a year ago. There is no specific reason for choosing that code name. The objective of Operation Kobe55 is very simple—cripple the Yakuza by identifying the traitors in our Diplomatic Service in Europe. Once they are exposed, the Shanghai syndicate will be set back. Professor Moriarty will continue to remain Europe's problem instead of becoming ours as well. This is our hope.

'The mechanics are more difficult—to infiltrate our own Diplomatic Service, identify the funding conduits and grab the plans of the syndicate before they can be operationalized. If diplomats can be compromised, politicians certainly can. By my estimate, we are some two years away from seeing a complete economic and political takeover of Europe by the Shanghai Triad, facilitated fully by our Yakuza and your Professor Moriarty. Funding is in place—which is why Sugiyama-san was posted to Berne. What was missing was that one person who could make the operation successful. Fortune has smiled on us in a most unexpected way. We believe that that person is you, Mr. Holmes.'

Holmes had not stirred during this discourse. His eyes were closed and he was listening with rapt attention.

'There is no question of hesitation. I must do this. What, specifically, are your plans? How will you support me? How many people know about this?' he finally asked.

'I am touched by your ready acquiescence, Mr. Holmes,' said Oshima-san after a moment's silence. 'Thank you. As of this instant, you are in the innermost circle of the Japanese government. Operation Kobe55 is now launched. There is an implicit assumption of utter secrecy and I will not insult you by asking you to take an oath.

'Including you, Mr. Holmes, there are only ten other persons who know about Operation Kobe55. Please read this list, which I will destroy after you have memorized the names.'

He handed over a sheet of paper with a list of names written in English.

1. The Emperor
2. Shigeo Oshima, Director of Intelligence Research
3. Hiroshi Sugiyama, Ambassador of Japan to Switzerland
4. Akira Otawa, Minister of Internal Affairs
5. Isamu Nishikawa, Minister of Finance
6. Yoshio Yoshida, Minister of Foreign Affairs
7. Hajime Sasaki, Chief of Secret Police
8. Kazuo Takenaka, Ambassador of Japan to France
9. Seiichiro Kasama, Consul-General of Japan to China
10. Miss Masako Nohara, Confidential Secretary

Holmes studied the names carefully. Then with deliberation, he folded the sheet and handed it back to Oshima-san, who tore it up and kept it aside for later destruction.

'Your confidential secretary,' Holmes remarked. 'A woman?'

'Yes. Masako was herself an intelligence agent and is probably the most brilliant woman in Japan.'

As far as Holmes was concerned, the only woman worthy of admiration was Irene Adler.[4] But she was from a different time.

'These are people with position and power. Presumably patriotic and completely in the clear.'

'Quite so, Mr. Holmes. But like you, I trust no one. In this business one simply cannot afford to. These ten individuals know about the objectives of Operation Kobe55. But only Masako and I have a complete view. Interestingly, she is the one with the

---

[4]   The reader is advised to refer to *A Scandal in Bohemia* for further information concerning the charm and intelligence of Irene Adler.

contacts in the Sumiyoshi-kai Yakuza clan and was responsible for unearthing the plot. Others are aware of some aspects, but again, in this business, the less you know, the safer you are.

'All persons on this list are aware of the existence of the others. Nevertheless, each one has only as much information as is necessary for him to carry out his duties.

'Let us now have lunch. You may find Japanese cuisine a little different from what you are used to, but I am hopeful you will acquire an appreciation for it soon. I will then have Masako brief you about the plan and I will ask Sugiyama-san to absent himself. For his own safety, of course.'

Masako Nohara

 The world belongs to the brave, my friend, as you said so many times when we strolled in your favourite garden in Fukuoka. They behave like Samurai, even without wearing their armour.

A note: *This is the account of Masako Nohara, Confidential Secretary to Shigeo Oshima. I spoke to her on many occasions over a number of years and additionally reviewed several confidential documents given to me by the Japanese government to confirm certain facts. What you will now read has her approval as being an accurate summary of many interviews.*

Ameya-Okocho, the cramped and crowded market of Tokyo is an area where the Sumiyoshi-kai Yakuza clan operates with impunity.

There is nothing to suggest, Dr. Watson, that this place is in any way special. It is like any other market anywhere in Japan, if not in Asia. It is not clean and orderly. The merchants lack finesse and the quality of their goods cannot always be trusted. Their language is coarse and they seem content to conduct commerce year after year at the very same place, with no discernible change in their economic condition.

But for those who can see past the obvious, there cannot be a better cover for the Yakuza. Look a little more closely and you will see many tattoo shops and plenty of men coming and going. Their upper bodies are often bare and they display their rather complex colourful tattoos more openly than at any other market. And if you look even more closely—which you really cannot without being noticed as a curious outsider who has no business being there in the first place—you might observe that many men have a smaller little finger than normal. Why? Quite simple—most have a missing digit, the result of the *ubitsume* ceremony. It is the evidence they flaunt of being a fiercely loyal member of a Yakuza clan. Even as a child, I found the ceremony and the purpose lacking logic. But I was never talkative and knew when to keep my thoughts to myself. This has always helped. In Japan, as in most countries, the value of women is minimal and regard for their opinions is not high. I have always found that advantageous in getting my work done.

Members of the Yakuza are not warped people with low intelligence; on the contrary, many are extremely intelligent and even excel in mathematics, music, and the arts. But for many reasons—a deprived socio-economic background, exposure to crime at an early age, or the glamour of being different and controversial and thus being looked at with fascination—they have resolved to become part of a group that attracts censure from civil society.

You ask about me, Dr. Watson. As a young girl growing up in Nagoya, to the southwest of Tokyo, I quickly discovered that I had an excellent memory. Faces, colours, patterns, numbers—I could not forget even if I wished to. My parents had a small garments shop and we had a comfortable life, though we were not rich. I had a brother who was not interested in school and dropped out soon enough to help in the shop. My parents saw that I was gifted and encouraged me. I excelled in music, sports, calligraphy, science, and history. But I was also quiet and preferred my own company. And I did not find the experience of being a girl very interesting. And I did not like wearing elaborate kimonos. These feminine pursuits were annoying and distracting. I preferred reading and thinking. I was keenly aware of my high intelligence and did not believe in false modesty. My family was proud of me.

I was sent away to Tokyo after I graduated from high school and joined Tokyo University, where I earned degrees in Mathematics and Economics. I had absolutely no time for the normal interests of most girls; I was pretty, but then beauty is only the applied mathematics of nature and I could not be bothered with it. Any male student who approached me turned away hurriedly as my absolute disinterest in him became evident in a few seconds. It is a universal truth, Dr. Watson, that men do not like women who are smarter than them. There was simply no question of getting married, though my mother, like all mothers everywhere, wished me to consider the possibility. I asked them to present an ideal match—there were none and the matter closed by itself.

My brother, Kazuo, was affectionate and protective and did not mind staying behind while I, his younger and more brilliant sibling, made a name for myself. He was very proud of me and rescued me from some strange circumstances I found myself in from time to time, where the natural frailty of a woman created complications.

I joined the Intelligence Research Department of the Japanese government after university as a special recruit. There were four of us—I cannot tell you their names, of course. After spending a year with Oshima-san and learning the art of thinking all over again, I was sent to be trained as a field operative. My natural circumspection, extraordinary memory, and absolute self-confidence made me the ideal agent. Intelligence-gathering is not about being in the thick of murders, as you obviously know. Economic crimes and the assessment of foreign threats to Japan were of particular interest to me. I travelled extensively—to Singapore, the Philippines, Korea, Formosa, China, the United States, France, England, and Russia. These journeys were usually undertaken in the garb of some innocuous position—third secretary for economic affairs or press attaché, for instance. I met ministers, journalists, other diplomats—but through all this, I was busy collecting information and storing it away in my methodical mind. I would send my missives to Oshima-san from time to time; I had learned the art of giving him precisely what he wanted in the form he appreciated for fastest assimilation. We both knew that I was far more intelligent than he was, but he was a paternal figure and was proud to be my mentor. In turn, I respected his judgment and experience.

In Paris, Dr. Watson, I happened to meet a French detective from the Sûreté, named François le Villard, at a diplomatic event.

I was quite taken by his intelligence, and also by the fact that he was charmed by me and not intimidated. He took me to the Louvre and to the newly opened Eiffel Tower and was gracious in every way. At some point, he mentioned the name of Sherlock Holmes, an Englishman with a great facility for inference and detection. He gave me several instances of his remarkable ability to think in a different way and I was reminded of Oshima-san. I also heard about a Professor Moriarty, who appeared to head a vast shadowy world in such an intelligent way that no crime of any consequence could ever be traced back to him. And yet, every police department knew that only *he* could have been involved. Even the instruments of the crimes were unaware that they had merely been used. I mention all this to tell you, Dr. Watson, that I knew of your distinguished friend a long time ago.

In one of my dispatches from Paris, I recall mentioning that Professor Moriarty was likely to be a person of consequence for the Japanese Empire and we would do well to keep an active dossier on him. Oshima-san could not act on the matter as there was too little to go on, but he did instruct the Japanese Embassy to send him information on the man whenever they heard something. It is unlikely that any information was ever sent; the professor lived in the darkest of shadows and was not interested in publicity.

Oshima-san recalled me to Tokyo in early 1888. At that time, I was using the cover of second secretary for economic affairs stationed in Shanghai and had accumulated a lot of knowledge about the opium syndicates. The Green Gang Triad, headed by Tsong Wang, had attracted my attention and I had just submitted a document to Oshima-san tracing the flow of funds to and from the group. The trade was facilitated by Indians and Baghdadi Jews in Shanghai and Hong Kong, but the actual deals and the running of opium dens and resultant crimes were all controlled by Tsong Wang and his group. I believed it was a matter of time before Tsong Wang looked at the Japanese market and felt it necessary to mention this in a couple of dispatches.

On receiving the summons, I left for Yokohama and went to meet Oshima-san in Tokyo. A young woman of authority was a curiosity and I was aware I was breaking every cultural norm. However, I did not care and neither did Oshima-san. We had no time to waste on pleasantries as we knew the possible implications of a minute's delay. It may be that intelligence-gathering is ninety-nine percent assimilation and inference but when action is called for, it must be decisive and a second's procrastination cannot be countenanced.

'Masako, we have a sensitive project. You may need to use your brother for the task I have in mind.'

'Explain, Oshima-san.'

'I am of the opinion that we have not adequately understood the Yakuza. Yes, we have friends among them. We know what they are smuggling, who they are extorting from, and what kinds of petty crimes they may have contemplated and committed. But generally, we are in a state of acceptance about them. I have been concerned that we are complacent and do not know about their future plans to the extent we should. Your report from Shanghai made it clear that we need to do something quickly. When I heard that Watanabe of the Inagawa-kai and Kiyono of the Sumiyoshi-kai had both travelled to Shanghai within days of each other, I sensed that something was amiss. It is not often that the *saiko-komon,* who run day-to-day activities of two large Yakuza clans travel to the same destination at the same time. Neither of them has been active in China and has no particular business interest there. Then why?'

'Why was I not made aware of their travel? I could have made enquiries in Shanghai.'

'Intelligence reached me only after they returned to Japan over the past week. Regret is pointless. Let us now work out a means to uncover their plans.'

'Your suggestions?'

'You need to infiltrate the two clans somehow.'

'How must I prepare? I know little about the Yakuza as I have operated principally from outside Japan.'

'Honda-san in Section Six is a former Yakuza operative who worked in a much smaller and now-defunct clan, the Kyosei-kai.

He will brief you about the cultures of individual Yakuza groups. He is reliable, but do not at this time mention that you have a mission. After that, we must find a way to approach one of the clan leaders, seeking assistance for your brother's business.'

'Yes, Oshima-san.'

'And oh, Masako, try to look feminine. It will help on this mission.'

'Yes, Oshima-san.'

I bowed and left. Independence in action is a chief requirement in my position. There was no question of anyone helping me at any stage, as I am sure you will appreciate, Dr. Watson.

Honda-san of Section Six, a group of undercover field operatives who liaison with criminal elements, gave me an excellent briefing about the methods of the Yakuza. He maintained contacts with old friends, some of whom were actually Yakuza members, and facilitated dialogues with them when necessary. He was never considered a real threat by the Yakuza and managed to function quite well.

I convinced Kazuo through letters that he needed to be more ambitious and expand his business. He agreed, after some initial hesitation, and came to Tokyo to meet me. We went to Ameya-Okocho together one afternoon in August to become familiar with the place.

Kazuo walked around the market introducing himself as a cloth merchant from Nagoya looking to move to Tokyo to establish a small business and enquiring if there was anyone who could help him. I walked beside him, demure in a *yuzen* dyed kimono with a particular design characteristic of Kanto. I bowed and spoke little.

By and by, Kazuo became friendly with a shopkeeper who was really more interested in me and kept up the conversation so that he could talk to me as well. He agreed to introduce us to someone who could help us. He asked us to come the next morning. But not before he offered us tea and asked if I was married.

We reached his shop in the morning and found another individual there. He was about thirty-five, with thin hair and cold eyes. We were introduced to him as people seeking to establish a new business in Ameya-Okocho. This man was Kobayashi and he was a member of the Yakuza, a fact that he did not seek to hide. I noticed his missing digit, and the shadows of his tattoos were visible through his shirt.

'Why do you wish to move from Nagoya?' he asked Kazuo. I had prepared Kazuo.

'Business is not very good and I do not think I have sufficient contacts. An ambitious man must spend time in Tokyo, I feel.'

'I do have a shop available for rent.' He named a price that was quite high.

I spoke softly and demurely and fluttered my eyelashes. 'We are not well-off, Kobayashi-sama. Please reconsider. We shall be indebted to you.'

With alacrity, Kobayashi reconsidered and soon enough a deal was struck. I expressed my gratitude and bowed many times in the most feminine and servile way possible. Once again, the shopkeeper and Kobayashi, who had by now softened considerably, insisted that we have tea. We did.

I set up the shop for Kazuo and invited the shopkeeper and Kobayashi to the formal opening and served them tea in an elaborate, traditional manner. We burned incense and prayed together for the success of the business. I presented them both with the best cloth we had purchased as part of our initial stock. I think it was English tweed.

Kobayashi became a devoted follower and came often to see me. He came with stories of his exploits and incidents of petty crime, in which he was the mastermind and everyone else was taken in by his supposed brilliance and absurd bravery. I listened to him with wide-eyed wonder and exclaimed every now and then in admiration, all the while thinking that I had yet to encounter a greater fool.

Before he knew it, he was ready to introduce me to his boss, Uchiyama, who supposedly controlled the business in the area. A man likes to have a pretty woman by his side as a symbol of acquisition and power. He probably thought that his influence would increase.

And so it did, for within weeks, Uchiyama introduced me to his boss who then introduced me to his boss. Because I was attractive and behaved in a coquettish yet conservative manner, the men did not take liberties with me and treated me with deference.

I finally met Kiyono-san, the *saiko-komon* of the Sumiyoshi-kai at a party organized by Uchiyama.

I bowed gracefully to him.

'My brother and I are grateful to you for your kindness, Kiyono-san. Our business is doing well and Uchiyama-san and Kobayashi-san have been most gracious. We wish we could express our gratitude in some way.'

Flattery gets you far, Dr. Watson. Caressing a man's ego opens many doors.

And so it was only a matter of time before Kiyono-san became enamoured and started spending a lot of time with me. I was by his side during his *Oichu-Kabu* card sessions. People thought I was his mistress, but really, I was not. Kiyono-san liked me and enjoyed the elaborate manner in which I would praise his business acumen. From time to time, when he was in a talkative mood and spoke of a problem here or there, I would offer a gentle suggestion which he greatly appreciated and then put into practice. He started referring to me as his good luck charm. All this within three months, Dr. Watson!

One day, he called for a meeting of some of his lieutenants at a gambling house. He requested that I be in attendance and serve *sake*. I agreed.

I recognized Takada, Murakami, Kobayashi, Itoh, and Sasaki, his most loyal core team. I served *sake* continuously and made efforts to be inconspicuous. The men appreciated the near-invisible attention.

'The Europe project is now to begin,' Kiyono-san addressed his team, ignoring me completely. 'Our plans are in place. Shirahata-san has confirmed that our contacts in the Japanese Embassies have been activated. Money is being sent to them.

You must now make plans to move to Europe immediately. Expect to be there for at least a year, if not two. Takada—you must be stationed in Rome. Murakami—Paris, Itoh—Berlin, Kobayashi—Berne, and Sasaki in London. You know what your occupations are to be. Await further instructions there. I myself will be travelling to Paris to meet the professor to formalize arrangements. I will meet each of you individually in Europe to check on your progress.'

'How sure are we of the Chinese?' asked Takada.

'I am convinced and so is our *Oyabun*. Our expertise is not opium itself. We are to provide the Chinese with the safe channels they need for trade. We have signed an agreement with the Shanghai syndicate. We collect twenty percent of the sales value in Europe. That should be substantial. We have been given a million American dollars as a guarantee of good faith.'

Kiyono-san rolled out several maps and the team discussed various plans over the course of the night. They were interrupted by a couple of young men who had just completed an *ubitsume* ceremony. Their faces were ashen. They had wrapped their severed digits in a soft white cloth and, bowing low, presented their package to Itoh and Sasaki respectively. Both nodded indifferently and bowed very slightly in return, acknowledging receipt. Blood still dripped on the floor. It was not a pretty sight.

I thus slowly collected the strategic plans of the Sumiyoshi-kai Yakuza. I also gathered that the Inagawa-kai was doing precisely the same, for the simple reason of redundancy in operations. I reported all this to Oshima-san, who was both delighted by my efficiency and extremely alarmed by the news I had given him.

He then set up the process for Operation Kobe55, but what we lacked was a single force capable of converting our plan into action. That vacuum was filled by the entry of Sherlock Holmes.

My parents suddenly fell ill around this time (as I told Kiyono-san) and I had to leave Tokyo for a few months to be with them. I promised to be back. But of course, first I spent time with Oshima-san, working out the details of Operation Kobe55. Kazuo continued his business and did well enough in Tokyo.

Bombay

I do not like cities, my friend. The paths of friendly winds are disturbed by ugly buildings. The vapours of the evil thoughts of small people collect and abuse the heavens. If you must visit Tokyo or Yokohama, do so, by all means. But leave quickly, before your soul is shackled. Return to your village near Nagasaki and rest on the morning dew of the meadow.

From a distance, the city of Bombay did not look particularly attractive. The buildings seemed haphazard and decidedly ugly. I was at the doorstep of India, a land of history and incomprehensible, fascinating culture, of maharajahs and mystifying religious beliefs, of complex languages and unusual music. It had been so many years since I visited this vast country and yet it seemed somehow familiar.

The captain had met each of us and told us that the ship would halt for just one day at Bombay for repairs and to restock supplies and would leave promptly at two o'clock in the afternoon the next day. Rooms had been reserved for us at the stylish Watson's Hotel,[5] he said, and our personal effects could be taken there with us. He had to file a police report about the disappearance of David Joyce and also communicate with the ship owners in Liverpool by telegram. Dr. James Israel would stay behind to assist him in the unpleasant paperwork. He would also be occupied with some minor repairs to the ship's boilers, he said.

'Voyage not on schedule! Please return promptly,' Captain Groves pleaded, 'Or we may have no option but to leave you behind. But do enjoy the city. Good hotel! Excellent! Organized a tour of the city tomorrow morning! After which you will be brought straight here. And then we leave!'

At about ten o'clock in the morning we slowly moved into our berth in the harbour. A few gulls greeted our entry with loud squawks, skimming on the dark restless waters. On the dock, workers were busy preparing for the ship's arrival.

---

[5] The name is merely a curious coincidence.

The others seemed equally pleased to welcome landfall and breathe freely without the tension and suspicion that had cast a pall on the ship. The *North Star* was soon moored and secured and the gangplank laid out. The two Japanese trooped down first, followed by Colonel Burrowe, Miss Bryant, Mr. Shamsher Singh, and us. After the formalities at Customs, we stepped outside the port area. Coaches were waiting to transport us and our effects and, as planned, Holmes and I were together. Mr. Shamsher Singh, Miss Bryant, and Colonel Burrowe were in another coach and the Japanese in a third. The journey to the hotel was brief. We asked for a large suite and everyone repaired to their assigned rooms in short order. I followed Holmes blindly.

We were escorted to a first-floor suite and refreshed ourselves. I now prepared to learn as much as I could about Holmes' mysterious reappearance in the guise of Simon Fletcher. By agreement, we had not discussed anything yet. Walls have ears even on ships and the priority was not conversation but simply staying alive.

Someone knocked on the door. Holmes opened it to admit a waiter with a large tray full of exotic dishes with unusual fragrances. 'This is welcome to Watson's Hotel,' said the beaming young man, bowing repeatedly and then departing. I was in no mood to eat, still coming to terms with the fact that I was in the company of a man whose death I had been mourning for so long. I was surprised at myself: how could I not have guessed his identity on the *North Star* all these days?

And suddenly it seemed that that large hotel suite in Watson's Hotel was 221B Baker Street. Holmes had found a chair quite similar to the one he was used to and had already settled down with his pipe. The two years of sorely felt absence evaporated in an instant.

'These many months have been most trying, Watson,' said Holmes. 'I have seen a great deal of the world and encountered the most obtuse and base human behaviour. Sometimes I marvel that society even functions at a tolerable level where people can speak innocently of the advantages of a civilized existence. The rule of law is the exception, sadly, perhaps a vain, futile, and feeble attempt to resist the overwhelming current of impatient needs, jealousies, and consequent violence. Crime is endemic. Evil is forever bubbling everywhere. We are deluding ourselves when we think there is a frame of law that good citizens should have faith in and that shall guide individual destinies.'

I had rarely heard Sherlock Holmes speak in this bitter vein.

'Doubtless you are shaken and confused by my sudden appearance and wonder at my whereabouts. You have a right to feel that I have been less than honest with you, Watson, and I am sorry that I did not communicate with you, even though I felt like doing so several times. Only my brother Mycroft and our friend Lestrade from Scotland Yard knew I was alive, apart from a few others, whose names I shall tell you soon. As to how I travelled from Meiringen to Bombay—well, it is a long story but needs telling. I certainly would wish you to chronicle it for your amusement some time in the future. First, a brief summary and let us then take stock of the situation.'

Sherlock Holmes proceeded to tell me about his miraculous escape at Reichenbach Falls and about an extraordinary journey through Russia to Japan with a subsequent extended sojourn in Europe under an assumed identity (as an American importer of spirits, including Japanese *sake*, their rice wine) and the events that led to his being a passenger on the *North Star* (returning to Japan in possession of sensitive information with criminal gangs hot at his heels, hoping to head them off).

The story appeared so fantastic that I wondered sometimes if Holmes was entirely deranged. Secret agents, a criminal organization—no, not one, not two, but three! Operation Kobe55, Oshima, Nohara, Tsong Wang, opium dens, Shanghai, Yokohama, the Meiji Restoration, Professor Moriarty—the whole thing was bewildering in its complexity! But then, Holmes was never one to fantasize, being something of a machine, not concerned with anything but objective facts. The reader is directed to subsequent chapters in this book for the details.

'Let us now come to the recent events that are most germane. I am Simon Fletcher on this trip, presumably, but Professor

Moriarty, sitting in Paris, will sooner or later deduce my true identity. I would not be surprised if he already has, based on reports he must be receiving at regular intervals. Of this I am sure—the Japanese belong to the Yakuza and Miss Clara Bryant, far from being a fading, gentle lady travelling to Shanghai to tutor the Japanese consul's children, is someone else. I do deduce a connection and even a lie, but shall not discuss it now. Colonel Burrowe—now who do you think he is, Watson?'

'I could not say, Holmes. Why are you suspicious?'

'It is in the nature of my business to be suspicious, Watson. I am surprised that *you* are not! You will recall he introduced himself as being in the Royal Horse artillery regiment, but you never, to the best of my knowledge, had any discussion with him on the ship about his experience with them. I, on the other hand, asked him a few questions very casually. If he had genuinely been in the Royal Horse, he would have known about the activities of that regiment in the Napoleonic War, who General George Campbell was, where the garrison was stationed in England, and so on. He could not even recall the colours of the Royal Horse regiment, which are blue with gold and red trappings. He responded to my friendly questions fluently, but in every case he lied, not being aware that I am quite familiar with military trivia. In brief, he had failed to do his homework, the hallmark of an overconfident master criminal who concludes, quite incorrectly, that a certain breezy fluency in speech and attitude will always cover a lie. That he was a soldier is not in doubt. But he was clearly not who he claimed to be.'

'So who is he really?'

'A general is only as effective as his advisors, Watson. This man is Colonel Sebastian Moran, formerly of the First Bangalore Pioneers. Incidentally, the Pioneers are the engineers of an army and a Pioneer cannot pass off as an Artillery man to the trained eye. He was decorated in Afghanistan and saw action at the Battle of Charasiab and then at the Battle of Sherpur, with a subsequent claim to fame as a big-game hunter. He is Professor Moriarty's right-hand man, having taken up a life of crime after he retired from Her Majesty's Army. Painful, yes, but such things do happen. A criminal streak lies dormant and can be triggered for some unknown reason, as a man of medicine like you would certainly appreciate, Watson; such was the case here, and very quickly he became Professor Moriarty's aide, commissioned to execute the most audacious and sensitive of operations. You may recall the sensational theft of the Marquis of Kintyre's sapphire ring, the bold assassination of the secretary of the Duke of Roxburghe, or even the shocking kidnapping of the young son of the ambassador of Slovenia. It was he who was behind those outrageous incidents. Military precision, the complete absence of any trace—why, I would even admire such a man if what he committed or abetted were not the gravest of crimes! But I digress.

'This is a dangerous group, whose purpose in travelling together is to track me down before I reach Tokyo. I think they have one other purpose, but I am not yet sure; we shall know soon. Inspector David Joyce had been assigned by Lestrade to watch my back and to observe the other suspicious passengers on the *North Star*, especially the Japanese. I am sure Colonel Moran and the Japanese killed him. I believe they have been under the impression all this time, and possibly still are, that it is Shamsher Singh who is Sherlock Holmes and have been looking for ways to eliminate him. That may explain the event in Alexandria. That knife was intended for him, but the man is no fool. He sensed danger and saved your life too in the process. I know this because I followed the Japanese when they left the ship after you and saw one of them throw the knife. I then wrote the note to you, asking you to be alert. As to Hashimoto, I knew him as a secret agent stationed at the Japanese Embassy in London, returning home.

'Do you recall, Watson, the Japanese characters on the sheet of paper that he told you about? Let me remind you.'

Holmes wrote the numbers on a piece of paper.

ヤクザ

'The numbers are "893", the "signature" of the Yakuza, if you will.

I will explain later what that means, but believe me when I say that it is of immense significance. It was I who slipped that paper under Mr. Hashimoto's door, alerting him to the likely impending presence of the Yakuza on the ship. I was already aware that the two Japanese might join us at Marseilles, having been tipped off by Lestrade. Mr. Hashimoto could never have guessed it was me who had given him the warning, I imagine. When he finally died, he left behind a clue for whoever was able to understand—he wrote the same numbers on another sheet of paper with his own blood to declare that he was killed by the Yakuza.'

'This is hair-raising, Holmes!'

'I am being chased, Watson, because I have information that will break the back of a criminal conspiracy with very serious objectives. I had to leave because my identity was compromised. If I reach Japan and inform the authorities, certain individuals will be severely inconvenienced and they will not be pleased. In effect, we can expect to be intercepted between here and Japan at every turn. By my calculations, we must reach Tokyo and hand over the information by the tenth of August, which is the arrival date of the *North Star* into Yokohama. The *Obon* holiday starts thereafter and most of Japan will be away on vacation for extended periods. It would be a dangerous time for us and perhaps for others.

'Many things will become clear as we travel and when we finally reach Yokohama, Watson. *If* we reach Yokohama. And then on to Tokyo, where I must meet my friend Mr. Oshima and give him the information he needs immediately. I will keep that secret even from you because it is highly sensitive and your very life may be in danger if it is found that you know things you should not. I know you will not mind.'

'Certainly, Holmes. I respect your judgment.'

'Thank you, Watson. Coming back to our current vexing situation—'

'What about Mr. Shamsher Singh, Holmes?' I interjected. 'Is he what he says he is, do you think?'

'I think that is the case, Watson. One can never be absolutely sure, of course, but I believe he is indeed an aide to the maharajah of Patiala. His bearing, language, knowledge, authority—everything indicates a man of great substance and command. My only concern is that he should not lose his life simply because Colonel Moran suspects him of being me.'

'What next, then?'

'The answer is clear in my mind, Watson, and I invite your opinion. I believe we should give Colonel Moran, Clara Bryant, and the Japanese the slip in Bombay. We should not continue our voyage on a ship where we have no advantage except, possibly, our wits. It is one thing to be courageous but quite another to be foolhardy and in a weak, unguarded position. If events happen on a merchant ship out in the sea, hundreds of miles from the outposts of civilization, there is no recourse and no protection. Shamsher Singh's strong presence will be missing too—he plans to be at the hotel for the rest of the day and then travel by train to Delhi and beyond later in the evening, if my memory serves me right. That is, provided he is not assassinated in the meanwhile. We should drop off at the last moment, feigning sickness, and take the next ship to Yokohama—which I think would be in a matter of days. Till then I continue to be the dull, uninspiring, and anonymous banker, Simon Fletcher.'

'Your reasoning is always sound, Holmes.'

'Thank you, Watson. Let us refresh ourselves and partake of a light meal, if you are so inclined.'

I stood up and went across to the table where the hotel waiter had placed the food earlier.

Holmes stepped forward and restrained me. 'Not so fast, Watson. Trust no one.'

He carefully took a spoonful of the fragrant rice pilaf and stepped out to the balcony of the room where a large number of pigeons happened to be resting. He sprinkled the rice on the floor and we waited. A pigeon came forward boldly to try out the rice grains while the rest kept their distance. In a minute, the bird was in distress and as we watched, shocked, toppled over, quite dead.

Holmes and I looked at each other. There was nothing to be said.

We shooed the other birds away and cleaned up the poisoned rice, placing the dead bird carefully in a small box.

'Well,' shrugged Holmes. 'I am sorry for the unnecessary death of the bird. But this validates our apprehensions. Someone does not desire that we should live. At the very least, they would like to incapacitate us. Perhaps we can use this to our advantage; we shall see. Let us go down to the lobby.'

We walked down and were relieved to find Mr. Shamsher Singh sitting at a table, leafing through a newspaper, which he set aside as we walked up.

'Ah, gentlemen! Welcome! Do join me for lunch,' he said, beaming at us.

We accepted his invitation. In the distance, I could see the two Japanese eating at a table and Miss Bryant and Colonel Moran at another, bent and absorbed in a discussion. They had not seen us.

We enjoyed our spicy and appetizing meal. Mr. Singh told us that he was leaving Bombay for Delhi and then going on to Patiala in the evening. 'It has been a long time away from home, gentlemen. I do miss the food and lively culture of my people, as you must your own by now.'

'The English are not known to be gregarious and spontaneous, Mr. Singh,' remarked Holmes, with a thin smile.

We spoke at length about our strange voyage from Liverpool. He expressed anguish about the two deaths on the *North Star* and the strange murder of the Egyptian in Alexandria. 'We must always be on our guard. Who can say when we shall be attacked and for what reason? The atmosphere here in India is deceptive. You may imagine we are a peaceful people steeped in gentle mysticism, but nothing could be further from the truth. Violence is around every corner. Trust no one.

'I hope you have a pleasant trip to Japan, Mr. Fletcher and Dr. Watson. I have always wanted to visit that country. Perhaps on your return you will do me the honour of visiting me in Patiala. You will enjoy the experience thoroughly, I assure you.'

'What time is your train, Mr. Singh?' enquired Holmes.

'At six o'clock this evening. The hotel kindly procured the ticket for me this morning.'

'I should like to see you off, if you have no objection. It would also give me an opportunity to see the city.'

'If that does not inconvenience you, I shall be delighted to have your company.'

I was baffled by Holmes' expression of warmth. Why would he take the trouble to accompany a relative stranger to the railway station? But I was too tired to think and instead concentrated on the meal. Sherlock Holmes and Shamsher Singh spoke about various matters such as the Cawnpore question, Governor-General Lansdowne's recent pronouncements, the ongoing military campaign in the Frontier areas, the turbulence created by A.O. Hume and other political issues rife in British India. I wondered how Holmes always had a reservoir of information on just about anything. We were finally done and walked back to our rooms. It was only about two o'clock in the afternoon, but I decided to rest briefly on a bed that would not, for a change, rock.

I woke with a start and realized that my brief nap had extended for a good three hours. Holmes was not present. He had left a note on the table: *Will see Shamsher Singh off and return shortly.*

I opened the windows and looked outside at the city. The pigeons had quietened down but the streets were still busy. It was noisy, dirty, and quite enchanting. Horse-driven carriages, women walking about in bright *saris*, dogs lying about disinterestedly here and there, cows standing and chewing indifferently—it was so very different from London.

I busied myself with my accounts and wrote out a letter to my wife informing her of my arrival in India, avoiding the mention of the phoenix-like appearance of Sherlock Holmes. It would have disturbed her and I realized that Holmes' existence still needed to be cloaked.

I suddenly heard a very subdued scratching. I turned toward the door; the sound was certainly from that direction. I saw the handle being tried very gently in an attempt to push it open.

'Who is there?' I cried out.

The sound ceased immediately and I heard the patter of feet running in the corridor. I rushed to the door, opened it and stepped out. No one was to be seen. I examined the lock on the door—there was clear evidence of fresh scratches on the metal.

I locked the door from the outside and went downstairs to report the matter to the young manager, Charles Atwood. He was extremely embarrassed and apologetic and came up to the room himself with a couple of staff. They examined the door and concluded that an attempt to break in had indeed occurred. He apologized again. 'A thousand pardons, Dr. Watson. I am shocked, extremely shocked! First time such a thing has happened at Watson's Hotel! I intend to institute enquiries…' He assured me that a guard would be placed outside for the remainder of our stay. I stepped inside and locked the door again, quite disturbed, hoping Holmes would return soon.

Holmes returned at about seven o'clock, after having seen off Shamsher Singh.

'What of the man outside, Watson?' he asked as he entered and shut the door.

I told him about the incident.

'Well, we certainly are not wanted by persons unknown, though I imagine I know who the persons are,' he said. 'I should have given you my spare revolver, Watson. Nevertheless, there is little likelihood of a recurrence, with both of us here now.

'I saw Shamsher Singh off at the Victoria Terminus, Watson. We had a very interesting conversation. He is, as you would agree, a most well-informed person. And the maharajah has an unusual interest in cars and a passion for polo, apart from having a large harem.

'I am fairly sure we were followed from the hotel for a short while. Once the pursuer—whoever he was—saw us at a safe distance, he perhaps assumed the room was without an occupant and tried to open the door. Did he want to search the room, perhaps? Do we have anything of value here except my Stradivarius? Well, we shall never know.

'I got an opportunity to see the city and make certain enquiries. There is no question of it now. We must not board the *North Star* and we must take the next ship to Yokohama. But we need a plan—I believe I have one, but I must think a while longer. We have limited time.'

'We are to be on some kind of a tour of the city tomorrow, arranged by the hotel,' I reminded Holmes.

'Interesting. Now that gives me an idea. I feel that it is unlikely that an attempt will be made on us in Bombay. An attempt to delay us by engineering an upset stomach is one thing. But yet another murder is a different matter. If we come to harm, their own plans to travel to Yokohama would be in jeopardy and the captain would have the right to refuse them passage on definite grounds of suspicion and safety. In fact, I am quite sure he would. I went by the *North Star* just now to see how things were moving along with the repairs and saw him conferring with the police. He told me he had reported the matter in detail and had hired some guards to take along for the remainder of the trip. I hinted that you were unwell. He suggested—with some enthusiasm—that if you continued to be in the same condition, it might be advisable to break journey in Bombay and take the next available passenger ship. I think he prefers to travel without passengers now and would be quite content with only cargo!'

We closed that eventful day with a thorough look at our accounts and made several entries in our personal diaries. Holmes had thoughtfully brought dinner for us from what he referred to as an 'Irani restaurant.' He said, 'We can't risk dinner here, Watson.'

Atwood knocked on the door and insisted that we come down to the lobby for a special concert he had arranged. He was very sorry about the attempted break-in and trying to do everything possible to make up for it.

'A concert of Indian music and dance just for you, gentlemen, compliments of Watson's Hotel. I feel you will enjoy it thoroughly. And I shall have two guards stationed here, fear not!'

Holmes was never one to decline an invitation to listen to music. We acknowledged Atwood's gesture and went down to the lobby. A few other guests had assembled, though Colonel Burrowe, Miss Bryant, and the two Japanese men were absent.

A small number of Indian musicians came in and sat down on a raised platform. Then, for an hour or so, we listened to a gentleman sing in a most peculiar way, waving his arms in the air from time to time, while keeping pace with a percussion instrument called the *tabla*. Sometimes he roared, sometimes he whispered. He grimaced, frowned, laughed, wept, leaped up in the air, bent backwards and held his hand to his ear as though he could not stand his own singing.

'What is he doing?' I whispered to an Indian gentleman sitting next to me.

'He is a famous classical singer, Sir, and he is singing,' he responded with a wide smile, in a tone of great admiration, while the man in question roared in a blood-curdling manner.

I sat back, in some confusion; there appeared to be some dissonance, figuratively and literally.

There was another bowed instrument called the *sarangi* which was being played by an old man who seemed to have fallen asleep, hunched over it. The sound of the *sarangi* was shrill, hideous, and positively alarming, if not devilish. The gentleman tried in vain to follow the hysterical outbursts of the singer, but failed repeatedly.

A young man was enthusiastically striking the *tabla* with vigour and smiling repeatedly at us in the audience, hoping to elicit our appreciation. At one point the singer seemed to point at me menacingly and his voice rose to deafening heights, almost as a threat, only to be followed by some kind of cajoling whisper. The audience seemed very appreciative, but I was mystified and even a little apprehensive.

I could make nothing of the chaotic formulation of sounds and near-violent singing, but Holmes seemed to enjoy it immensely. There was no sheet music and yet the troupe seemed to carry on and on, with a particular sequence being some kind of a refrain. I found it a bit tiresome, while Holmes was spellbound. After the concert, he went up to the musicians and engaged them in conversation, asking about the instruments and the music. I was glad when we finally returned to our suite, where our guards were waiting for our return. I had developed a blinding headache.

Much later, I was told that the singer was famous for a musical form known in India as *thumri,* and the exposition was essentially romantic, an explanation I found bewildering.

The next day promised to be eventful. Holmes discussed his plan and I agreed that it seemed daring and viable.

The following morning, having packed very carefully, we went down to the lobby of the hotel and joined our fellow passengers in the dining hall. The two Japanese were at another table in deep conversation. Burrowe had not yet arrived. Clara Bryant was at her charming best, greeting us effusively and speaking of a shopping expedition she had been on the previous evening.

'A colourful city, Dr. Watson. Full of interesting sights and markets. I visited a place called Crawford Market and picked up quite a few antiques. A very fascinating country, don't you think?'

I appreciated the fact that she was so full of energy at her age and stage of life. 'It certainly seems so. You do enjoy your shopping, Miss Bryant! I remember our little adventure in Alexandria.'

'Oh yes!' she said, with a most attractive smile. 'But where have you been, Dr. Watson? I saw you at lunch yesterday, I thought.'

'A delicate constitution, Miss Bryant. Something I ate seems not to have agreed with me.'

'Oh dear!' She shook her head with genuine concern. 'That's India and the tropics, you know. You can never be too careful. I always carry some bicarbonate of soda with me—would you like some?' I noticed that she had the most expressive blue eyes.

'I have already had some, thank you. Still a bit woozy but I do need to recover and make sure I travel on the *North Star* this afternoon.'

'You are a brave man, Dr. Watson!'

Holmes spoke. 'That he certainly is. Did you know we had an attempted break-in at our suite last evening? Dr. Watson here had the presence of mind to thwart the attempts of the scoundrels. Didn't I warn you about the natives? Just can't trust them!'

'I'm shocked! But that's rather uncharitable, Mr. Fletcher. I think the people here are quite nice,' said Miss Bryant warmly. 'How do you know it was a native?'

Holmes shrugged. 'Who else could be so audacious? Mr. Singh warned us too, just before he left.'

'He left?' exclaimed Miss Bryant, surprise in her eyes. 'What a charming gentleman he was. I never had a chance to say good-bye.'

'Yes, he left yesterday for Delhi. Almost an Englishman, I thought. His language, his manners—quite elegant,' I remarked.

Burrowe joined us at the table and expressed happiness that we would be moving on in the afternoon. 'Can't wait to get to Penang and kick back in a hammock!' he said.

Conversation was desultory. We were to take a brief tour of the city before returning and departing for the dock. I grimaced occasionally and held my stomach and everyone looked at me sympathetically. I refused to eat much and sipped a little tea.

'Your name is very familiar, Dr. Watson,' said Miss Bryant suddenly. 'Why do I feel I have heard it before?'

'I could not say. But perhaps you have read my chronicles of the adventures of my late friend Sherlock Holmes.'

'Ah yes!' said Colonel Burrowe. 'He died some time ago, didn't he? A bad business in Switzerland, if I recall.'

'Quite so. We were close friends. A most astute and intelligent individual.'

'Was his body ever found?'

I shook my head. 'No. It is a most tragic situation.'

'Ah, I see the coaches are here. It is time for our little tour of Bombay. Will you be joining us, Dr. Watson?'

'I wouldn't miss it for the world,' I said, with a forced laugh.

We boarded the two coaches the hotel had arranged for us and were off. The two Japanese and Colonel Burrowe were in one and Holmes, Clara Bryant, and I were in the other.

We went to various points of interest—Juhu Beach, the Mumba Devi Hindoo Temple (just from the outside), the Haji Ali Mosque (again, from the outside), and many more. At Chowpatty Beach, a number of vendors suggested we partake of a local delicacy called *bhel puri*. Only Holmes and the Japanese were willing to take the risk (the process of preparation appearing unsanitary to the extreme) and were quite appreciative of its merits. Meanwhile, I continued groaning and clutching my stomach.

I finally declared, in a weak and feeble voice, that I would go back, rest for a short while, then head straight to the *North Star*. It was already about half past ten. The expedition was to take another hour, it appeared. Miss Bryant was dismayed that we were leaving for the hotel just when we had reached the fascinating Chor Bazaar (a place where thieves resold their ill-gotten acquisitions furtively at a modest profit and which, I was alarmed to discover, was a place where some of Queen Victoria's stolen violins had resurfaced—but I digress). Holmes was most solicitous and helped me climb back into the coach and we made our way back to the hotel. As the horses galloped away, he looked back for a second. Clara Bryant was speaking with the colonel, while the Japanese had disappeared into the market.

'Colonel Burrowe is no fool, Watson,' said Holmes, his face set and grim. 'He knows who I am. Having me around was comforting for him. In our absence, he will sense that there is some game afoot. Your histrionic abilities are quite remarkable, by the way. I must recommend your talent to the Shakespeare Theatre when we return to London!

'Now we rush to the hotel and take a coach to the *North Star*. Every second is of importance!'

We reached the hotel and brought our luggage down to the lobby. As we settled our accounts, we informed Atwood that we were leaving early for the *North Star*.

Atwood was anxious and solicitous. 'I hope your brief stay was pleasant, Mr. Fletcher. I am so sorry for the incident yesterday. Dr. Watson, are you sure you wouldn't like to be examined by a doctor? I can arrange for one immediately.'

'Thank you but I must decline. This voyage is a must, I'm afraid. I shall rest on board. Thank you again.'

We moved on and the coach reached Bombay port where we alighted. We tipped the coachman after our luggage had been offloaded and bade him good-bye. We busied ourselves in examining our effects, while Holmes covertly watched the coach's departure.

'The coachman is out of sight now,' said Holmes. 'We must act!'

He engaged a much humbler local contraption, a horse-drawn *tonga,* onto which we loaded our effects. Then we moved on quickly in a direction away from the port, with no chance of being intercepted.

A note: *Some years later, I ran into Atwood at the Reptile Gallery of the Natural History Museum in London. He had not changed much and was as ebullient as ever. He remembered me quite well, and recalled the way Holmes and I left for the port.*

He said that the other group returned shortly to Watson's Hotel after a tour of the city. As they alighted, they enquired about us.

He told them that we had insisted on departing for the ship for Dr. Watson preferred to rest on the ship. Miss Bryant asked him to check if the coachman had indeed dropped them off at the port. She seemed very pleased on hearing a confirmation. For some reason, Colonel Moran was not equally enthusiastic.

Atwood said to him that it was always a pleasure to see such camaraderie amongst passengers. He supposed such long voyages fostered friendships.

'Indeed,' replied Colonel Moran grimly, walking into the hotel.

'A queer bird, the Colonel, Dr. Watson,' said Atwood, returning to the present. 'I wonder what became of him.'

A Journey Through India

魂   *So old is that land, that soul of humanity, my friend, that we must ask the stones and the breeze if they know its age. Pray to the Buddha in Kyoto and he will tell you to travel to India and pray to him there as well. Shall we go?*

'Not a moment to lose, Watson!' shouted Sherlock Holmes, as we raced away from Bombay port. 'Check our luggage again, I beg of you. There is a train to Calcutta from the Victoria Terminus in forty minutes. I purchased the tickets last evening when I went to see off Shamsher Singh. We must leave before it is discovered we are not on the *North Star!*'

We had slipped away from our inquisitive and rather malevolent fellow passengers. I imagined that Moran would be chagrined by our deception and would suffer from a bout of apoplexy. 'But the man is clever, Watson. It is never a good idea to underestimate him or Professor Moriarty. Let us see what happens.'

Holmes was entirely undisturbed by the chaos, noise, and smell about us. As for me, India was overpowering even at that tense moment. The *tonga-wallah* found space in front where there was none. Dogs, cows, other *tongas,* the yelling of the rickshaw drivers, the endless shouting and click-clacking of vehicles, the extraordinary mass and swirl of humanity, the absolute unconcern of people as they crossed the narrow roads, seconds and inches away from certain death—it was overwhelming. I saw some holy men sitting right in the middle of a pavement ignoring the pedestrians who in turn went past them without complaint. Even though I had seen action in Afghanistan and was minimally acquainted with Karachi and Lahore, I had never really seen this side of life in India.

But during the mad dash to the Victoria Terminus, Holmes was the picture of equanimity. The violent shaking of the *tonga* left him unperturbed. He sat regally, his chin sunk in his chest, in a classic position of repose that signified he was thinking. He could as well have been sitting in a hansom cab in London or in his chair at 221B Baker Street. His acute mind was processing facts, finding solutions, eliminating worthless information, determining the best and most optimum course of action.

'Pray hold on to my Stradivarius firmly, my dear fellow,' he remarked over the babble of noise about us. 'It is a delicate whimsical instrument unused to such turbulence, heat, and humidity.'

'With my life, Holmes. Lead the way, I shall follow, violin in hand!' I shouted, almost thrown off the *tonga* as we briefly descended into an oversized pothole.

'Do you have any view of the classical music of India, Watson?' he suddenly asked just as the carriage passed over yet another large pothole with a sharp jolt and complete indifference to our well-being. 'I found the concert most enchanting.'

'I have no idea, Holmes,' I yelled, holding onto my hat and my sanity. 'I don't understand their music and followed nothing last night. All they seemed to do was shout!'

'An unfortunate conclusion, Watson. I have quite the contrary opinion,' said Holmes in a disapproving tone.

'An unusual country, Watson,' he continued, in his normal tone. 'The music is an acquired taste, but is quite enchanting. The Hindoos have mixed religion and melody and created a powerful concoction. I hope to research this matter and write a monograph once we conclude our journey and of course, to try their melodies on my violin soon. Then again, there is the little challenge of reaching Tokyo in one piece as quickly as possible.'

'Holmes!' I cried, exasperated. 'How can you think of monographs at a time like this?'

'There is no time, my dear Watson,' said Holmes in an even voice, unperturbed by the annoyed neighing of the horse as it passed by a cow emptying its bowels desultorily in the middle of the road, 'when I do not think of monographs. Knowledge must be captured and liberally distributed. That is my chosen means for the dissemination of whatever I glean from my experiences.'

The *tonga-wallah* was shouting at the top of his voice, demanding space. Other equally choleric individuals shouted back. I could barely hear myself. Next to me was a man considering the musical notions of the natives!

We reached the Victoria Terminus and while Holmes paid the fare for the *tonga*, I collected our effects and proceeded to the platform where our train, the *Bombay-Calcutta Mail*, was waiting to depart. The station was absolutely choked with humanity and the streets of Bombay looked deserted in comparison. We pushed and shoved our way through, ignoring the beggars who had seen us and hoped to benefit from our munificence. Holmes moved quickly, not perturbed in the slightest. In a few minutes, we found the first-class carriage and our coupé and settled down. Holmes shut the windows even though the weather was sultry. 'A precaution, Watson. Who knows who is watching us?'

In a few minutes, the train left the chaos of the station and settled into a slow but steady rhythm. Holmes opened the windows and we both looked out as the train moved through the colourful city of Bombay. We spent some time in silence, gathering our thoughts about the extraordinary events of the previous day.

'We may have given them the slip for now, Watson, but we should assume nothing and must continue to be on our guard,' said Holmes grimly, sitting back in his berth.

'I agree,' I said. 'It will not be long before they discover we never boarded the *North Star*.'

Holmes took out a map of India from his pocket and unfolded it. He pointed to Bombay with his pipe and traced the likely journey.

'Our train takes us to the rail junction of Itarsi, then Jubbulpore and onwards to the Central Provinces and the Mughal Sarai[6] junction near Benaras. From there we continue to Calcutta and assess our next steps. I am not yet clear if we are being followed but I shall leave nothing to chance. We should consider

---

[6] The words translate to 'Resting place for the Mughals.' The Mughals ruled India in the period immediately prior to the establishment of the British Empire.

a disguise at the next opportunity—we are far too visible and news of two Englishmen travelling in the hinterland is certain to cause comment.

'Yet, Watson, this brief interlude does give us some time to assess the facts and devise a stratagem. How do we reach Tokyo as soon as possible and meet Mr. Oshima and give him the information that is needed for him to act? Professor Moriarty is no fool; unless he has conclusive proof, he will not believe that we will board the next ship to Yokohama from Bombay. Therefore, I believe danger awaits us everywhere. His network certainly extends into India. He may intercept us, arrange unfortunate accidents, lure us into traps. Ah, a very sharp adversary indeed!'

He puffed at his pipe, his eyes far away. Some more time passed in silence.

I too sat back, thinking over the situation. The entire journey from Liverpool had been a continuous series of unexpected events. Mr. Singh, Miss Bryant, my murdered Japanese friend Hashimoto, the events in Alexandria and then Bombay. The inexplicable behaviour of the tattooed Japanese and the unexpected revelation of Miss Bryant's Japanese connection. I reflected philosophically. Nothing is as it seems. The yardsticks of conduct in one culture are vastly different from those in another. I see someone—but is he who he says he is? Can our eyes and other senses be trusted? Do we train ourselves to see what we would like to see? What are the various shades of grey in conduct, in relationships, and in the meanings and import of words? Why was I convinced that Shamsher Singh was Holmes when indeed he was not? Why was I unable to discern that Simon Fletcher was in fact Sherlock Holmes? What is the truth about anything? And so my thoughts meandered. I opened an old issue of the *Times of India* that I had picked up in Bombay and started reading it absently.

The train moved on, the click-clack of its passage a pleasant backdrop to my thoughts. After a half hour or so, Holmes spoke.

'Your wife is a brave and resourceful woman, Watson. She has the ability to look after herself.'

'Yes, yes, that she is, you are right…but how in the world did you know I was worried about my wife, Holmes? This is uncanny!' I was stupefied.

'If I tell you how I deduced this fact, you will say that it was absurdly simple, Watson.'

'Assuredly not, Holmes. You wound me!'

'We shall see. I saw you read the article in the *Times of India* that reported the death of Mr. Hashimoto on the *North Star*. Let me read it again for you.'

From our London Correspondent: Readers would recall our recent dispatch in regard to the mysterious murder of Mr. Kazushi Hashimoto, a Japanese businessman returning to Yokohama on the *North Star*. The singular circumstances relating to the discovery of the crime have already been detailed in these columns. Our correspondent has since learned that Dr. John Watson, the physician and erstwhile confidant of the late Sherlock Holmes, shared the cabin with Mr. Hashimoto and was reported to be quite shaken by the shocking incident that took place not twenty feet away when he was asleep in his bed. The investigation of the matter continues in Alexandria under the supervision of the redoubtable Inspector G. Lestrade from our Scotland Yard. Our sources tell us that the Japanese gentleman may actually have been a diplomat travelling under an assumed identity, though we do not have a confirmation of this point. Further, if true, we cannot advance any conjecture as to why such a stratagem might have been necessary. We shall endeavour to keep our readers informed of further developments in this regrettable case.

'This, Watson, obviously caused you alarm as you deduced that your wife would have possibly read the same news article. We are reading this several days after the report was dispatched from London. I saw you double check the date of the newspaper and then your eyes drifted to the ceiling as you calculated the number of days. Then you closed the newspaper—you had a worried look. You then looked at your pocket watch for quite some time. I am aware that your wife presented it to you and you attach great sentimental value to it. Then you closed your eyes for a short while and shook your head. I concluded that your thoughts were with her.'

'Absurdly simple, Holmes!'

'Precisely as I had foretold,' Holmes responded with a tight smile.

'I would recommend you post her a letter from the next station if you have time, merely to reassure her that you are well. Do not give details.'

The attendant, an old man, thin and tall, with rheumy eyes, came in to check on our well-being. He was rather obsequious, as is usually the manner with such employees. His name was Rahman Khan, he said in broken and heavily accented English.

'I help you. What you will have for dinner tonight, sahib? Vegetarian? Non-veg you want, Sahib?'

'Vegetarian, please,' said Holmes. I glanced at him in surprise.

Rahman Khan stepped out with much bowing, promising to return in half an hour after looking at his pocket watch. He bent down to pick up a piece of paper that had slipped to the floor and handed it over to Holmes. Then he left.

'Vegetarianism, Holmes? You surprise me! You always relished your beef, bacon, and eggs!'

'Watson, at a time of unplanned travel and danger, when you need your strength more than anything else, it is safest not to consume meat and chicken. You have yourself commented on the hygiene here.'

'True, Holmes. Tropical diseases and a debatable sense of cleanliness, especially in public, are things we must guard against.'

'Moreover, Watson, I have recently developed a new perspective on the concept of vegetarianism. I have concluded that given a choice, it is altogether more rational and ethical not to destroy animal life for personal consumption. Perhaps I have been influenced by my sojourn in Asia, or even more specifically by the spiritual observations of many Eastern religions that see no challenge in equating all forms of life, giving no advantage to humanity. However, I would not wish to debate this with you at this point. I have begun a personal journey. Let us see how far I progress.

'Be that as it may, you are aware of my view that eating little actually stimulates the brain and encourages thinking.'

'Quite so, Holmes.'

Rahman Khan returned with our dinner and laid out the cutlery and plates. There was some local bread, a yellowish *dal*—a kind of lentil soup—potatoes with spinach, a kind of spicy chutney, and some salad. It was appetizing fare.

'An interesting man, our friend here,' commented Holmes, while dining. 'Have you any view of him, Watson?'

'Other than that he is probably about sixty years old, none.'

'I can tell you more. This is a man who has seen better days, likes to rear pigeons, and was probably stabbed in his stomach in his youth.'

'Holmes! This is impossible!'

'Certainly, my dear Watson. I will not insist. But surely, there is no other explanation for why his shoes have almost worn out, but he still polishes them well, or that he not only possesses a pocket watch—which must be rare enough—but an Emery no less. It is not hard to see that he rears pigeons—you can see plenty of down on his uniform and I can smell on him the faint aroma peculiar to the bird.'

'Now that you mention it, it seems quite obvious. But being stabbed in the stomach?'

'Once violated, flesh never fully recovers its suppleness. You saw him bend down with some difficulty to pick up a sheet of paper. You could say it was age, but in fact he wanted to avoid straining his abdomen. His shirt rose as he bent and I caught a glimpse of a long scar.'

'I thought you would say something clever, Holmes, but this deduction seems very pedestrian.'

'Indeed? Then why did you not guess?'

'I am not too well, Holmes,' I replied, weakly.

'Of course, of course, Watson! Nourishment is necessary, after which your mental faculties would undoubtedly be in excellent condition.'

Holmes and I ate and felt much better after the chaos of the day.

At about this time, as the train passed through the interesting countryside and towns on its way from Bombay, I started feeling a sense of unease. I checked and found that I had developed a fever and found it advisable to lie down on the berth. Holmes was very concerned and insisted that I change into my pyjamas and rest.

Very soon, I broke into chills and began sweating profusely. There was no doubt—I was now quite likely very ill with malaria. I guessed that I must have contracted it in Alexandria. Thankfully, I had brought with me some Warburg's Tincture, which used to be standard Army issue during my time in Afghanistan. I had some idea about the ailment and how to tackle it, due to personal experience during the campaign there. And now, with the constantly changing climes, the Jezail bullet made its presence felt in my shoulder.

I passed the night restlessly. Holmes ministered to me generously, ensuring that the berth was comfortable and that I took regular doses of the tincture. Rahman Khan was extremely worried and brought boiled water and towels regularly.

'I call doctor next station, sahib, and he give you the medicines. You will be better soon, sahib!' He was quite agitated.

I reassured him that I was a physician myself and not unfamiliar with tropical diseases. Nevertheless, I was disappointed that I had fallen sick at such an inopportune time, when Holmes needed me.

'Would it not be wiser, Holmes, for you to proceed and for me to return to Bombay and then London? Your mission is too critical for me to hold you back.'

'On the contrary, Watson, I cannot complete this mission without your support. We have at least one complete day before we reach Itarsi. We shall decide then. But for now, not another word.'

The steam locomotive continued its journey into the night, belching smoke and whistling loudly. I fell into a restless slumber as the fever fought the tincture. Holmes smoked his pipe quietly in a corner, his thoughts in Paris, Bombay, and Japan.

Meanwhile, in Europe, Professor Moriarty stared at the telegram that had just been handed to him.

'Holmes and Watson disappeared without a trace at Bombay Port! They take their eyes off him for a minute and he's gone! First they said it was some Singh! Now they say he was that dull banker and they never guessed all along. Imbeciles!' He shook his fist in the general direction of Bombay.

He wrote out a long telegram to his assistant Colonel James Burrowe c/o the *North Star*, Singapore port, expressing his strong and considered opinion about the colonel's gross incompetence and asking him to return immediately to the European continent. Then he opened the railway map of India, the Indian Railway time table, and a map of Asia. He thought long and hard about what Sherlock Holmes might do and then he wrote out another telegram to a trusted associate in Bombay with detailed instructions on the steps he would need to take.

Bodh Gaya

敬 *When you accept you know nothing after years of study and experience, then begin the search for the teacher who knows more than you. The blanket of time slowly covers us with darkness, my friend. But the teacher in our heart fills us with light and we are not afraid.*

I woke the next morning after an exhausting night. The symptoms of malaria were now unmistakable. I was not yet in a delirium but would soon be. The fever came in regular gusts. My body was considerably weakened and I could barely sit up without Holmes and Khan to help me. Their patience and solicitude were remarkable and moving. I could not imagine how we would complete the five-day journey in this condition. I was determined not to burden Holmes in any way, but knew better than to press home the point at this stage.

The train pressed on, stopping at stations intermittently. The smoke from the locomotive did not make things easier, but certainly the countryside did provide respite. Nature has showered its bounty on this fascinating country; every hue of green, the most glorious vistas, colourful little villages and towns with charming temples representative of the inhabitants' faith. The scenes were therapeutic but just barely so. I knew I would probably need medical attention beyond my own ministrations. But I calculated that I would be able to carry on thus for at least the next two days.

Holmes swung between extreme solicitude for my condition and savage frustration at being unable to come up with a plan for how we could reach Tokyo as soon as possible. Neither of us knew a soul in India; to take the help of the authorities would be to reveal our identities, which was an impossibility. We simply had to travel incognito to our destination.

The Indians are a naturally curious people. They must enquire into every aspect of their fellow passengers' lives. No one takes offense at being asked about their family, their source of income and domestic challenges. A train journey in India, as I learned, was a great communal event, with stories, songs, and food being shared without a second thought. Though we were travelling in first-class, which afforded some privacy, it was not absolute and we received frequent visitors. The ticket collector, various attendants, and other passengers in our compartment—everyone wished to visit us and give suggestions and reassurance. But Holmes' commanding presence and the protective attitude of Rahman Khan ensured that we were not particularly bothered.

Holmes used this opportunity to fraternize with the passengers in the lower-class coaches whenever he had a chance to get off and on during the train's frequent stops. Rahman Khan had taught him a few words of Hindoostani and Holmes, being a quick and perceptive student, was able to speak a few broken sentences very soon. Moreover, with his usual foresight, Holmes had acquired John Gilchrist's *A Grammar of the Hindoostanee Language* and occupied himself whenever possible with thumbing through its pages and making notes, while ensuring he checked the usage and colloquial aspects of various words. He would disappear for brief periods and return to check on me whenever the train stopped at a station, which happened very frequently.

'There is no better way for us to become anonymous in a strange country than to appear to speak the language with confidence, Watson. I intend to ensure that our dependence on an interpreter is reduced as we traverse through India.

'In the adjacent coach, Watson, are several Hindoo *sadhoos*— religious mendicants—dressed in ochre robes that proclaim their religious intent. I was impressed by their minimalistic view of life and their emphasis on detachment and simplicity. They were most generous to me, sharing their perspectives on a wide variety of matters. From time to time, they broke out in religious chants, beating drums and cymbals. Somewhat noisy, but positively colourful.

'A curious people, the Indians,' he remarked at some point. 'At once hyperbolic, solicitous, taciturn, ignorant, philosophical, wise, creative, practical, indifferent, accepting, fatalistic—a very singular race. Our knowledge of India has been largely second-hand, from tales passed on by those who spent a few years here and had a sheltered existence. There is no substitute for actually interacting with the people, eating what they eat, trying to think like they do and never being patronizing. By and large, they are a people with unusual intelligence but strangely lacking in ambition and quite comfortable in their beliefs. If they sense they are being seen as curiosities, their behaviour changes to one of tolerance, masking contempt very well.'

'A very broad and liberal perspective, Holmes,' I mumbled, lying drenched in sweat on my berth.

'I had the occasion to listen to a young man sing a song in the next coach. I feel inclined to try it out on my violin, Watson, with your permission.'

'Of course, Holmes, it would be therapeutic, I am sure,' I said, my voice a mere hopeless whisper.

Holmes took out his violin and tuned it. Then he applied bow to strings and extracted an unusual melody. Not Chopin, not Paganini—something quite different and yet haunting and plaintive. I thought it spoke of the land and was perfect for the setting we were passing through—green hills, a blue sky with a sprinkling of cumulous clouds and a peculiar smell in the air that was so typical of this country. I do not believe I had heard such a strange and gentle tune before.

'Interesting, interesting…I see possibilities…yes…,' muttered Holmes, putting away the violin and bow in due course.

'My dear Watson,' mused Holmes, 'what is it about music that makes for systematic thinking? I have applied my mind to the matter. Music is merely very refined mathematics. A note by itself has no meaning unless seen in the context in which it appears. The distance between its predecessor and the next note, the extent of silence, the pitch, the volume, the cadence—now a note has much more to say. The human mind is imperfect. Mathematics and music are much more factual. Give me a musician, Watson, and I will show you a man who knows the value of details.'

Then he once again wiped my brow and ensured that I was comfortable before administering a dose of the tincture. He had an unusual bedside manner that was extremely reassuring.

A couple of days passed and we were soon in the Central Provinces and then Mughal Sarai, which was developing as an important railway zone. There would certainly have been a physician here who could have examined me. However, I felt fit enough to continue and did not wish to break the journey. We passed by the holy river of the Hindoos, the Ganges. By this time, Holmes had become quite knowledgeable about the river and the culture and had processed every little scrap of information he had absorbed. He kept me enthralled with stories about the religious and cultural practices of the people, the significance of the river, and the local food habits. He also picked up the accent, gait, affectations, and colloquialisms of the people and, with Rahman Khan's help, acquired some local clothing—a *kurta* and *dhoti*, as they were called—and learned how to wear them. But I could see that his mind was actually in Tokyo all the while.

Meanwhile, Rahman Khan confided that he had indeed belonged to a wealthy family which had fallen on bad times many years ago. A grim life full of debt and hardship had replaced one of extreme affluence. And sure enough, he enjoyed raising pigeons on the terrace of his home near the town of Patna. But Holmes' gentle query about his injury unsettled him; his pupils dilated with fear and he shrank back, almost dropping his tray. The wound was obviously still raw. Holmes did not press him—everyone, he said, had a past they did not discuss—and reassured him that we meant no harm.

At Mughal Sarai station, an incident occurred that convinced us that Holmes' fears were not baseless. Holmes was always cautious at large stations. He conjectured that Professor Moriarty would not have been entirely convinced that we had taken the next ship from Bombay. 'And if I thought of taking a train and crossing India to travel to Japan in an entirely different way, there is every likelihood that Professor Moriarty would have as well.'

As the locomotive whistled to announce its departure from Mughal Sarai and slowly eased itself out, we heard a commotion at the entrance to the station from a distance of some two hundred yards. We saw three civilians, who appeared to be Englishmen, rush onto the platform and look up and down at the departing train, shouting directions to each other. One of the men ran toward the first-class coach. In one fluid movement, Holmes, who had been smoking his pipe and looking out of the window in a desultory manner, was completely transformed. He sprang from his seat, pushed me down on the berth and quickly shut the windows, leaving a crack open to observe the movements of the men. Fortuitously, the train was moving too quickly by then for any of the men to board, but there was no doubt—Professor Moriarty was searching for us. We would have to be on our guard. Someone else would certainly be waiting for us at the next major station, Patna.

'Once again, Watson, we see the astonishing reach of Professor Moriarty. This is a game of chess, in a manner of speaking. He anticipates my move, I anticipate his. We were not seen, but he will not rule out anything unless *he* is sure. But my dear fellow, I do you an injustice. You are unwell and I must not cause you any alarm.'

Ignoring my protests, he resumed puffing his pipe as the train picked up speed. He took out the map of India and looked at it carefully. He then called in Rahman Khan and asked him a few questions in broken Hindoostani. Rahman Khan's responses elicited satisfied nods from Holmes, and I could see that he had thought of a possibility. He gave Rahman Khan some instructions and sent him away.

'How are you now, my good fellow?' he asked with gentle concern. On rare occasions such as this, my fine friend showed signs of being human.

'Holmes, another night or so and you will have me at your service.'

'Excellent, excellent! The ever-reliable Dr. John H. Watson! Our attendant is most trustworthy and resourceful and is on a

small mission on my directions. Sleep well tonight. Tomorrow
will bring danger.'

He then explained his plan in detail. I was amazed by the
sheer audacity of his thinking.

Professor Moriarty read the wire with mounting frustration:

SEARCH OF BOMBAY–CALCUTTA MAIL BEFORE
PATNA REVEALED NO SIGN OF HOLMES AND
WATSON. THE ATTENDANT SAID TWO EUROPEAN
MEN HAD ALIGHTED AT JUBBULPORE BUT NEI–
THER FIT THE DESCRIPTION. SEARCHED THE
ADJACENT COACH JUST TO BE SURE. HINDOO
SADHOOS IN OCHRE ROBES WERE SINGING RELI–
GIOUS HYMNS WITH THE PASSENGERS. NO EURO–
PEANS WERE SEEN. AWAITING INSTRUCTIONS.

'Holmes, you are clever, very clever. But I am not done yet,'
hissed the professor.

We had shifted to the adjacent compartment and when the
train arrived in Patna, we alighted with the sadhoos and merged
into their chaos. Rahman Khan had instructions to handle our
luggage separately. We boarded the slow train to Gaya, a town
due south of Patna, assisted by Khan, to whom we shall always
be indebted. I was now almost completely fit, though tired and
dehydrated to some extent. We sat in the fourth-class compartment with dozens of other passengers, all of whom were quite
deferential to two holy men travelling to a place of pilgrimage.
Holmes had already acquired a more than rudimentary grasp
of the local dialect and had completely dissolved into India in
his manner of speaking. He later made light of this superhu-
man effort, saying that the diction, lexicon, and grammar of
Hindoostani were entirely logical. His rectangular violin case
and our other luggage was camouflaged or hidden in other
ways. He took up the offer of smoking the local drug, *charas*, in

a smoking pipe called *chillum*, and convinced our co-passengers that I was dumb and unwell, thus sparing me the possibility of any interaction. He was entirely at home.

As far as I was concerned, his astonishing skill as a master of disguise was in evidence in the most profound way. The brown complexion, the long matted hair, the crushed and unwashed robes of the *sadhoos*, the local mannerisms—none in our circle of acquaintances would have ever believed that two upstanding men with rooms at 221B Baker Street and memberships in exclusive clubs in London might be seen in such garb, sitting on the floor of a filthy coach on the slow train from Patna to Gaya.

On the Bombay-Calcutta Mail, the resourceful Rahman Khan had obtained the ochre robes, sacred ash, and matted locks from his sources and, within a couple of hours, we had both been transformed. He understood that we were in danger and readily assisted us in moving our effects to the next coach, which happened to have several *sadhoos*. He even refused to accept any *baksheesh*, insisting that it was his duty.

We reached Bodh Gaya, a Buddhist pilgrimage destination associated with the enlightenment of the Buddha. Holmes felt it would be wise to rest here for a few days for two reasons: to shake off our pursuers and to allow me to regain my energy. We walked the distance to the temple complex, hoping to find acceptable lodgings. Only a few years prior to our arrival, Sir Alexander Cunningham had made a serious attempt to rescue this temple from utter ruin. I found it quite splendid.

The complex was full of Buddhist pilgrims from various countries. Most had shaved their heads and possessed oriental features. I gathered many were from Tibet, Burma, Siam, Ceylon, and China, where the faith had taken deep root. I myself was quite unfamiliar with the precepts of this religion.

As we passed two Buddhist monks, Holmes suddenly stiffened and gripped my wrist. 'Look, Watson, did you notice anything? One of the monks had a missing digit! What do you infer?'

I shook my head. 'I am sorry, Holmes. I do recall the two Japanese on the *North Star* had missing digits too, but what that means, I cannot say. At best, I infer from their faces that they are possibly Japanese.'

Holmes abruptly turned around and went back to the monks. I followed. He was attempting to converse with them in Hindoostani, enquiring if they knew of a place where we could stay the night. The monks were friendly and soon it became clear that they could speak English better than Hindoostani and I saw, with some surprise, Holmes laugh heartily, quite unlike the taciturn, sardonic detective I was so used to.

Holmes introduced us as *sadhoos* from Delhi. 'We have come to spend some time at the feet of Buddha,' he said in accented and broken English. 'Where we can stay?'

In equally broken English, but with a distinctly Japanese accent, one of the monks responded, 'Please share our small room. It is honour for us.'

They were delighted when Holmes spoke a few words of Japanese. I could not follow the conversation, which, subsequently became a bewildering mixture of English, Japanese, and broken Hindoostani.

One of the monks, who introduced himself as Hiroshi Ota, explained that they were Japanese monks who had arrived at Bodh Gaya a few days ago as part of a pilgrimage and had taken rooms close by. The other, older monk introduced himself as Akira Fujimoto. Both were from the ancient Kinkaku-ji temple of Kyoto, they said. Holmes accepted their offer of hospitality and, in short order, we accompanied the monks to their dwelling, a small but comfortable facility for pilgrims operated by a Buddhist religious group.

I asked Holmes to explain.

'Watson, it is a curious coincidence that we meet two Japanese monks in Bodh Gaya. What is even more curious is that one of them is almost definitely a former member of the Yakuza. I refer to Akira Fujimoto, the older monk. Observe his urbane and reserved manner. This is no ordinary person. His eyes are thoughtful and he speaks little, letting the younger monk handle matters. This is usually a sign of someone who has enjoyed authority in the past and is unused to executing actual tasks. I must get to know him better. We spend a week here, Watson. You must complete your convalescence and we must be ready to move on after. Today is the fifteenth, if I am not mistaken. I would like to be in Tokyo by the first or so. Let us make every attempt.'

Holmes was soon on very friendly terms with the two Japanese monks. He did not feel it prudent to reveal just then that he was familiar with Japan and knew a great deal about the Yakuza. But within a couple of days, Akira Fujimoto opened up to Holmes on his own and revealed that he was on a journey of transformation, almost literally. Hiroshi Ota and I became friendly as well and we strolled through the temple complex together. I spoke no Japanese or even Hindoostani, and he spoke no English, so we managed, very effectively, through extravagant gestures and smiles.

In the interests of brevity, I quote here from Holmes' notes:

Mr. Fujimoto and I became fast friends in short order. He was no fool. He guessed quickly that we were not really sadhoos but he had a gentle sense of humour and saw no harm in letting us keep our little secret; he was not curious and was quite at ease with himself and his past. He was not ambitious any longer and was on a spiritual quest of discovery. We warmed to each other and he also guessed that I had a greater interest in Japan than I was willing to reveal. I consider it an extraordinary quirk of destiny that I met Mr. Fujimoto in such circumstances. It puts my perspective of Operation Kobe55 in a different light, something that I had not considered entirely seriously till that point.

He was born on Kyushu Island, like many Yakuza members. His childhood had been ordinary and he had never really excelled in anything except mathematics. He could not get into a university and slowly drifted into crime. He said that he had once been part of a Yakuza clan, the Dojin-kai, and had almost become the *kumicho*. His career in the Yakuza was fairly prosaic; he had been a gang leader and then responsible for certain activities in Fukuoka City (he did not specify the activities and I did not feel it was germane to press him). He had had only one digit cut off in an *ubitsume* ceremony, which presumably implied that he had made few mistakes for which an apology was thought necessary. He managed the finances of his clan for many years and was also responsible for money laundering. As he aged, he was given the task of liaising with the Japanese government's Domestic Intelligence Department. This task was given only to the most diplomatic, suave, practical, and patient (and, I might add, intelligent).

What did such a role mean, I asked. It was simple yet very important, replied Mr. Fujimoto. Generally, it was necessary to keep the Domestic Intelligence Department in good humour. 'I would keep them informed of the general nature of our activities—what we were doing and where. As long as there was no subversion and there were no extreme social implications, the police would leave us alone.

'Occasionally, I had to intercede when someone senior was actually charged with a grave crime. Then I would organize the legal team, arrange for the bail money and attend to related matters. You could call me a troubleshooter. I myself was never involved in any serious chargeable crime, so my role was legal and useful.

'In exchange for looking the other way, we would also undertake missions on their behalf. For example, extremely covert operations overseas, perhaps in Korea or China, where some vital Japanese interest was threatened. I recall, for instance, handling the financing and logistics of an operation to assassinate an official in the Korean court who was actively working against Japanese interests. At another time, I provided the support needed to get a corrupt but influential government official out of Japan and to Hawaii, thus providing the government with the excuse that they could not act against the official. These are merely two instances.'

About two years ago, Mr. Fujimoto had had a change of heart. He had recently became a grandfather and felt that a personal spiritual quest was in order. He reflected on the matter of living a clean life a great deal and visited monasteries in Kyoto. He took to writing *haikus* and philosophical essays and spent time at Kinkaku-ji, an extremely revered Buddhist temple, learning how to meditate. He sought retirement from the Yakuza and was granted his wish. An interest in the teachings and the life of the Buddha spurred him on and he went through a spiritual renewal ceremony to become a lay monk. After that, he and the younger monk, Hiroshi Oto, decided to spend some time travelling to various spots of Buddhist significance. He had managed to travel to Calcutta via Hong Kong and Singapore and was delighted that he had achieved a major milestone in his life.

He wrote a *haiku* for me in the Japanese *Kanji* script as a gift, which I later had translated.

Let the winter's snow
Fall on your memories
The Buddha's blessings

We discussed his work further in liaising with the government. His chance remark—'Life will soon change in Japan and perhaps in the world'—piqued my interest. He was completely candid; though he had retired a couple of years earlier, he had kept in touch with his old friends, he said. He said that the Yakuza had infiltrated and completely compromised the Japanese Diplomatic Service—he spoke of the Korean assassination, which while technically a mere 'facilitation,' was in fact executed by a junior diplomat.

He said that various ministries were also riddled with Yakuza sympathizers who were often extreme nationalists too and not entirely pleased with the winds of transformation being ushered in by the Emperor Meiji. He gave me the names of many influential persons in the government who either ignored the Yakuza because they sympathized with them or were actually part of the organization. He was fairly sure that 'something would happen soon.' He was quite aware that the Yakuza was working closely with the Shanghai Triads and that the goal was quite complex.

He then lapsed into a long and rambling soliloquy about life being a complete illusion and referred to the Buddhist concepts of Maya, Dharma, and Nirvana. These matters, while interesting in their own way, were not relevant to my objective and I have not written them down. Nevertheless, from a purely philosophical perspective, I found them intriguing and worth additional research at the Library of the British Museum, should I ever return to London.

Do not get the impression that Mr. Fujimoto was an indiscreet, garrulous person. He had simply reached a peculiar inflection point in his thinking which made him wish to unburden his soul of any information unnecessary to his new quest. Moreover, my notes above are not the result of any one long conversation, but the collation of several brief ones.

I expressed my desire to visit Japan one day. Mr. Fujimoto gave me a long and searching look and finally smiled. He said he hoped such a thing would happen and wondered if it had already taken place.

At that point, I revealed our real identities and explained our circumstances, though I did not go into unnecessary details. He then insisted on writing a letter of introduction, which he said I could use gainfully at the Kinkaku-ji temple in Kyoto should an occasion arise; I would be afforded hospitality and protection. I do not anticipate such an eventuality, but I nevertheless accepted the letter politely.

◇◇◇

We spent a fine week at Bodh Gaya. The bracing air and physical activity helped my recovery. Holmes did not consider it advisable for us to abandon our disguise till we reached Calcutta, though. We looked at the map again and concluded that travelling back to Patna was hazardous. We decided to take the road to Calcutta through the towns of Dhanbad and Asansol and then plan our next move toward Japan.

And so we did, after bidding good-bye to Hiroshi Ota and Akira Fujimoto, who proposed to continue their pilgrimage. They were planning to travel to Lumbini, near Nepal, where the Buddha was born, they said, and to other places on the pilgrimage circuit. We wished each other well.

The journey to Calcutta was arduous; we completed it in about two days without incident. We travelled by road to Dhanbad and took a train to Howrah, the railway station serving Calcutta. We were extremely tired, but quite aware that perhaps our journey had barely begun.

Calcutta

 You often argued with me, when we were young fools in Kobe, that logic is less important than passion. No. There is logic and music in a blade of grass, in the song of a hummingbird, in the sigh of a lover.

We reached Howrah Station, the main railway access point of Calcutta, around noon. The Hooghly River, over which we passed, is an offshoot of the Ganges that retains the mystique of its source. The July heat and the humidity of Calcutta affected us greatly, but my first impressions of the city were favourable—even if my description of it won't be. It was different from Bombay and even more crowded. The air hung heavy with a concoction of smells, mostly offensive, but interesting on the whole.

The teeming mass of humanity belied description; poverty and utter deprivation seemed rife. The area was, I was told, in the midst of an extended drought of extreme severity and thousands from the hinterland were travelling to Calcutta to find a means of survival. I was moved by the plight of the hopeless and starving and the deep, silent stares of the emaciated children. But there was little I could do, being on a different mission that could not afford the slightest digression.

Holmes had an idea that we would find good rooms and remain inconspicuous in the Armenian Street area, which was filled with immigrants from that distant country—a quite surprising fact. We found rooms at the Rose Lodge that were comfortable, though we had to change our garb at an intermediate spot in order to avoid refusal. Holmes still insisted on a disguise for himself; he made himself up to look several years older. He bought a pair of spectacles for me and I was transformed into a scholar. We now looked like two English gentlemen—and since there were hundreds in Calcutta, it was fairly simple to assimilate. We checked in as James Smith and John Brown; not very original, but as inconspicuous as we could imagine.

We considered our options after lunch. The manager, Mr. Abel Petrosian, proved to be a genial and talkative soul.

'Ah, gentlemen, you wish to travel to Shanghai? Excellent! Admirable! A fine place, home to so many of our Chinese immigrants here! Let me suggest some options.

'The first way, perhaps the fastest, is to take a passenger ship to Singapore and then travel upwards to the northeast. The second way is to travel to Rangoon on the same ship, then head due east overland to Bangkok and finally resume the sea journey. This sounds arduous, but you will actually save time. During the monsoon, however, the overland road is nothing but a sea of mud and I would not suggest you go there. There is a third option that involves travelling to Dacca, then on to Kohima in the Naga Hills, Burma, China, but that is considered highly risky and there is every possibility that you will be subject to an attack on your persons—no, no, I would not advise that! I strongly recommend that you take the sea route to Singapore. If you like, I can arrange for first-class tickets. I believe there is a passenger ship, the *Isabella*, to Singapore in two days. I recommend it highly.'

'Two days seem considerable, Mr. Petrosian,' said Holmes, after a moment's hesitation. 'But I suppose there is no alternative. If you could arrange for passage for two on the *Isabella*, we would be indebted. Going to Singapore makes eminent sense.'

'Your tickets will be in your hands by this evening, gentlemen. Now, I do suggest you take a tour of this interesting city. If you wish, I can arrange a coach to take you around.'

Holmes declined. 'I think we shall walk around, Mr. Petrosian. I hear there is considerable musical influence in this town. Could you guide us to someone who could elucidate?'

'Ah no, Mr. Smith, this is not the refined and cultured music that you are used to. The music of India is primitive, barbaric, and quite disorganized. I would not recommend it at all. There is no philharmonic or conservatory of music here, sadly.'

'I'm afraid that is not quite what I am looking for, Sir. Well, I shall find out. Good day.'

As we stepped out Holmes remarked, 'There is no question of going to Singapore, of course, Watson. This is a talkative man not given to circumspection and it is best to give him an incorrect impression about our true plans. We shall travel on that ship, but get off at Rangoon or elsewhere and take the land route. There is no doubt in my mind that Professor Moriarty would be scanning the Singapore port. Well, let us discuss that later. I—we—shall be frustrated by a forced rest of two days, but we might as well make the most of it and soak in the culture.'

We explored Calcutta for a short while. The city was unusually filthy, with evidence of grinding poverty and decay. Neither of us was deterred. There was a different kind of life here, full of emotion and energy. We decided we rather liked Calcutta.

We strolled through the European Quarter. I had rarely seen Sherlock Holmes in such a relaxed frame of mind, though I was quite sure his gigantic brain was ahead in Tokyo.

We stopped at a large bookstore in an area called College Street. The owner came up and introduced himself as Mr. Shyam Chundur Mookerjee. He was a slight man and spoke excellent English.

'Perhaps you can give us an idea of what we could see and experience in Calcutta for the next two days, Mr. Mookerjee? In particular, I would be keen to be introduced to a local musician.'

'A local musician, Sir? An unusual but wise choice! We are certainly proud of our music and musicians. Would you like to meet someone specific?'

'Perhaps someone who could teach me for a few hours. I have seen that music sharpens my mind. I am a violinist, albeit a dilettante.'

'Unusual, unusual! But commendable.' Mr. Mookerjee was quite flustered by this peculiar request from an Englishman.

A young Indian gentleman in Western attire stepped out from behind a large bookshelf. He had a regal bearing and intelligent eyes, with hair parted in the middle. He bowed gravely.

'Gentlemen, excuse me. I happened to overhear your conversation with Mr. Mookerjee, quite inadvertently, for which I do beg your pardon. I may be able to assist you in your endeavours if you permit me.' His English had no accent. Mr. Mookerjee stepped back in deference.

'My name is Rabindranath Tagore, gentlemen. I am a regular patron at this establishment. If you could step behind here, there are some comfortable seats where we could converse in private. Mr. Mookerjee, perhaps some tea for your esteemed visitors?'

'Of course!'

We introduced ourselves to the gentleman as visitors in Calcutta who would soon be on our way to Singapore. I was quite content watching Holmes adapt to our surroundings so easily and converse with natives of all classes; this young man of aristocratic bearing, suggesting a man of independent means, would likely be an interesting individual to be acquainted with.

Holmes puffed at his pipe. 'I am a violinist, Mr. Tagore, perhaps merely an itinerant one. Nevertheless, if I could be instructed on a few select local compositions, I believe it would be time well spent. I propose to write a monograph on the adaptation of the violin to the music of India one day.'

Mr. Tagore looked at us very carefully. 'A most noteworthy and desirable objective, Mr. Smith. I may be able to help you. The music of India is demanding, however, and may not be appreciated and absorbed over a matter of three days. Some take decades before declaring a mild appreciation for its underlying complexities. Nevertheless, a very brief introduction is certainly possible. As it happens, I am a lover of music myself and do compose music that is of a somewhat lighter nature, but I have an assistant, Mr. Sen, who is a classical musician of some eminence and could impart some training for a few hours, should it be convenient.'

'I appreciate your courtesy. And what would be his fees?'

'None whatsoever! A visit from Sherlock Holmes to my humble home would be fee enough.'

It is not often that I have seen Sherlock Holmes let surprise show vividly on his face. He took the pipe out of his mouth and stared.

'I beg your pardon, Mr. Tagore?'

'Come, come, Sir! I am certain—*quite certain*, Sir—that I am speaking with Mr. Sherlock Holmes, the eminent private detective. It is an extraordinary coincidence that I am meeting you here in a bookshop in Calcutta. I lived in England for a few years and your famous face is quite familiar to me, though you seem a little older than I had imagined—excuse my poor manners! I was privy to the manner in which you handled a certain case involving the Treaty of Pondicherry. Your intervention prevented extreme embarrassment to the French governor-general and some other individuals. I am also aware of your role in retrieving the missing diamonds of the Princely State of Gwalior. Your name and fame precede you, Sir. And this, of course, must be Dr. Watson.' He bowed. 'Please tell me if I am wrong.'

Holmes regained his composure. 'I must compliment you, Mr. Tagore. Let us drop this pretence. I can, of course, completely count on your discretion. I am here on a mission of great secrecy and shall leave in two days. If news of our identity is made known, I am afraid the consequences would be disastrous.'

'In that case, Mr. Holmes, permit me to take charge of your affairs. I will proceed to my home in an area called Jorasanko, north of Calcutta, to make arrangements and organize myself. And if you will permit me, I shall like to send word to my good friend Mr. Jagdish Chandra Bose to join us there. He is a lecturer in Physics at Presidency College and is involved in several controversial forays into the world of science, for which, I confess, I have no talent. I know that he is an admirer of yours and would be sorely disappointed not to be able to avail of this opportunity to meet you. Mr. Mookerjee here will give you a brief guided tour of the city and then provide you with reliable transportation to my residence. You will then be escorted back to your hotel later tonight. Does this plan suit you?'

Holmes nodded and, within minutes Mr. Tagore departed after giving Mr. Mookerjee instructions. Mr. Mookerjee organized a brougham and we embarked on a brief but interesting tour of the city.

We visited a Kali temple, which turned out to be an unsettling experience. The place was dirty, noisy, and extremely crowded and we had to exercise care, as dozens of urchins and beggars made futile attempts to divest us of our money, clothes, and belongings. The priests—referred to as *pandas,* if I recall—were particularly persistent in their manner, to the point of being unpleasantly intrusive, and promised salvation for monetary considerations, a matter in which we evinced no interest. Goddess Kali, depicted as a rather ruthless eradicator of evil, appears central to the culture of Bengal and the city is named after her. Devotees sacrifice all manner of animals to propitiate her rather startling idol at this temple; this can be a very unpleasant sight. We left quickly.

I erred in making a slightly uncivil remark about the natives and their beliefs. 'Such heathen customs, Holmes!'

Sherlock Holmes shook his head disapprovingly. 'Heathen? Tut! A most uncharitable comment from you, Watson. Doubtless our own beliefs guided by the Church of England will not stand the test of scrutiny from the lens of their perspective!'

'Yes, you have a point, Holmes,' I said, suitably chastened.

As we travelled to Jorasanko to meet Mr. Tagore (after picking up Holmes' violin from our hotel and dropping Mr. Mookerjee back at his bookstore), we passed by a motley group of Bengalees of the labour class waving red flags and raising slogans outside a factory on the outskirts of the town. We had never seen such a sight before and Holmes requested our driver to drive by slowly to enable us to observe the event closely.

At regular intervals, the group, as a body, would clench their fists, raise their right hands and shout something loudly, which invariably ended with the expression '*Moordabad,*' which I understood later is condemnatory and hopes for death for the person or persons who are the object of their ire. Holmes directed some enquiries at the driver, who responded, presumably explaining what the matter was.

'Why are they upset, Holmes?' I asked, quite fascinated by the sight.

Holmes sank back in the seat as the coach gathered speed. 'It would appear that the Bengalees are an excitable people, Watson. Easily agitated about issues big and small and prone to endless argumentation. For a moment, I thought we were witnessing some form of political protest, which is indeed the case, but the coachman tells me that the gentlemen were, in fact, additionally leading a labour disturbance. In essence, they were protesting against working conditions and their pay, which they believe is altogether too modest. Their suggestion is that working hours be reduced and the pay increased, a proposition that they hope the mill owner [for it was a mill the gentlemen were standing outside] will consider favourably.

'Doubtless you are aware of the influence of Karl Marx, presently comfortably interred at the Highgate Cemetery in London. He made a powerful case—though, I would personally argue, an erroneous one—for common ownership of land and industry and the notion of socialism. I would hazard a guess that the citizens of this area are quite taken by this utopian ideal and look forward to an equalization of economic conditions. While I would not challenge the premise of the demonstrators, being unaware of the specifics, I also conjecture that the disturbance is some form of political catharsis. I wonder if we are witnessing the beginning of some stirring changes, Watson, in the very concept of the British Empire. Time will tell.'

By now, we had reached Jorasanko and after dismissing the cab, we entered the rather large and beautiful building where we expected to meet Mr. Rabindranath Tagore. We were welcomed elaborately and most warmly and then escorted to an inner room. In a moment, Mr. Tagore entered the room, greeted us with great warmth, and made the most courteous enquiries about our well-being.

He sat opposite us on an oversized chair made of teak and studied us carefully with his intense eyes, his fingers drumming the wooden arms. 'Mr. Smith and Mr. Brown? Well, well! You could have done better! In any case, I am delighted, Mr. Holmes, to learn about your interest in the culture of India. Someone did mention that you had written a monograph[7] on the dead language of Pali, which is considered the final word on the matter. I hope to give you any additional information that is within my capacity to provide.

'And you, Dr. Watson,' he said, turning to me. 'How I envy you your excursion to Afghanistan of which I have read so much! Yes, it was war and doubtless unpleasant, but I am a romantic man, Sir, and think of Afghanistan in a certain dreamy way—strong and proud Pathans, beautiful women, Kandahar, mountains, the famous city of Kabool…'

'May I?' enquired Holmes, taking out his pipe after some additional pleasantries.

'Of course! And ah, here is Jagdish!'

An Indian gentleman in his late thirties, in Western attire, rushed in, panting slightly. He started speaking in Bengalee with Mr. Tagore, but arrested himself when he saw us and continued in English.

'Gentlemen, my apologies, I have just concluded my classes and was delayed. I—'

Mr. Tagore raised his arm in greeting. 'Jagdish! No need to apologize! Let me introduce you to Mr. Sherlock Holmes and Dr. John Watson, newly arrived from England. Gentlemen, this is Mr. Jagdish Chandra Bose, a man with a remarkable penchant for scientific enquiry, who, I dare say, will make a name for himself very soon.'

Mr. Bose bowed to us and we shook hands.

'Mr. Tagore is too kind. I am just a humble student of science. And I am delighted to meet both of you. I used to read about

---

[7] I recall that I felt a sense of doom and *déjà vu* as the existence of one more example from an apparently bottomless pit of monographs written by Holmes on every possible arcane subject became known.

you while I was a student at Cambridge, Mr. Holmes, obviously through the wonderful efforts of Dr. Watson here. Lord Rayleigh, my professor there, spoke often about your scientific methods and urged me to review some of your cases to see how the application of scientific methods could solve some kinds of criminal situations.'

I observed Holmes study this interesting gentleman carefully. Mr. Bose was obviously of an excitable disposition, his eyes darting here and there. Of medium height and average build, wearing rimless spectacles, he radiated a certain magnetism and energy. He made for an interesting contrast to the more reflective Mr. Tagore.

Mr. Bose sniffed the air. 'Tobacco. An unusual variant—not from India. Possibly Brazilian? No—a subtle Virginia.'

Sherlock Holmes was delighted. 'Quite so! You know your tobacco, Mr. Bose!'

Mr. Bose shrugged. 'Merely the result of having spent time with others in London who were quite obsessed. And I have read a couple of your monographs on the distinctive nature of various kinds of tobacco ash. Really sir, your range of interests is fascinating!'

'More monographs, Holmes?' I asked wearily. Holmes pretended not to have heard my cry of hopeless misery.

'I am, after all, a scientist, gentlemen, and may be forgiven my questions. As I understand from Mr. Tagore, you are travelling in a roundabout way to Japan on a sensitive mission, all the way from London. Is that correct?'

He saw our hesitation and continued hurriedly, 'I can only assure you of confidentiality, for whatever that might be worth, Sirs, but it happens that I too have some knowledge of Japan and may be able to suggest a few lines of enquiry. But that is entirely up to you.'

'Have you heard of the Yakuza, Mr. Bose?' asked Holmes.

'Yes, I have. And if it is them you seek, you obviously know it is a difficult and dangerous business. But I am sure you have thought it through. It is the fear of violence from organized gangs that is the apparent deterrent to probing from the outside. But since their value systems are invariably convoluted, you will find a weak link based solely on some principle of irrationality that ties them together. That is my suggestion for your line of enquiry, not knowing much more about your mission.'

Holmes nodded, his eyes already gazing into the distance, weighing this sage advice and various facts he was privy to.

Servants flitted in and out, serving us tea and local sweets. ('The Bengalees have quite the sweet tooth, Watson. People of extremes in every aspect of behaviour,' Holmes had earlier remarked.)

Mr. Tagore said, 'Mr. Holmes, let me take a moment to tell you about my family, though I am not ordinarily given to boasting.

'The Tagores have been landed *zamindars* in this area. We are quite prosperous, perhaps due to the canny business sense and political adroitness of prior generations, particularly my grand-father Dwarkanath Tagore. Incidentally, his business empire spanned many areas, such as jute, tea, and coal production, and even shipping and banking. But it was in the trade of opium that the large bulk of our fortune was made and the family had very strong connections with the East India Company, which in turn had ties with China. I will not detain you with details of our family wealth, but to this day we have properties all over India and even in England. Indeed, my grandfather is buried, contentedly we hope, in Kensal Green.'

I saw Holmes stiffen at the reference to opium and China.

'I myself received some form of education in England, but cannot boast of an excellent academic record. I have strong views on the matter and I intend to prove in due course that the lack of formal education need not come in the way of a rich and fulfilling life. However, I digress. Allow me to turn the conversation to my friend.

'Since I lack a scientific disposition, I am unable to engage in a discussion on the astonishing new ideas propounded by him.' He looked up at Mr. Bose and said, 'Perhaps I should let my young friend take over the conversation now. His English superiors keep him at a distance, his colleagues have other interests and his students lack the spirit of enquiry he sorely desires to see in them. I think he will enjoy an argument with you on some aspect of science.'

'It would be a great privilege to listen to the perspectives of Mr. Bose,' said Holmes, politely.

I did not share Holmes' enthusiasm and could not understand why he was getting diverted into scientific discussions when, on his own admission, it was imperative that we find ways to think about reaching Japan and staying ahead of our ill-wishers.

The restless Mr. Bose stood up and walked about the room, his head bent and his hands clasped behind him. He was evidently an intense man with many weighty matters on his mind.

'Yes, I am a man of physics, Mr. Holmes, Dr. Watson. After gaining my *Tripos* at Cambridge and then a degree from London, I returned to India. I am presently a member of the faculty at Presidency College—'

'Not treated very well, sadly,' remarked Mr. Tagore. 'There is reason to suspect our brown skin—'

Mr. Bose waved his hand impatiently. 'It is not relevant. Small men resent the potential and race of others and I personally do not care for popularity.'

'I am, however, currently grappling with issues related to plants. And now, Mr. Holmes and Dr. Watson, I must ask you a question, quite distinct from the world of electromagnetism, which is what I teach at Presidency. What is your opinion of plants? Do they possess sentient life?'

'Yes,' I volunteered. 'But the implied comparison can be challenged.'

Holmes did not respond immediately. He puffed at his pipe for a moment and said, 'Please elucidate. I believe you are trying to say something that we have not yet understood.'

'Do they live with awareness? Do they experience death?'

'Yes,' said Holmes.

'Would you compare their lives to ours?'

'To the extent that we, *Homo sapiens*, are believed to be at the apex of animal development and claim that we can reason and feel emotion—I would say that no, it would not be correct to compare plant and human life,' said Holmes slowly, puffing at his pipe.

'It seems almost heretical to make the claim of equivalence of human and plant life, Mr. Bose. We are quite convinced we are superior in every way and would not tolerate any opinion to the contrary, as it would put emotive issues like religion on the table. This is a world that does not even accept the equivalence of human and animal life. What is your proposition, Sir?'

'I say I am embarking on a journey to prove that plants, too, feel emotion and pain. My initial experiments demonstrate very clearly that if presented with certain stimuli, plants respond in a manner similar to us.'

'My dear sir!' I exclaimed.

'Most remarkable! And can we see a scientific validation of your theory?' said Holmes, ignoring my outburst.

'At this moment, no, Mr. Holmes. I am building a machine called a Crescograph, which I hope will demonstrate that plant physiology has curious similarities to our own. This should take a few more months. If you happen to be in Calcutta, it would be my honour to have you examine the machine and witness my experiments personally.'

'Sadly we shall not be here then, but we shall certainly follow developments with interest.'

Mr. Bose's intensity was quite overpowering. 'The scientific spirit of enquiry must banish notions of superiority and not be fixated on one absolute ideal of what the term "life" means. How brainwashed we are, gentlemen! Never challenging, never questioning self-serving axioms dinned into our heads from a young age. We live on oxygen. Others may not—could they thrive on nitrogen, perhaps? We have a cardiovascular system. Others may not. We reproduce in a certain way. Others may reproduce in different ways. We have a view of the meaning and experience of time. Other life forms may think differently.

Who decides which is more advanced and correct? I have even shown that plants react to music!' It was difficult to contain this passionate man.

Mr. Tagore spoke. 'Yes, quite a remarkable experiment that I was witness to and in which I participated, as a matter of fact. Jagdish asked me to sing my songs to some plants he had brought with him. When I did, some died while others experienced terror![8] Ha ha ha!'

We laughed politely at Mr. Tagore's little joke, though he himself was quite taken by it and kept chortling for a few minutes.

'Well, Mr. Bose, I am certain there is merit in what you say. You may or may not convince me with your theories, but I am certainly convinced that you are a man born too soon. I hope I shall have the pleasure of corresponding with you.'

I heaved a sigh of relief. This pointless conversation was finally coming to an end.

But then Holmes continued, 'Mr. Bose, tell me about your work in physics.'

I almost cried out in frustration. When would this end? When would we discuss Japan? Mr. Tagore observed my restlessness and hurriedly placed some sweets in front of me.

'These *rosogollahs* are remarkable, Dr. Watson,' he said in a soothing voice. 'I must insist that you try one.'

I did and was silenced. They really were quite remarkable.

'I am a researcher of radio waves, Mr. Holmes. I have been

---

[8] My audacious—and perhaps, some may argue, attractive—editor, foisted on me by Messrs Poisoned Pen Press, wanted wholesale cuts claiming that the modern reader sought crime and not botany, missing the point entirely, due to her being immature, and, after all, a woman. The point of this narrative is to chronicle the interesting discussions and experiences Holmes and I had during our adventure. The modern crime-seeking reader, easily bored with scientific enquiry and seeking unwholesome racy entertainment is advised to gift this book to an acquaintance with more finely honed sensibilities, or return this book to the commercial establishment from where it was purchased and apply formally for a refund. The intelligent and mature reader is requested to stay on and read carefully, as he will doubtless benefit.

attracted by the work of Heinrich Hertz in the issue of invisible electromagnetic waves in space—'

'The German professor from Karlsruhe,' remarked Holmes.

'Quite so. How pleasing that you have heard of him. He worked on Maxwell's theory. You seem to know all this, though we are speaking of developments of only the past ten years or so. Now, this theory says in essence that it is possible to transmit signals through walls, via what we shall call electromagnetic waves. Wires are not necessary. You can imagine the world of possibilities that opens up.'

I was astonished, but Holmes was the picture of equanimity. 'Unusual, but not impossible, I imagine.'

'Naturally, like Tesla and many other pioneers, we are faced with skepticism and even derision. I have a small lab—it will suffice—at the Presidency College. I am convinced that this is an entirely new area of science waiting to open up. But I am unable to attract funds and attention.'

'Genius is always met with skepticism. I am sure you will not give up.'

'I am grateful that you are not dismissive. To begin with, I need the opinions of men of logic such as yourself on creating a vision for the future application of such electromagnetic waves. People are attracted by applications, not theory alone, I have come to realize.'

'Have you approached the Royal Society? What is the opinion of Oliver Lodge? I heard him speak once on the existence of Maxwell waves.'

'Indeed, I am in correspondence with the Royal Society, but the whole process takes a long time and I am impatient by disposition. I am now designing a microwave receiver and transmitter, but there are challenges…'

'…Hertz…'

'…galvanometer…antenna…'

'…coherer…crystal detector…'

And thus the discussion turned scientific and to my discomfiture, I soon found myself bewildered, distracted, and utterly bored. Mr. Tagore, too, was finding it difficult to keep up and, much to my amusement, the distinguished gentleman fell asleep in his chair, snoring loudly, while not ten feet away two men of science discussed the quirks of a new theory.

With an effort, I kept my eyes open. Sherlock Holmes was speaking.

'…wireless telegrams would soon emerge, I believe. An Italian scientist Marconi is presently discussing this matter with the Home Office, if I recall. My brother Mycroft mentioned that there was interest at the highest places. You must, I believe, patent these discoveries of yours.'

'I am not driven by lucre, Mr. Holmes. Whatever I discover must be in the public domain. I refuse to profit from it.'

'A noble perspective, no doubt. But you may face problems in funding future experiments if you do not take precautions.'

'Perhaps, but I am prepared. Science belongs to humanity, not to the scientist. There is no room for ego.

'I dream of a wide series of applications that I imagine may change the world one day. Electromagnetic communication—perhaps a device through which the public can listen to the music of my good friend Mr. Tagore. Perhaps the speeches of the prime minister. Or the emperor of Japan.'

'The mind draws its own boundaries, Mr. Bose. I believe such a day as you describe will come. I see that it may be possible for police departments to exchange information through wireless devices, discarding the inefficiencies and eccentricities of the telegraph bound by Morse Code. Though I wonder what would happen if my criminal adversaries, such as Professor Moriarty, were to take possession of such science.'

'I do not feel, Mr. Holmes, that such discoveries must be limited to select groups simply because of the fear of its misuse, its benefits must touch humanity at large!' exclaimed Mr. Bose with passion.

I was impressed by Mr. Bose's obviously sincere, though perhaps slightly naïve, altruistic nature.

Holmes shook his head. 'There we perhaps disagree, Mr. Bose. My assessment is that the abilities of the public to use the benefits of science in a constructive way are limited. I am by no means one to advocate denying convenience, but appropriate authorities must first explore and certify, and only then let the benefits of science and engineering percolate to the citizenry. I say this only from the perspective of pure logic, having observed the behaviour of all manner of people in my career—the common man who lives for today, the criminal who seeks to maximize profit through illegal means as soon as possible, the woman who covets a necklace and would go to any length to get it, the merchant who profits by arbitrage because he has an unfair advantage...'

Mr. Bose's eyes flashed. This was bait that he could not ignore.

'Autocracy! Who decides?' Mr. Bose cried, his voice rising in anger. 'Who gave these authorities the right to decide what is good for the public and what is not? Is this not how autocrats and dictators keep power—by limiting access to knowledge on the specious theory that they possess the ability, power, and right to discriminate? And who can decide that they have used knowledge and science wisely? Mr. Holmes, the first application of science has invariably been on the battlefield. We would rather kill with better cannons and guns using the principles of science. No, Mr. Holmes, no! I have no patience for the self-serving votaries of regulation and control!'

Mr. Tagore was suddenly awake, the raised voice of Mr. Bose having penetrated his siesta. He observed his guests with bleary eyes.

'Let us agree to disagree, Mr. Bose,' Holmes responded in a conciliatory tone. 'Both of us have travelled on different roads and have reasons to believe what we believe. What we should do is celebrate science and the scientific temper. No doubt we shall see the application of your discoveries soon. Naturally, I am forced to wonder if a day might not come—very soon—when information will be shared easily and almost instantaneously anywhere in the world, making it much smaller in a manner of speaking. What if information about the Yakuza, the Thuggees, and the Mafia were made available to investigators around the world in seconds instead of months, if at all?'

I was unable to control my laughter. 'My dear Holmes! I too am a man of science in my own way—but surely there must come a time when fantastic ideas must be challenged?'

'Watson, what is possible? What is probable? How much do we know? How much do we not know?' asked Holmes. 'I am surprised at you, my dear fellow, that such a refreshing idea could provoke such a hot-blooded response from you. Perhaps the effect of malaria continues in some insidious manner. If this discussion were happening a hundred years ago, you would perhaps have been outraged by the suggestion of the principle of the telegraph. Yet we—you!—frequently send wires without a second thought. When you chronicle this episode and if it were to be read a hundred years hence when the world is entirely different, you may look rather ridiculous, Watson!'

I recall feeling outraged and perhaps my face showed my strong feelings as I searched for a sharp retort.

'Some more Bengalee sweets, Dr. Watson?' interjected Rabindranath Tagore, seeking to soothe tempers.

I accepted a peculiar-looking white sweet called *sondesh* with some hesitation and nibbled at it tentatively. The taste was quite enchanting. 'Pray, carry on, gentlemen,' I said, my anger subsiding in seconds, 'while I conduct a prolonged scientific enquiry into the secrets of this sweet.'

My attempt at humour was well received and the others broke out in laughter. I proceeded with my enquiry in earnest, while their voices rose and fell around me.

Holmes' voice suddenly interrupted my consciousness. 'And now, Watson, if you are quite done with those Bengalee sweets, perhaps Mr. Tagore would be kind enough to introduce me to his musician acquaintance, Mr. Sen, from whom I may pick up a few pointers on music.'

I was embarrassed to discover that I had consumed almost the entire plate of sweets in barely ten minutes!

After the good-natured laughter subsided, we went out to a small building in the garden, where we found a thin, dark gentleman waiting for us. He wore a *dhoti* and seemed rather nondescript at first glance, but made up for it with a bright and genuine smile a moment later. He was seated on the floor on a carpet behind a harmonium and stood up as we entered and brought his palms together in a *namaste*. After some initial exchange in Bengalee between him, Mr. Bose, and Mr. Tagore, he spoke.

'Meester Holmes, I am Binayak Sen, teacher of music. I teach you some music if you like!'

Sherlock Holmes bowed courteously. 'Thank you for the privilege. You will find me a poor student. A few suggestions on the basics of Indian classical music are all I ask, if not inconvenient. And I have here my violin.'

'A violin!' exclaimed Mr. Bose. 'Excellent, Mr. Holmes! Physics in action in every possible way, would you not say? May we have the pleasure of hearing you?'

Holmes removed his violin from the case. 'Hold on to the music sheets, Watson. They are irreplaceable.'

He took the violin to his shoulder and applied bow to strings and, after a few minor tuning adjustments, played the instrument with a verve and sensitivity I had rarely heard from him before. He played some Welsh tunes, then the "Devil's Trill" of Tartini, and then a soulful composition of his own. The atmosphere in the room was transformed; Mr. Bose and Mr. Tagore had closed their eyes and were quite lost, swaying as their bodies kept time. Mr. Sen observed the deft movements of Holmes' fingers very carefully and nodded vigorously in appreciation.

We clapped when Holmes concluded and bowed.

'Outstanding, Mr. Holmes! A true application of the beauty of science!' cried Mr. Bose.

'Very poetic,' remarked a subdued Mr. Tagore.

'Bhery good, bhery good!' exclaimed Mr. Sen, rubbing his hands in glee.

'Thank you. I am now at your service.'

'You please sit down on carpet in front of me and we begin the simple Indian music lesson,' commanded Mr. Sen.

With great difficulty, Holmes managed to sit cross-legged on the carpet in front of Mr. Sen. Mr. Bose and Mr. Tagore followed. I expressed my inability to sit on the floor owing to my overall lack of flexibility, and a chair was found.

Mr. Sen placed his fingers on the keys of the harmonium and produced a peculiar, though not unpleasant combination of sounds.

'We first create atmosphere. *Raaga* is emotion and atmosphere. First we tune your violin, then you follow what I play on harmonium. Is it all right?'

Holmes followed Mr. Sen's instructions and tuned his violin carefully. ('An unusual combination of notes Watson, not native to the violin as we know it,' he commented later. 'But appropriate for their music. A clever adaptation. It was quite difficult to avoid making comparisons while playing, but I did my best. The fingering, arpeggios, the bowing—our technical conventions do not find easy applicability here.')

Then Mr. Sen began teaching Sherlock Holmes the basics of Indian classical music. The experience was enjoyable for all of us, watching the world-famous investigator struggle to understand the thick accent of Mr. Sen, while extracting unfamiliar notes and cadences.

Holmes proved to be a quick learner, however, and the cries of joy from Mr. Sen seemed to indicate that he had found a promising student. This went on for a couple of hours, with neither student nor teacher showing any signs of tiring and all kinds of peculiar melodies and language emerging. *Raagas, Swar, Vadi, Samvadi, Aarohon, Abarohan.* I took notes, of course, and Sherlock Holmes told me later what his interpretation of these words was.

The class came to a close, and Holmes and Mr. Sen acknowledged each other's competence with pleasure. A lavish dinner awaited all of us, with several Indian dishes being brought in, one after the other in rapid succession. My fondness for the local sweets had become a talking point in the kitchen and I kept finding new dishes appearing mysteriously in front of me. I consumed them in as inconspicuous a manner as possible, finding myself unable to resist.

Meanwhile, Holmes was in an animated discussion with Bose on his left and musical discourses with Sen on his right. Mr. Rabindranath Tagore played the perfect host, involving all of us in his conversations and ensuring we were fed well.

We said our good-byes and departed for our hotel around midnight, very satisfied with our day. Mr. Bose and Holmes promised to be in frequent touch and he wished us well with our plans to engage with the Yakuza, once again advising us to concentrate not on the apparent but on the implied and exaggerated.

'A boastful enemy is your best friend, Sirs, since he is given to overconfidence,' observed Mr. Bose as we shook hands.

We were suffused with contentment. Music and science (and Bengali sweets) had enriched this strange journey and we felt refreshed as never before, ready to take on the formidable dangers ahead.

By mutual agreement, Mr. Sen came to the hotel the following morning and spent all day guiding Holmes in the nuances of Indian music. Holmes told me later that he knew quite well it would be impossible to learn anything of significance of the vast ocean of Indian music in a few hours, but he was satisfied that he had had an excellent introduction. His violin-playing somehow became more emotional and subtle.

Many years after his formal retirement, when he took up beekeeping in Sussex, he would often invite me to visit and would invariably play charming little tunes that brought back memories of those two remarkable days in Calcutta.

Angkor War—
Saigon—Nagasaki

 It seems only yesterday that we played in the forests of the Hakko mountains. The trees smiled when we laughed and shouted and hit each other with love. Today, our grandchildren do the same. I have already started seeing the ghosts of my ancestors in this house.

We departed without incident that night from Calcutta for Singapore on the *Isabella* as planned, boarding the ship at separate times. Holmes was in the garb of an affluent Bengalee *baboo*, wearing the local *dhoti*, while I pretended to be an English planter returning to my rubber estate in Sarawak. Nothing could be ruled out. The game of chess was being played furiously across continents. The past two days had been extremely interesting, what with Holmes' newfound mania for the classical music of India. Our encounter with Mr. Tagore had been inspiring as well. 'Mark my words,' Holmes had said, 'we will hear more of him soon.'

But now we had to move rapidly to Tokyo to meet Mr. Oshima. We had equipped ourselves in Calcutta with the clothes and medicine we might need for the residual part of the journey. Holmes was quiet and non-communicative and was not interested in the voyage itself. We moved to our first-class cabin and, in due course, it was filled with the acrid smoke of tobacco mixed with a local narcotic, *ganja*, derived from cannabis. I busied myself with the accounts and with updating my diary before bed.

We had been informed that the passage to Singapore would take approximately ten days, with halts at Rangoon, the port of Myeik toward the south of Burma, and George Town in the State of Penang in the Straits Settlement. The journey was uncomfortable for the most part, with the monsoon in full force. We were buffeted by gales and strong waves and the occasional heavy shower. This suited us quite well as we were confined to our rooms and thus avoided contact with fellow passengers.

But Sherlock Holmes was soon pacing the rolling floor of our cabin furiously.

'There is no doubt, Watson. Moriarty would have anticipated our every move. He would certainly have the port of Singapore watched. In a day or so, he would have checked the passenger manifest of the *Isabella* and, becoming suspicious about two men travelling to Singapore, he would have sent a wire there.'

Holmes took out a map of the area and placed it on a table. 'Watson, our objective is now twofold. Get to Yokohama and thence to Tokyo as soon as possible and also evade the traps of Professor Moriarty. There is one option, though dangerous, especially since you have only now recovered from malaria. And that is to completely avoid Singapore. We can do this in one of three ways. Get off quietly at Rangoon and travel to Siam, then to Saigon. Or at Myeik, which appears closest to Bangkok. That journey will be the toughest, given the terrain and the mud and slush we can expect. Finally, we can get off at George Town, but we would have given our adversary far too much time to prepare. No, we must take our chances at Rangoon or Myeik.'

'It should be Myeik, Holmes. There appears little option. Those disembarking at Rangoon would also likely be watched. Myeik appears to be a small port.'

'Capital! The matter is settled, then! I see that we are to arrive at Myeik at about six in the morning. Let us feign sickness and get off. The ship will weigh anchor after only fifteen minutes at the port. That is our window!'

We reached Rangoon but kept to our cabin. A number of passengers disembarked and a handful embarked. I watched from the porthole for any sign that we were being sought. I did see two Englishmen standing at the passenger gate beyond the Customs shed, looking carefully at everyone who exited. There was no way to determine their purpose.

We were soon on our way to Myeik, a distance of some three hundred nautical miles. The Myeik archipelago is known for its breathtaking beauty, we were told, but we were too preoccupied to take particular note; in any case, Holmes was not a man to consider Nature's pulchritude even at the best of times. We had no idea how, but we knew we had to shake off our pursuers here. And as the *Isabella* eased into Myeik's harbour, we feigned acute sickness and prevailed upon the captain to let us disembark, promising to resume the journey the following day on the next ship.

Our plan worked. We disembarked at the sleepy little port just before dawn, clutching our stomachs and our luggage, escorted by a concerned captain. Except for a couple of porters and an official, the place was deserted and quiet and not very used to visitors. The Burmese are a friendly people and, as the *Isabella* weighed anchor and moved away in the direction of Singapore, we recovered our health miraculously and made enquiries as to how we could move swiftly to Bangkok.

The Burmese official, Mr. U Mya Sein, very courteously offered us breakfast and said that the fastest, if rather arduous, option would be to travel by mule through the mountains which, he informed us, were experiencing heavy rains. The jungles were thick and dangerous but the path was known and he would put us in the hands of a good guide. We agreed and were equipped for the journey in a couple of hours.

We entered the jungle right outside the port. Our journey went as smoothly as one might expect while going through a tropical forest. Our guide had thoughtfully provided us with a thick oily cream that had a distasteful smell that would deter insects. He also provided us water. But nothing could have prepared us for the sweltering, stifling heat and the intermittent cloudbursts. Holmes was a picture of equanimity as always and discussed various cases from the past to pass the time. He was unusually garrulous and even rather gay.

'Certainly you will recall, my dear Watson, the case of Sir George Hastings and his encounter with the blackmailer Charles Milverton. You know my methods—I tried to put myself in Milverton's shoes and imagined what options he would consider. He squeezed the last drop from his victims but occasionally miscalculated the limits of tolerance. When that happens, a person enduring blackmail may be perfectly content to endure the consequences of not succumbing. And then when you consider the case of the naval attaché of Sweden and the missing engineering blueprints, you wonder how careless people in positions of responsibility can be—leaving those documents on his table right next to an open window, accessible to any passerby.

'Let it be said, Watson, that a certain class of criminals are extraordinarily creative, deriving energy from the finer things in life—authorities on Anatolian *kilims*, connoisseurs of Shiraz wines, experts on Ming vases—do you remember that rogue philanderer, Baron Adelbert Gruner? Artists, sculptors, violinists, pianists, poets. It is a matter of profound interest and deserves scientific analysis. Perhaps such men view sophisticated crime as another art form. They go from success to success, pleasantly surprised by the naiveté of men who literally suggest ways in which they could be taken advantage of, until they finally meet their match. Their Achilles heel is their growing arrogance and overconfidence—I referred to that earlier in the case of Colonel Sebastian Moran passing as Colonel James Burrowe, and the manner in which he lied on board the *North Star*.'

And in such manner Sherlock Holmes carried on, unperturbed by the strange odours and sounds of the tropical jungle, the jerky rhythmic movement of the mules, the insects that came to enquire, the oppressive humidity and the noisy presence of the monkeys and birds all around us.

The lush flora of the jungle was a pleasant distraction—colours and shapes that I had not imagined. Holmes advised me not to touch anything. 'Looks are deceptive, Watson. You certainly recall the case of the Vanishing Horseman, in which so many perfectly intelligent members of a reputable family in Norwich were collectively convinced that horsemen were marching through their house during the day—a striking case of mass hallucination, reminding us of how suggestible our minds are. On investigation, we found that the family was being given doses of *Datura stramonium,* or devil's trumpet, by the cook. That plant you see there, Watson, is the culprit. The purple bell-shaped flowers and shoots contain a hallucinogen that could quite easily prove fatal. And there is the lovely castor bean plant, otherwise known as *Ricinus communis.* The flowers are attractive and fuzzy and the large leaf pleasantly purple. A single bean can cause nausea and disorientation and the accumulated toxin causes a painful and lingering death. But of course, you are a man of medicine, and you may already know this.'

Holmes collected several leaf and flower specimens along the way, saying—to my exasperation—that he hoped to someday write a scholarly monograph[9] for private circulation titled *The Flora of the Malay Peninsula.* We also had a couple of minor encounters with the snakes of the region and I may be excused for mentioning an incident where I possibly saved Sherlock Holmes' life.

As we rested at one location, Holmes sat on a large boulder by the side of the narrow path near a running stream and smoked his pipe. I walked about; it was getting on in the day, we were still about two hours from the village where we were to spend the night, and my limbs were stiff. At Holmes' feet was a large accumulation of dead leaves. As I walked toward him, I noticed a slight rustling and a movement in the heap, barely two feet from Holmes. I shouted out a warning.

Without a moment's hesitation, Holmes jumped right up on to the boulder in a single fluid movement. We saw a large brown snake with black triangular markings raise its head in enquiry, look at Holmes disapprovingly, and then move slowly away.

'A Malay pit viper, Watson! *Calloselasma rhodostoma*, if I am not mistaken. A single bite would have kept me in a state of acute agony for days if untreated. Necrosis and possibly death! My dear fellow, I owe you my life!'

'Holmes, I have lost count of the number of times you saved me from fatal consequences. Think nothing of it. Let us move on.'

We crossed the mountainous terrain by and by, once side-stepping an enormous sedentary Burmese python along the way, and entered Siam. The journey ended soon after at the

---

[9] I did not read this monograph as I felt it was one monograph too many.

outskirts of the large city of Bangkok where we dismissed the guide. Holmes was in no mood whatsoever to break the journey unless absolutely necessary. So once again we consulted our map.

'The most judicious course, Watson, is to avoid large cities, where there is every likelihood of a mishap. It would be better to move eastward into areas where the British Empire has minimal influence, though that by itself guarantees nothing, given Professor Moriarty's reach. Our best course is therefore to travel to the French Protectorate of Cambodia and then into the other French territories of Indochina. From there, we take a sea route to Macau, a Portuguese colony where we shall perhaps find friends, and then onward to Japan.'

We passed through Bangkok where I visited the post office to send a brief letter to my wife. Holmes went back to his disguise of a Bengalee *baboo*. I, too, reverted to my rubber planter guise, but we took no chances and avoided being seen together as far as possible. Though the city seemed lush and interesting with many Buddhist pagodas, which I would otherwise have liked to visit, we simply had no time. We hired a coach to take us from the city to Siem Reap, a town of some antiquity in Cambodia. The road was in surprisingly good condition and we passed through pretty terrain. I made note of various sights, while Holmes kept to himself, smoking the local brand of cigarettes, the quality of which he derided quite often.

After a journey over two or three days, punctuated by frequent changes of horses, and passing through the picturesque towns of Bang Pakong, Sa Kaeo, and Aranyaprathet, we finally reached Siem Reap in the evening, where we decided to rest for a day, given that we had had no break in our journey since we had started from Calcutta. The town was small and pleasant, as were the people, who spoke the Khmer language, distinct from the softer Thai. The Cambodians were darker but more affable and relaxed.

We took a room at the only (and rather primitive) lodgings in town, where the manager, Mr. Suvann Chea, spoke some French, a language that Holmes and I spoke tolerably well. Mr. Chea was most hospitable and insisted on serving us some tea and surprisingly fresh—and unexpected—croissants as light refreshment.

We understood that the city was the gateway to a much larger complex that was the foundation of Cambodian culture. The manager recommended that we visit the ruins of the local temples about three miles away, collectively called Angkor Wat, the next morning, while he arranged for our onward journey. Holmes readily accepted the suggestion.

'Is this wise, Holmes?' I remonstrated. 'Speed is of the essence! Is this the time to set out on an expedition to admire the local architecture?'

Holmes raised an eyebrow. 'I appreciate your spirit and dedication to the pursuit, Watson, but I would like you to consider several facts. One: We are sorely in need of rest and mental distraction. A jaded mind and tired body are unequal to the challenges that lie ahead. Two: We are in a place of extreme historical significance that we may never visit again. And three: We have no choice since transport will be available only in the afternoon.'

I was not entirely convinced, but I withheld comment. Holmes proceeded to make a rather sharp and hurtful remark. 'You seem to resemble, in certain ways, precisely the same kind of reader whose flippant attitude you have deplored on countless occasions. I can see that you hope to chronicle this adventure someday, in the event we survive and you wish to entertain and provide a sense of restless action, desiring perhaps that the average citizen in Birmingham, Glasgow, or Norwich has a jolly time. We do not live in a book, Watson! This is real life where practical considerations must prevail over petty excitement!'

'You do me a grave injustice with your cruel taunt, Holmes!' I cried, my face flushed. 'My literary efforts may be modest, but will one day be regarded as a tribute to you and your intellect. I was merely anxious about the possible loss of time and its effect on your mission.'

'Indeed, Watson? In that case, I withdraw my unnecessary remarks. In the meanwhile, have some of this excellent Darjeeling tea and this fine croissant.'

We slept well and after an early breakfast left for Angkor Wat on fresh and sturdy horses. We settled our accounts with Mr. Chea and asked him to keep a couple of carriages ready for us to travel (*'back to Bangkok,'* said Holmes smoothly). Mr. Chea assured us that arrangements would be made and we should not worry.

A guide, assigned by Mr. Chea, explained that the complexes were presumably the world's largest, spread over hundreds of acres, cutting through thick tropical jungle; indeed, many of the temples had been reclaimed by the flora. They seemed an amalgam of Hindoo and Buddhist cultural influences with representatives of the immense Hindoo pantheon and the Buddha in various esoteric forms. We walked around the rather spectacular ruins. We saw some friezes of the ancient Indian myth, the Ramayana, which Holmes—who said he had once written a well-received monograph on the esoteric aspects of the worship of the monkey-god Hanuman, prominent in that story[10]—observed were subtly different than the original myth prevalent in India.

Holmes also commented on the mathematical precision of the architects. "These were people short in stature, Watson, but tall in intellect and mathematical enquiry, clearly conversant with the subtleties of trigonometry. Note the extraordinary angles of the rise of the sides of the temples, and the precise width of the stairs."

'Trigonometry is not my forte, Holmes,' I said.

'Quite so, my dear fellow, quite so, I had forgotten,' said Holmes, his face expressionless.

We also visited the Terrace of the Leper Kings, the charming temple of Bantey Siri and a number of other fascinating buildings, all in states of disrepair and neglect. As we walked through the buildings, finding our steps gingerly, snakes of various kinds slithered away. We saw at least a couple of huge pythons and many others; none were interested in us, to our relief.

'I find the significance of these temples equals the accomplishments of the Greeks and the Egyptians, Watson. I pity

---

[10] I do not know who received this monograph, but I am quite certain it was not I.

our ignorance of such rich cultures of the past. I wager that these temples, once formally made known to the world, will be counted as some of the greatest ever constructed by man.'

I agreed, 'An extraordinary experience indeed, Holmes.' I had started becoming a bit restless.

'And you see the marked influence of the culture of India extending into this country. The temples have inscriptions in Pali, in which I have had some interest in the past, as you may recall. One inscription said that the temple had been consecrated with the waters of the Ganges, India's holiest river. What do you think of that, eh, Watson?'

'Admirable, Holmes, but I would rather keep moving on toward Japan, if I had the choice!' I said, quite agitated now.

'Tut, Watson! You typify the restless, anxious Englishman far removed from his bowler hat, his club, cricket at Lords, and *The Times*, unable to appreciate the beauty of the moment of heathen cultures. I frown upon your attitude!'

'And I frown on yours, Holmes! Perhaps the heat of this place has reduced our perceptual acuity. I am uneasy and wish we were elsewhere instead of commenting on Pali inscriptions and the Ganges!'

We reached the remote and magnificent Ta Prohm temple, which was in the process of being reclaimed by the unforgiving jungle, then the temple of Bayon with the multiple faces of Avalokiteshvara, and then the main and truly breathtaking temple at Angkor Vat. The structure was easily some two hundred feet high with an angle of about sixty degrees. It was not an easy climb—a good two hundred feet perhaps—and inadvisable for anyone with a fear of extreme heights and lacking physical fitness. The steps themselves were very narrow and we had to climb sideways. One misstep would have meant instant death. At the top were various large statues of the Buddha made of granite and some representations of the Gods of the Hindoo religion as idols or in friezes. Holmes sketched the reliefs and the view and took a few notes. We also took in the spectacular view from the top of the surrounding lush jungles.

After another tortuous climb up the main temple at Angkor Wat and then a frightening, almost-vertical descent, I sat down on one of the granite slabs at the base with my back to the temple to remove my hat, wipe the sweat off my brow, and catch my breath. The agile and sure-footed Sherlock Holmes had already reached the bottom several minutes ahead of me. I felt quite pleased by this little digression and felt relieved that I had descended without incident. Holmes was a few feet in front of me looking at the surrounding flora while our guide was a hundred feet beyond him readying our horses for our journey back to Siem Reap.

The air was thick with history and mystery; I could not have asked for a more pleasing experience. A brilliant blue, yellow, and red butterfly flitted by slowly and rested on my elbow. Everything seemed quite perfect.

Holmes sensed my arrival and turned toward me and the temple, looking up at the remarkable structure.

His face froze with a look of absolute horror.

'Watson!' he cried and sprang toward me, grabbing my shoulders and pushing me away. As he did so, a massive boulder thundered past, passing straight through where I had been sitting and smashing against the steps and pulverizing a few smaller rocks lying at the base.

Holmes pointed upwards and shouted, 'Watson, there! There! Do you see him?'

I got a second's glimpse of a dark face peering down from the very top. Then it disappeared.

'Not a moment to lose, Watson! That was no accident! You were right to be so agitated. We have been discovered! We must leave immediately!' Holmes was in his element—every protective and aggressive instinct at its height, nostrils flaring, every sinew of his body taut, in an absolute state of readiness for any eventuality.

Climbing quickly onto our horses, we galloped away at top speed from Angkor Wat. From behind, we could hear shouts and the pops of revolvers being discharged. The distance was too great however, so we were never in any real danger. We rushed back to Siem Reap.

'We have at best a twenty-minute advantage—the time they need to descend and give chase. Speed is of the essence!' shouted Holmes as we galloped.

At our lodgings, Mr. Chea came out to greet us as we rushed in.

'*Ah, messieurs, vos amis de Bangkok vous cherchaient! Vous ont-ils trouvés?*'

'*Je crains que non, Monsieur Chea, pourriez-vous les décrire?*'

'*Deux messieurs—des Anglais, je dirais. D'une trentaine d'années, environ. Ils étaient accompagnés par un jeune garçon Cambodgien. Ce n'était pas plus de trente minutes après que vous soyez partis. Ils ont dit qu'ils arrivaient de Bangkok et avaient hâte de vous voir.*'

'*Nous ne nous sommes pas rencontrés, malheureusement. Nous partons immédiatement pour Bangkok, Monsieur Chea. Merci de le leur faire savoir.*'[11]

Our carriages were ready, just as Mr. Chea had promised they would be. Sherlock Holmes paid the coachmen the fare to Bangkok. He asked one to proceed without passengers as quickly as possible, saying that a friend would be waiting by the road some fifty miles ahead. Within minutes, we followed the first carriage. About a mile outside Siem Reap, we arrived at a fork where one road led to Bangkok and the other to Phnom Penh, the capital of Cambodia. Holmes directed our coachman to take the Phnom Penh road and turn our carriage into a wooded area where we jumped off, returned to the road, and hid behind some bushes.

'Let us lie low now, Watson, and check to see if our simple stratagem has worked.'

---

[11] 'Ah gentlemen, your friends from Bangkok were looking for you. Did they find you?' 'I'm afraid they did not, Mr. Chea, could you describe them?' 'Two gentlemen, English I would say. Perhaps thirty years old. They were accompanied by a young Cambodian boy. They must have come not more than thirty minutes after you left. They said they had arrived from Bangkok and were most eager to meet you.' 'We did not meet, regrettably. We shall be leaving immediately for Bangkok, Mr. Chea. Do let them know.'

We crouched behind the thick vegetation and watched the road with bated breath. The trail cloud of dust made by the earlier carriage on the way to Bangkok was still visible. Within fifteen minutes, we heard the sound of galloping horses and a rushing carriage. They rushed past, taking the road to Bangkok and we heard someone shouting loudly, 'Faster! Faster! The dust beyond! We can't let him get away this time or he'll have our heads!'

The reference was, obviously, to Professor Moriarty, our malefactor in Paris. As the dust settled down and the sound of the thundering coach became distant, we re-entered the road and proceeded toward Phnom Penh.

'We have bought time, Watson, but not much. That was an exceedingly close encounter and confirms once again that it is possible for a man sitting in a study in Paris to watch our movements as though he were hovering invisibly just above us. We now head south toward Phnom Penh and then move sharply east into Vietnam, to the port of Saigon. There we take a Chinese junk, if one is available, to Macau.' Sherlock Holmes had clearly done his homework.

The coach was comfortable and the road passable, and except for a change of horses every few hours or so, the four-day journey was swift and uneventful. The splendour of the Cambodian countryside made no difference to Sherlock Holmes, but I looked at the green fields and ancient temples along the way with considerable appreciation. Some shops by the wayside offered fried and roasted crickets, the local delicacy, which we politely declined to sample. By and by, sometime early on the fourth day, the coachman announced that we were about to reach a crossroads. To the right would be the road to Phnom Penh and to the left would be a smaller road heading to Saigon. We turned left and after several hours, neared the old and charming city of Saigon.

We changed our disguises at a wayside guesthouse where we ate, as well. And now, with some help from our friendly coachman, we were transformed into two Chinese merchants. Holmes' abilities in the art of disguise were extraordinary; the elaborate robes, the pigtail, the eyes and the complexion—everything was exact. He had picked up a smattering of Mandarin while working on a case at the London dockyards and he used it now confidently. We reached Saigon and, wasting no time, went to the port and made enquiries about a ship proceeding to Macau. It was a busy port with plenty of traffic, and within a couple of hours we were on the *Tek Hwa Seng*, a modest Chinese junk plying to Hong Kong via Macau. We had dismissed our Cambodian coachman after paying him a handsome amount for his trouble; this must have been the longest and strangest journey he had ever undertaken, with an Indian native and an Englishman transforming into Chinese merchants before his eyes. We were now the Chinese timber merchants Wang Tao (Holmes) and Li Hongzhang (I, as Wang Tao's mute friend), returning to Macau.

While we waited, I wrote and then posted a brief letter to my wife, not giving her any hint of my whereabouts, merely saying that all was well and I would communicate with her again very shortly. I thought a telegram would be dangerous. Yes, the letter would take longer, but it would perhaps bring comfort when it arrived.

We walked about the city for an hour. The French influence in Saigon was very evident; the relatively new Notre-Dame Basilica stood out conspicuously over the city. For a moment, we felt we were in Lyons. The Quan Âm Pagoda, on the other hand, was quite different and distinctly Vietnamese and Chinese in its design and colours. Holmes insisted on us sitting in a corner and meditating briefly, following the example set by other Chinese; it would have been inappropriate for us to not do so, given that we were now masquerading as Chinese. We then boarded our ship.

The *Tek Hwa Seng* was well furnished and not very crowded and had about fifty passengers with only three first-class cabins. The journey was not expected to take long and the conditions were favourable. We breathed a sigh of relief as the junk slipped out of the port and headed straight for Macau with a possible halt at the Paracel Islands in the South China Sea, a water body known for its deadly typhoons.

'You see once again, Watson, the extraordinary reach and ability of Professor Moriarty. Nowhere are we safe. The analogy to chess that I had made earlier—quite accurate, would you not say?' mused Holmes as he smoked his pipe, an accessory quite incongruous with his ornate Chinese *changshan* attire and pigtail. We avoided any unnecessary contact as our linguistic difficulties would become obvious and arouse suspicion.

'In my opinion, we have actually gained at least seven days by getting off at Myeik and cutting across to Saigon by land. Yes, it has not been comfortable, but I believe we have learned several things. First, that Professor Moriarty will never give up. As we speak, he is possibly poring over a map of this area and making arrangements to head us off. His resources are incalculable and things may possibly become worse now as we head toward China, where we shall fall into the operating region of the Opium Triad. But we simply must press on—there is too much at stake.

'And, of course, we have learned a lot about the flora of this area and passed through the remarkable lost world of Angkor Wat. If this regrettable matter is brought to a close, I hope to spend time writing monographs[12] for private circulation on the botany of the area and the architectural insights of the early Cambodians. But now, let us rest and regain our energies.'

The *Tek Hwa Seng* made excellent progress over a couple of days and, other than a minor squall past the Paracel Islands, we experienced no discomfort. Holmes and I avoided stepping out as far as possible. He spent time organizing his notes and leaf specimens. Occasionally he would take out his violin and check the tuning, but avoided playing with the bow since there was the distinct possibility of exciting comment. He also looked at the many pages of a musical opera, the score of which he said had been written by a promising young composer in Prague with whom he was acquainted. I admired Sherlock Holmes for

---

[12] Holmes' mania for monographs certainly called for a separate monograph.

the ability to so easily distract himself. I was, of course, secretly pleased that he had no recourse to cocaine.

'The maritime expertise of the Chinese is quite remarkable, Watson,' said Holmes, puffing at his pipe. 'They were seafarers and brilliant naval architects. Many hundred of years ago, they built ships with five masts, weighing in excess of two thousand tons. To our eyes, the square sails and design seem strange, but they were effective for long journeys. Their Admiral, Zheng He, if I recall from my enquiries at the Library of the British Museum some years ago, was a gifted sailor with an open mind, who combined scholarship, ambition, and action, the traits of all successful leaders. We have much to learn from the Chinese, Watson. Paper and gunpowder are only two examples of their ingenuity. Their literature must be singular.'

'I was unaware that you were making enquiries about Admiral Zheng He and the Chinese at the Library of the British Museum, Holmes,' I said, slightly weary.

'You are unaware of many things, Watson,' remarked Holmes cruelly, adjusting his pigtail.

'Now, as far as this matter is concerned, while I believe we shall be safer once in Japan, danger certainly awaits us at Yoko-hama, which would be the natural port of call for most ships. If we are thwarted there and detained by Professor Moriarty's men, we are lost. We should therefore attempt to enter Japan in an unexpected manner. While I cannot say that we have shaken off Moriarty's men just yet, it is likely he is somewhat chagrined by his lack of success. Macau offers a more interesting possibility for us, being an enclave of Portugal. From there I propose that we find a way to enter Nagasaki, a small town in the southwest of Japan, which also has a strong link to Portugal.'

After the initial good weather, we did run into a few trying squalls along the way, but the ship was sturdy and the captain experienced. We covered the distance from Macau to Nagasaki in good time, continuing in our disguise as Chinese merchants. The ship stopped at Shanghai for two hours; we stayed on board, not interested in tempting fate. The ship moved on, without incident. Finally, at dawn on the 29th of July, 1893, we eased into the charming Nagasaki Bay.

Nagasaki is a prosperous trading city in a picturesque setting. It was once the gateway for Europeans who wished to trade in Japan. The Portuguese and the Dutch, in particular, left a lasting impression, particularly with their architecture. The hills surrounding the city were verdant and I looked at them with pleasure as we moved into the harbour.

Holmes stood at the railing with me, watching the dawn break. He was in a philosophical mood. 'Do not be deluded by the apparent tranquillity of this scene. We shall now confront the matter that has consumed me since I fell off the cliff at Reichenbach Falls. And that which has received your complete attention for the past two months.

'We are now at the most dangerous stage of our journey, Watson. We have stayed ahead of the *North Star*. The two Japanese on board the ship must be apprehended as it docks in Yokohama, or the consequences will be shattering. I will tell you why.'

We disembarked at the port and were waved through since we looked Chinese; the community has a large presence at Nagasaki and has trading rights, which give them certain advantages.

We were finally in Japan.

In Paris, Professor Moriarty stared at yet another cable.

TARGETS DISAPPEARED ON THE WAY BACK TO
BANGKOK FROM SIEM REAP. ATTEMPT FAILED
AT ANGKOR WAT. AWAITING INSTRUCTIONS.

He drafted a wire to his associate, Tsong Wang, in Shanghai.

Kyoto

夢

It is safer to live in dreams, my friend.
There we shall meet the lovers we never had. We can listen
to the most wonderful music there, that which does
not deserve to be played in the real world.
Yes, your suggestion is excellent.
I shall leave tomorrow. Perhaps I shall meet you in my dream
and we shall sing songs for the ghosts.

After refreshing ourselves in Nagasaki, at lodgings that a friendly Japanese gentleman at the port had recommended, Holmes and I considered our plan of action. Every security agency was likely to have been compromised and it was necessary to maintain absolute secrecy. Oshima-san, according to Holmes, was possibly the only person we could fully trust.

'I would venture to say, Watson, that we shall not find safety till we actually enter the building that Mr. Oshima operates from. The focus of all the forces must now be on Japan. I have deliberately not kept in touch with Mr. Oshima all this while. Who is to say who is monitoring telegrams in Tokyo? And yet, time is of the essence. We must reach Tokyo very quickly. I must ring Masako Nohara and consult with her.'

We had stepped outside, after discarding our Chinese guise, to visit Meganebashi Bridge, a local attraction that our hotel manager said was a place of exquisite beauty and tranquility. Holmes needed a place for quiet deliberation and a smoke. Both of us wished to stretch our limbs and feel the earth after the extended voyage. The city was certainly beautiful, with Dutch and Portuguese churches, Buddhist temples, manicured gardens, and well-designed roads. The people were singularly courteous.

We dropped in at the pleasant British Tea House for a quiet cup of tea and to find our land legs. It was a quaint little place and I felt a touch of nostalgia, momentarily feeling that I was in London.

We then found the nearest post office and Holmes placed a trunk call to Masako Nohara. Their conversation was brief and to the point. We continued toward Meganebashi Bridge.

'Developments, Watson. Perhaps significant,' said Holmes, as we walked. 'Miss Nohara says that Mr. Oshima has suddenly taken ill with symptoms of food poisoning after a meal at a restaurant and is currently recuperating. He will be back at work on the fifth. She recommended we keep to the interior till then as the Yakuza would certainly expand their search to include all ports of entry. It appears that someone made enquiries about us at Saigon just yesterday. Also, the Emperor of Japan is away north in Sapporo and will also return on the fifth. She advises us to plan to reach Tokyo only on the sixth to be on the safe side and not communicate with her any further till then. In brief, we must lie low. We still have a slight time advantage over the *North Star*, so her advice is sound.'

While he smoked his pipe, leaning on the railing of the bridge, I opened a map of Japan, planning our logistics. 'Holmes, the journey from here to Tokyo touches the cities of Fukuoka, Hiroshima, Okayama, Kobe, Osaka, Kyoto, Nagoya—'

Holmes stopped me. 'Watson, what was that you said? What are the cities we shall be passing by on our way to Tokyo?'

'Fukuoka, Hiroshima, Okayama, Kobe, Osaka, Kyoto, Nagoya, Shuzuoka…'

'Have we not heard the name of one of those cities in the recent past, Watson?' Holmes asked, his brows furrowed.

I shook my head. 'No, Holmes. I have no recollection. The only Japanese we have met thus far were Mr. Oto and Mr. Fujimoto at Bodh Gaya. I did not speak to Mr. Oto, much less discuss the cities of Japan.'

'But I spoke at length with Mr. Fujimoto, my dear fellow!' Holmes was positively excited now. 'And I now recollect! Mr. Fujimoto and Mr. Oto were monks from the Kinkaku-ji temple in Kyoto. And he gave me a letter of introduction to the chief priest. There is not a moment to be lost. We need sanctuary wherever we can get it. Let us take the next available train to Kyoto, Watson.'

We rushed back to the lodge, where Holmes verified that he had the letter from Mr. Fujimoto.

I was apprehensive. 'We cannot read the Japanese script. Are you quite certain this is a letter of introduction, Holmes, and not something that would put us in difficulties?'

'An astute observation, Watson. That thought did cross my mind. But given the disposition of Mr. Fujimoto and the length of the letter, it seems probable this is a letter of introduction. We will have to take our chances. Let us make haste!'

On enquiry, we found that the most convenient route was overland to Fukuoka, with a ferry transfer to the Honshu mainland. From there, a number of convenient trains were available that could take us all the way to Tokyo. We traveled to Fukuoka and then took an overnight train to Tokyo through Kyoto, after a quick visit to the telegraph office, from where I sent a wire to my wife. Holmes also sent out a couple of wires, though he was quite tight-lipped about it.

The train was slow but comfortable and spotless. We had already started developing a favourable opinion of these interesting people and their elaborate culture.

'A mania for precision and timeliness similar to the Germans, but perhaps more colourful,' Holmes observed dryly. 'I was also pleasantly surprised to learn from our efficient hotel manager, Mr. Yamamoto, that Nagasaki has an English language newspaper called *The Rising Sun and Nagasaki Express* and the editor, Arthur Norman, is a Freemason. I have brought a slightly dated copy with me. Perhaps you would care to peruse it and tell me if there is anything there that may be of interest. Meanwhile, I shall shut my eyes and listen to you.'

I was pleased to read an English language newspaper after so long. 'Let me read out the headlines, Holmes:

'*Emperor to visit Nagasaki within a month* (Ah! We shall miss seeing him then, Holmes)...*Guy de Maupassant dies of syphilis in Paris on 6 July* (Hmm, reported late. How did we miss that, Holmes?)...*King Kamehameha III of Hawaii declares 31 July as Sovereignty Restoration Day* (Now what is that about?)...*Tension grows between China and Japan over Korea* (Why, I wonder. Well, we shall read momentarily)...*Daniel Williams successfully performs the first open-heart surgery without anaesthesia* (This verges on the unbelievable, Holmes, but the progress of medicine must be applauded, yes indeed!)...*The first cultured pearl has been extracted by Kokichi Mikimoto* (How wonderfully exotic, Holmes! I wonder if I can get one for my wife)...*Senior priest at Kinkaku-ji temple found dead in mysterious circumstances* (Tragic indeed!)...*Morita-Za kabuki production of* The Tale of the 47 Ronin *received with acclaim* (Now what is *kabuki*, Holmes? And what an unusual title!)—'

'Stop right there, Watson!' exclaimed Sherlock Holmes, sitting up, his eyes alert. 'What was that about the Kinkaku-ji temple? Was that not the place our two Japanese friends were from?'

'Yes, Holmes. The report says a senior priest there was found dead. Let me read it out for you.'

Kyoto—From our special correspondent

Mystery surrounds the death of Ataru Hayashi, one of the distinguished senior priests of the Kinkaku-ji Temple in Kyoto. The temple is the seat of the Shikoku-ji school of Zen Buddhism. Hayashi-san was the Chief Custodian of several ancient relics and manuscripts and was considered an able administrator, brilliant musician, and scholar.

Last Sunday, after the evening prayers, Hayashi-san retired to his private chambers, mentioning to others that he proposed to practise on his *koto* for a while, meditate, and then retire for the night, a routine he was known to follow. The next morning, when acolytes knocked at his door to serve him tea, there was no response. After repeated attempts to elicit a response failed, the chief priest was informed and he authorized the opening of Hayashi-san's room. The priest was found dead on the floor of the living room, his eyes wide with terror and with froth encrusted around his lips. A *koto* with its strings cut was found next to him. Two cups of tea were on a small table nearby, indicating a possible visitor. An inventory revealed that no object in his custody had been stolen. Japan's top criminal detective Shinji Kurosawa has been assigned to this case and we have been assured of rapid progress in the matter, though there are no immediate leads. We shall endeavour to keep our readers updated.

'Well, well! Now that is a remarkable coincidence, Watson. The very temple we propose to visit is the scene of a crime! The report, though extremely brief, has two or three interesting points I wish to look into this further, should I have the opportunity.'

'Yes. The cups of tea and the *koto* with the severed strings, Holmes?'

'Watson, you excel! But I am also intrigued by the comment on his visage. Why was he terrified? That, of course, may also be symptomatic of poisoning. Perhaps you recall the case of The Devil's Foot in Cornwall. What might have been the reason, Watson? Well, one can conjecture, but perhaps not on this trip.'

Destiny would have something else to say, however. We reached Kyoto by mid-morning and set out to the Kinkaku-ji temple, a well-known landmark in an already enchanting ancient city that was once the capital of Japan. The attire of the people, the designs of commonplace objects, the sweeping arcs that high-lighted the reliefs of the temples, the emphasis on minimalism and nature—I was quite fascinated and made several apprecia-tive comments. Even Holmes, usually indifferent to beauty, was constrained to remark that the city appeared to contain the very essence of Japan.

We had long since discarded our Chinese disguises. Holmes, however, took care not to wear his close-fitting travelling cap and cloak as he would have certainly been conspicuous. We appeared to be two European gentlemen going about our business in a town not unused to foreigners.

We presented ourselves at the gates of the Kinkaku-ji temple and sought an audience with the chief priest. This proved fairly easy—cards were not necessary. It was clear, however, that the events of the past few days had cast a pall over the occupants. Dozens of monks of all ages were walking about at that time, perhaps right after scheduled prayers. But their manner lacked

the exuberance I would have expected to see in a group of acolytes. They were whispering, their brows creased with worry.
Not one was smiling.

We entered the grounds of the exquisite temple, which we
understood was almost six hundred years old and was built to
honour the Buddha. The fourteenth-century temple was gold-
plated and located in the midst of sylvan settings, with a beautiful
lake as a counterpoint to the main structure. The temple was
also referred to as the Golden Pavilion and lent itself to a certain
serenity; the reflection in the tranquil lake, Kyôko-chi, was visu-
ally soothing. The three stories each had separate significance and
the monks' quarters were adjacent to the main building. Certain
relics of the Buddha added to the temple's perceived sanctity.

We were escorted to a large room for an audience with the
chief priest, Akira Arima, and asked to remove our shoes and
take off our hats. I was struck by the room—there was absolutely
no sound. Several priests sat motionless in postures of contemplation against the walls and large drapes hung down from the
ceiling. There were several Buddhist motifs. The overall mood
was sombre.

The elderly priest presented a picture of dignity and intelligence. His English was excellent with only the slightest Japanese
accent.

'Gentlemen, I welcome you to our temple,' he bowed.

'We are greatly honoured, Sir, and thank you for this audience,' replied Holmes, bowing low. I followed his example. 'My
name is Sherlock Holmes and this is my friend and confidant, Dr.
John Watson.' I was surprised by Holmes' unexpected candour,
then realized that the letter of introduction probably contained
our real names anyway, so it made sense to be truthful.

'We are presently in a state of mourning, as you may perhaps
know. I regret we cannot extend even normal courtesies to you.'

'Yes, we have heard of the event and would like to express
our condolences.'

'Thank you. Perhaps you are from a newspaper. I do not have
much more to add to what you have read—'

'No, we are not. We have just arrived from India and have a letter of introduction from Mr. Akira Fujimoto, who is affiliated with your temple and who we met at Bodh Gaya.'

'*So desu ka*? Indeed?' responded the priest and accepted the proffered letter from Holmes. 'I am pleased to hear that.'

At this point, I shall transliterate the elegant words of the chief priest (*busso*), who later kindly gave me his written notes and reflections on the events that transpired after we met him.

From the Notes and Reflections of Busso Akira Arima: The suddenness of the passing away of my good friend Hayashi-san certainly shook me. Even though we teach our acolytes about the transient nature of life and the need to accept the inevitability of death, I must confess that I was deeply grieved, in particular because his death was unnatural and seemingly without cause. I spent long hours contemplating the Buddha and reciting the Amitabha Sutra, as did the other monks and acolytes.

Hayashi-san was an exceedingly fine man with the perfect balance between spiritual pursuits and the need to navigate the material world satisfactorily. He had the keys to all the safes and cupboards that housed our invaluable scrolls and artefacts, going back six hundred years. He was responsible for accounts as well and handled our treasury with diligence and scrupulous honesty. He also took care of our properties elsewhere in Japan. Never had a word been whispered about him in any manner that was not respectful. He was quiet, reserved and always spoke in a soft and gentle voice. He sought neither recognition nor reward and gladly accepted any assignment I asked him to undertake. Indeed, I recall sending him to Mongolia as a representative of the temple to a conference on the interpretation of the *Ratnakuta Sutra*, which expounds the advantages of the Middle Path.

He was a great scholar and mentor with absolutely no worldly ambition. And so he had become respected and gained influence without seeking it. He was my best friend and advisor, though I did not see him as a natural successor since he did not have that rare element of authority and ambition required in a leader.

And how can I ignore his musical virtuosity? Hayashi-san was a brilliant *koto* player, with a remarkable knowledge of Buddhist music and of the instrument too. His music helped all of us meditate with greater focus; we were often in a trance as his sublime notes caressed our souls and delivered us to the feet of the Buddha. The notes from his wonderful *koto* skimmed the waters of this lake, feeding off the moonbeams, asking us to chant our holy sutras with care and love instead of as an exercise in mindless repetition, thus savouring the essence of the teachings. His music added even greater dignity and grandeur to this most respected temple, Kinkaku-ji. It was said that had Hayashi-san not been a monk, he would have become a renowned *koto* player.

Like so many extremely gifted and creative people, he loved colour, form, substance, and shape. He believed with sincerity that repeatedly painting the Buddha in various states of blissful contemplation was in itself an evolved form of meditation. He was in charge of the painting classes and very gently taught students the subtleties of colour-mixing, the use of brushes, the introduction of light, the selection of the medium and so on. The hesitant, self-conscious but eager student, unsure of his abilities; the mature, gifted student with deep knowledge of dimensions and aspects; and the dilettante—Hayashi-san had something for everyone and gave them a gift they were always grateful for. Alas, I myself never had any talent in that area, so I cannot say more except that the evidence of his brilliance can be seen on every wall of this temple. The Buddha—the peaceful, closed eyes, the clear forehead touched by *Nirvana*, the gentle compassionate smile, the fingers, the life-like hair; many dozens of Hayashi-san's paintings will live here forever, inspiring the seeker, calming the troubled mind and guiding the artist. In blue, in red, in orange, in black—each different and each the same. Each exemplifying perhaps one or the other sutra. The gold you may see in this temple is merely real. The true gold is in the essence of his wonderful paintings; he has created an astonishing legacy that future generations of Buddhists in Japan shall cherish. His life seemed so complete and rich. Perhaps you can understand why I never wished to burden him with the additional ugly responsibility of leadership; his was a beautiful soul and his destiny was to spread the message of the Buddha through his music and painting.

I had prophesied many years ago that a calamity would strike Kinkaku-ji, though I was unsure of its nature. And so it did. One fateful morning, many young acolytes created an unprecedented disturbance outside my quarters. I emerged and questioned the boys. One of them said that Hayashi-san was not responding to knocks on his door and they were concerned. Would I give permission to enter his room, they asked; the door was not locked, in any case. I rushed to Hayashi-san's quarters, knocked and called out loudly. Finally convinced that there was a problem, I pushed open the door.

Hayashi-san was sprawled in the middle of the living room, dead. He was lying on his back and his face was contorted in a terrible grimace. His eyes stared at the ceiling in utter horror, and foam had dried on his lips—it was a terrible sight. Beside him was his beloved *koto*, its strings inexplicably cut and a wire-cutter placed alongside.

I ordered that no one touch his body and sent word to our resident physician, Nara-san, who arrived in moments. He examined the body and said that Hayashi-san had been dead for at least six to eight hours. He suggested we call the police, for which I issued instructions.

Police personnel arrived quickly along with Detective Kurosawa, who impressed me as a man of few words and high intelligence. He examined the room carefully and observed that it appeared that Hayashi-san had had a visitor the previous night, judging by the two cups of tea on the table. He was puzzled, I could see, by the fact that we insisted that the door had been shut but not locked. The windows in his quarters had metal bars and the ventilators in his room were too far above and too narrow. The other person could have left the room only by the front door, but the event was unthinkable, since it was not the norm to visit the quarters of any priest after dusk, much less have tea with him. Moreover, all of us were emphatic that Hayashi-san never entertained any visitors at any time. Had there been visitors, we would have known. It was impossible to keep such an event secret.

In my presence, Kurosawa-san conducted a thorough search of Hayashi-san's rooms and did not find anything missing. All the keys were precisely where they always were. There were a few scrolls that Hayashi-san had borrowed from our library—they too were safe and in immaculate condition. There were some other books from the office, mostly of accounts.

There was one unusual addition, however, which I shall talk about later.

Kurosawa-san took charge and asked that nothing be disturbed. We respectfully removed Hayashi-san's body, so we could prepare it for the funeral, and sealed his room. All the monks were plunged into grief, as Hayashi-san had been a venerated priest, particularly loved for his music and painting. I found it difficult to contain my own feelings, but I had to demonstrate the behaviour expected of a chief priest and therefore went about without any great show of emotion. We began the funeral preparations immediately; I took personal charge of the matter and concluded the ceremonies appropriately. The local officials had also come and the matter received some publicity.

A day after the funeral, with all of us still reciting the *Amitabha Sutra* and otherwise continuing our mourning, we received two Englishmen who introduced themselves as Mr. Sherlock Holmes and Dr. John Watson. They had with them, quite surprisingly, a letter of introduction from Fujimoto-san, a dear lay monk who had embarked on a pilgrimage to Bodh Gaya several weeks prior, as part of a personal quest for atonement and forgiveness for a life spent in the pursuit of incandescent objects of acquisition. He had been accompanied by Oto-san, a younger monk.

The letter the visitors presented was interesting.

Respected Arima-san,

I am indeed blessed that I was able to travel to the land of the Buddha without incident and with your permission. Oto-san is a fine companion and very caring and we managed to travel uneventfully through Shanghai, Singapore, and Calcutta. We did have some difficulty in reaching Bodh Gaya, but the journey was tolerable. We found shelter at a dharamshala and have spent several days absorbing the grace and wonder of the land where the Buddha himself walked. Indeed, I have spent hours contemplating the Buddha at the Bodhi tree and felt the vibrations of the enlightened soul.

I am sending this letter through the hands of two extremely interesting and trustworthy gentlemen, Mr. Sherlock Holmes and Dr. John Watson. I sense that they wish to travel to Japan soon and they may need assistance. Mr. Holmes, the taller one, speaks some basic Japanese, while Dr. Watson does not. They met me disguised as Indian monks, but I realized they were not so and are possibly policemen or government officials on some sort of mission. This I have guessed because of my past interactions with the government, of which you are aware. They finally admitted to being Englishmen on a sensitive mission. These are good men, in my opinion, and deserve your consideration and protection.

As always, I regret the life of crime I was associated with, but I am also happy that you, Arima-san, helped me to confront the consequences that I may face in my next incarnation. I wish to break the cycle of illusion and adopt the path of truth by confessing my misdeeds at every opportunity and, when my time comes, I hope to receive forgiveness at the feet of the Buddha.

We propose to leave soon for Lumbini and Sarnath. With the blessings of the Buddha, perhaps we shall return to Kinkaku-ji in six months.

Respectfully Yours,
Akira Fujimoto

Fujimoto-san was a former member of the Yakuza, who had been at the periphery of that organization and had developed spiritual interests some years ago. As you may know, we do not judge a person by his life; we are all in the grip of Karma and must consciously work toward breaking the cycle of cause and effect.

I looked at the tall gentleman with the sharp nose and intense eyes. I saw extreme intelligence and wisdom and could also see why Fujimoto-san was so impressed. I too instinctively felt that this was a person of great discernment who was likely to have the skills needed to understand the reasons behind the unfortunate event.

'Can you help us' I asked him, 'in determining how and why Hayashi-san's life ended in such a manner?'

'If your local investigators would not object to my presence, I would be honoured to do so.'

'I shall speak to the inspector. I know him.'

I ensured that our guests received the best care and refreshments. After that, I summoned Kurosawa-san and asked him to allow the gentlemen access to the crime scene, introducing them as my dear friends who had lately arrived from Nagasaki.

Mr. Holmes examined the room very carefully. The force of his magnetic personality was such that it became clear that he was in charge of the investigation.

'What was the nature of Mr. Hayashi's duties?'

I described them in detail.

'Who are the priests who live on either side of his quarters?'

I summoned Shimuza-san and Saito-san, lay priests both.

They denied having heard anything and confirmed that they would have known if anyone had entered or left the room. There is almost no sound here, they said, as we spend most of our time in private contemplation. Hayashi-san was not in the habit of inviting anyone for tea.

'I see that the tea cups are still here.'

'Yes,' said the inspector. 'I left instructions that nothing be disturbed. It is now three days since the event. I was proposing that the room be cleaned up.'

'One cup has completely dried up while the other is half-empty. Does that not strike you as significant, Watson?' Mr. Holmes asked his friend.

'Perhaps the guest was not a tea drinker.'

'Quite unlikely. It would probably be bad manners for a guest to not sip some as a matter of form. No, you have missed the point here. Let us delve further.'

He examined the cups carefully and then turned to the inspector: 'Could we have a chemical analysis done of the contents of the cups?'

'Of course.'

'Was there a post-mortem?'

'No.'

'How will you determine the cause of death?'

'At this time, we believe Hayashi-san was shocked by some news and had a severe heart attack and died. There was no physical wound on his body. The possibility of poison does exist, given the appearance of the corpse.'

'Were you a frequent visitor, Mr. Arima?'

'Not frequent, but perhaps once a month.'

'Is there anything you see here that is different?'

'Yes,' I said, gesturing. 'This painting.'

On the opposite wall was an extraordinary painting that I had never seen before Hayashi-san's death. That in itself was not surprising, since Hayashi-san was a prolific painter who worked on many pieces simultaneously and I was not usually aware of what he was doing. What was surprising was that this was not a painting of the Buddha.

It was a painting of a woman.

The painting was a portrait, about three feet in height and two feet wide. It was clearly the work of Hayashi-san in the prevalent Nihonga style, but it was uniquely different from his other pieces. The unsmiling woman was not particularly beautiful; many women look more attractive in real life than in portraits. And perhaps that was what made it special. The painting looked more real than anything I had ever seen before. Life pulsated on that canvas, but it was grim and not liberating. She was young, perhaps twenty, and her eyes had an infinite sadness in them. She was looking slightly to her left.

Let me attempt to describe it further. I am not gifted in the use of words and if I stumble, please excuse me.

I saw the unmistakable genius of Hayashi-san. But I was embarrassed. It was a very private painting, full of frustration. No, do not misunderstand me.

She had on an unusual kimono, light green with a delicate flowery motif, and wore no make-up—now can you imagine a painting being able to make such a statement? Her hair was set neatly in the style of the times and yet she was timeless. Behind her was a brilliant blue sky, full of furious white clouds, pushing against the canvas, wishing to burst out. Though red was not really visible, it could be sensed—a peculiar understated emotion soaking the canvas.

The painter had transferred a message of deep love onto the canvas. But the woman clearly did not reciprocate. His love had been found unworthy or unsuitable, perhaps. And as the painter had painted her, her rejection had become progressively firm and so the painting was not static. It described a string of tormented moments, of the painter and of the subject. And we could almost *hear* the woman breathing.

I was absolutely awestruck by what I saw, as was Dr. Watson.

'I have not known Hayashi-san to paint anything but the Buddha!' I finally said.

'Perhaps this was a woman he knew,' remarked Dr. Watson. 'He dies facing the painting. Very melodramatic!'

Mr. Holmes stepped up to the painting and studied it and the frame very carefully with a magnifying glass. Then he attempted to lift it and gave up after a couple of tries.

'So you say that this painting is new.'

'I have not seen this before. It may not be new, but I know he never displayed it. I am quite sure of that.'

'Ah. The painting may be old. But I see that the frame is new.'

'The face is somehow familiar,' said Detective Kurosawa, frowning. 'I have seen it recently, but I do not recall where.'

Mr. Holmes examined the late priest's effects and the account books very closely. He removed a slip of paper from the pocket of the priest's kimono, which had been kept folded on the bed after the funeral.

He handed it to me and asked me what it was.

'This is a ticket to a recital by the great *koto* player Yatsuhashi Miyagi at the Minamiza Auditorium, a place used for *kabuki* and musical performances. This was on the day prior to his demise.'

'Was he in the habit of attending concerts?'

'Oh yes,' I said. 'He was a great connoisseur of music. He had a deep unspoken passion for its spiritual significance and was himself a brilliant *koto* player.'

'Did he perform in public?'

'No. Music was, to him, a personal matter. But I know that he was extremely gifted.'

Mr. Holmes' eyes moved to the *koto* with the broken strings, still lying where it had been found. He bent down and looked at the cut strings and the metal cutter very carefully and nodded. His eyes were reflective as he stood.

'Why would he cut the strings?'

'I do not know,' I replied. 'It seems an impossible thing for him to do. Practically sacrilegious.'

'Not necessarily, not necessarily. There is an element of finality in the act.'

'Did he maintain a personal diary?'

'I could not say. Let me look.'

I went to his desk to look over his documents. Finding nothing, I looked behind the desk and saw a crumpled piece of paper.

'Ah, here is something!'

I picked it up and smoothed it out.

'This is in Hayashi-san's handwriting. Let me translate it for you.'

> '*Music is nothing but heaven itself. When I play, I touch heaven.*'
>
> '*Miyagi is inferior, yet people applaud. This too is an illusion.*'
>
> '*I am a mere monk who no one knows. And he—utterly amateur and worthless as a player—he is worshipped. How can he play thus?*'
>
> '*He always knew I was better. His father threatened my poor mother and forced her to make me a monk. What option did she have?*'

'Emiko! Emiko!'
'I have spent a life in contemplation and music. To what end?'

'The entries appear disconnected,' I remarked, 'though I get the impression of a man in the grip of a negative emotion. This is strange because I do not recall seeing him upset. Of course, we have a very set routine and spend a lot of time in meditation. It is possible our ability to observe worldly events has dulled.'

'Perhaps we get a glimpse of the psychology of the man, in spite of what you believed him to be,' murmured Sherlock Holmes. He paced the room, frowning, head bent.

'What does "Emiko" mean?' Dr. Watson asked. 'Is that a name?'

'Yes,' I said. 'A woman's name. Though I could not say who she might be.'

'I just remembered something! I attended the same concert last night,' interjected Kurosawa-san suddenly. 'And now I recall why that painting seemed familiar. I saw an older woman there in the front row who had some resemblance to the woman in this painting. I am sure of it. I never forget a face.'

'Capital! This opens a new line of thinking,' murmured Mr. Holmes. 'Detective Kurosawa, may I ask you to please check on a couple of points?'

He scribbled something on a slip of paper. Kurosawa-san glanced at it, nodded, rewrote the text in *Kanji* and passed it on to an aide.

At this point, another detective entered the room in a hurry and spoke to Kurosawa-san.

'We have made a breakthrough. Three witnesses claim to have seen Hayashi-san and Miyagi-san after the concert. They overheard Hayashi-san inviting him for tea!' Kurosawa-san was excited.

'From this you conclude?'

'We must hold Miyagi-san immediately on suspicion!'

'What is the case?'

'A ticket to the concert. Three witnesses who overheard the invitation to tea. Two tea cups. The death appearing to have been caused by poison.'

Sherlock Holmes looked dubious. 'Well, well, I am not completely convinced, but I do not have much more to go on. Something does not seem quite right. Every instinct protests. Meanwhile, when do you expect to know about the contents of the tea cup?'

'By this evening.'

'Excellent. Shall we meet again at eight? Is it possible for you to avoid detaining Mr. Miyagi till we have had a look at the results?'

'Yes. That is not a problem. I shall be back.'

Kurosawa-san and his aide left the monastery after sealing the room again.

'Miyagi-san is a very accomplished and famous *koto* artist. For him to be arrested on suspicion of murder would be sensational, of course,' I said.

'Yet something is not quite right.'

'If the scrap of paper showed that he was jealous of Miyagi-san, why would he invite him over for tea? Why would he even attend his concert?' Dr. Watson enquired.

Sherlock Holmes halted in mid-stride. 'Watson! Now that is a remarkably astute observation! A musical monk visits the *koto* concert of someone he believed to be his inferior, uncharacteristically invites the artiste to tea, writes apparently incoherent sentences suggesting jealousy and depression and is found poisoned. Inexplicably, his *koto* has broken strings. And what of the discovery of a hitherto unknown painting of a woman? Is a picture emerging? No? Well, let us withhold judgment. We may be close to the answer.'

We waited in my office for the report to come in. Sherlock Holmes sat back in a chair, lost in thought, his eyes far away. Dr. Watson looked at the ancient manuscripts and objects of art and history that were on the shelves. We discussed the history of the temple and the kinds of studies that the monks pursued. I was pleased to note the gentleman's interest in our religious beliefs and in our temple.

Kurosawa-san came in precisely at eight.

'Well?' asked Mr. Holmes eagerly. 'Was I right?'

'Yes,' nodded Kurosawa-san. 'Perfectly right. We checked. Miyagi-san and Hayashi-san were students of the same *koto* teacher at the same time. Miyagi-san belonged to a prosperous Samurai family, while Hayashi-san was of much humbler stock and was raised by his mother who was very poor. They knew each other well but were not friends and, in fact, disliked each other intensely. Hayashi-san was considered the superior musician, but he abruptly chose the life of a monk, perhaps because Miyagi-san's father spoke to his mother and, in those days, absolute obedience to a Samurai family was taken for granted. Miyagi-san pursued a career in music. He married his teacher's daughter, Emiko, and she was at the concert last night.'

'That answers many questions. And the tea cups?'

'A confirmed mixture of arsenic and an unidentified chemical suggesting a hallucinogenic in one cup. Nothing in the other.'

'The other being the half-empty cup?'

'Yes. How could you have guessed?' Kurosawa-san gasped in admiration.

'Nothing but logic, Mr. Kurosawa. In itself, the case is now quite clear, gentlemen, and provides yet another odious glimpse into the sinister workings of the human mind. So, Mr. Kurusawa, do you have a better view now?'

'No, Holmes-san. In fact, I am even more confused now.'

'Let me help you. But may we take another look at the painting?'

'The painting? How is that relevant at this time, Holmes-san?'

'Oh, I think it is very relevant. If nothing else, it will confirm my conjecture.'

The painting was brought in.

'Permit me to remove the frame,' said Mr. Holmes, his eyes shining.

With a pocket knife, he gently removed the painting from the frame.

Behind were several small packets of papers, tied together with a string. He handed them over to me.

'Please read the papers, Mr. Arima. I think they are connected to the matter and I would like your confirmation.'

'How did you know these papers would be there?' asked Kurosawa-san, shocked.

'I guessed, but was not entirely sure. I noticed the fresh scratches on its sides, showing that the painting had been newly framed. When I tried to lift it, the painting seemed slightly heavier than what I would have expected, with a slight but definite tilt toward the right. I saw some paper coming through the edges there. Someone had been trying to hide something and not done a clean job. Let us review the contents. I may be wrong, but even if I am, it should not alter the facts materially.'

I untied the strings and opened the papers. In a moment, it was clear that these were letters. These were expressions of love from Hayashi-san toward Emiko. I shall give only two examples, because the love of a man for a woman is private and must be respected as much as possible, even after his death. Here is a small extract from one, which I translated into English and read out for the benefit of Mr. Holmes and Dr. Watson.

Emiko,

   These words will never be read by you and yet I must write them. I have painted you and I feel you here. It is enough. I am now just a monk and my life is slowly passing by. Why did you marry Yatsuhashi? You knew that my koto sang poems of love for you. You knew that he was inferior. Yes, I was poor but I thought you did not believe that to be important. But was it?

   To paint you and to play the koto…music and colour and love…

   I have composed a beautiful tune in your memory. I shall never play it. The world shall never hear it. But it is my masterpiece. I have never conceived of anything more pure. If I meet you after we die, I shall play that piece for you. The heavens shall be silent forever after.

And here is an extract from another.

Emiko,

   I turned sixty-two today. Forty years have passed since I last saw you. Every day I look at your painting. Every day you look different. I share your life, unseen. Did you have children? Should they not have been mine? The clouds in the painting are quieter today; perhaps it means that you are at peace. But a few days ago, I felt you were upset about something and the clouds were very restless. I asked you what the matter was, but you looked away again and did not reply. You have not spoken to me for forty years.

   Will you speak to me tomorrow?

All of us were deeply moved upon hearing the tragic, searing tale of unrequited love. Finally, Mr. Holmes spoke.

'And so, gentlemen, I hope the matter is now clear. Mr. Hayashi was not killed—he committed suicide, but wanted it to be seen as a murder. How and why? For this we must consider the psychology of the man.

'Mr. Kurosawa says that Mr. Miyagi and Mr. Hayashi learnt the *koto* from the same teacher and were not well disposed toward each other. His notes point to a feeling of extreme jealousy over the fact that a less-accomplished artiste who was his musical rival made a name for himself, while he was perhaps forced to become a monk. He joined this temple and was anonymous for the most part, at least as far as the outside world was concerned. And even more significantly, he loved a woman—Emiko—who rejected him and married his rival. Over a lifetime, jealousy and bitterness consumes him. He visits a concert and sees the woman he has loved all his life. Rage finally overwhelms him and reason is discarded. This is his only chance to act and ruin the career and life of his adversary—by staging his own murder and making it appear that Mr. Miyagi had something to do with it.

'He goes to the concert and later asks his adversary to visit him for tea. Why, when there was no question that Mr. Miyagi would accept the invitation, given their past animosity? Arima-san specifically said that he always spoke softly. Yet he, quite incongruously, invites Mr. Miyagi in a loud voice. Why, Watson?'

'I cannot imagine why, Holmes, unless there was someone within earshot he wanted to inform.'

'Precisely! Because he *wanted* people to hear him. He *wanted* people to remember that there was an invitation extended to Mr. Miyagi! The man has made lightning plans and wants to seize the moment.

'Now he returns to Kinkaku-ji in a ferment and continues with his routine but with his mind clear on what is to be done. He brings out his painting and frames it, after inserting his love letters behind. He cuts the strings of his *koto* in a gesture of closure—there is symbolism there; remember that he is at heart an artist with an enhanced appreciation for the dramatic. He pours tea in two cups, so that it would appear that someone had tea with him. He puts arsenic in his tea cup and none in the other and drinks from his own. Then he lies down and lets the poison takes its terrible course. He probably calculates that the police will not find arsenic in the other cup. A scrap of paper is conveniently found—I would even conjecture it was placed there deliberately—hinting at a long festering streak of extreme hatred and the fact that Mr. Miyagi's father manipulated his career.

'The ticket provides further clues in the direction of Mr. Miyagi. He ensured that his invitation to Mr. Miyagi was heard by several persons. The cut strings of his beloved *koto,* something no one could imagine that he would do, to suggest a vicious spiteful rival. It does not take much to conclude, based on circumstantial evidence, that Mr. Miyagi murdered him. He will, at the very least, be harassed severely and will be looked at with suspicion till he manages to clear himself, if at all, because I do not know the nature of the laws that protect the alleged accused here in Japan. His career will be ruined. In Mr. Hayashi's mind, killing himself is worth the cost and would bring about some kind of warped closure.'

'The half-cup?'

'Evaporation over the period of a day, nothing else. The full cup of tea became a half-cup!'

'The look of terror on his face?'

Mr. Holmes shrugged. 'I imagine it was the hallucinogen or a realization that he could not reverse his action. We shall never know.'

'Excellent, Holmes-san!'

Kurosawa-san bowed. 'There is no doubt about what you have said, Holmes-san. We have no basis for holding Miyagi-san. A man's reputation has been saved just in time.'

I was distressed, however. 'Holmes-san, in one way I am glad that an innocent man has been exonerated. But it is a matter of anguish that a close friend orchestrated his own death with such cruel intent. We at the temple are contrite. His action has brought dishonour to us. How can anyone accept the idea that a monk with such a great reputation would be consumed by the desire to harm someone else?'

Mr. Holmes was reflective. 'An idea may take a lifetime to mature. Jealousy grows over the years and can consume you, as I have seen. A motive for murder may be completely irrational. We eliminate the most obvious ones and then the bizarre and improbable become likely. A man hides behind the cloak of a respectable priest at a famous temple for years. His mind is preoccupied by the whats and whys of a life gone by. A glorious musical career. The love of a woman. He could have neither. The seeds of bitterness lie within, waiting for exactly the right time to germinate. I have seen this again and again, and you may even recall, Watson, the time we were engaged to handle the case of the attempted assassination of the Prince of Bavaria. Contrary to what one may think, the majority of premeditated crimes are committed by people over the age of fifty. They have spent years nurturing a certain bitterness about past events and people and have rationalized their plan of action. I believe such was the case here.'

We were in a sombre mood at dinner. There was no feeling of satisfaction. I knew it would take me a long time to reconcile to the fact that a close colleague had a side I knew nothing of. A brilliant priest, able administrator, outstanding musician, and painter—he was now gone, in such an awkward way, fumbling to bring down another talented man, who he believed had thwarted him in music and in love. He may have succeeded if not for the intervention of this gifted Englishman. I am grateful to Fujimoto-san for having introduced him to us.

The newspapers reported that Hayashi-san had committed suicide and there was some talk about it, but it died down after a few days. The real reason for the suicide was kept secret; no real purpose would have been served by revealing it anyway. Miyagi-san went his way without knowing how close he had come to disgrace. Neither did Emiko ever know the role she had played in Hayashi-san's death. On Holmes' advice, it was decided that the beautiful painting of Emiko be wrapped, sealed, and stored in the archives of the Kinkaku-ji temple and unsealed only after one hundred years; that is where it is today.[13]

Arima-san was the perfect host. Our stay at Kinkaku-ji allowed us to consider our situation. Meanwhile, the priests began a fairly elaborate set of rituals for the departed soul and I sat through the ceremonies, looking on with fascination.

Sherlock Holmes was busy preparing for the short trip to Tokyo. Kinkaku-ji had been a safe haven in one way, but we could no longer afford to wait. It was time to leave. The *North Star* would soon dock into Yokohama. We could still be apprehended before we completed our mission; it was impossible to tell who on the ship was Professor Moriarty's man.

Then with the generous assistance of Arima-san, we were on our way to Tokyo on an overnight train. Holmes first took the unusual step of sending a wire to Miss Masako Nohara, the private secretary to Oshima-san, requesting her to meet us at the Tokyo Central station the next morning, on the eighth of August.

---

[13] Enquiries have been made in the year 2014 by the office of the publisher of Poisoned Pen Press to trace the painting in the vast archives of the Kinkaku-ji temple. The curator first indirectly confirmed the existence of such a painting but has thereafter declined to provide further details. The secrecy is mystifying.

Tokyo

 Why do we like each other, my friend? Simple: you did not complain when I threw snow at you. You smiled at my happiness as the rain fell on my face. When the salty breeze from the Sea of Japan whistled through our hair, we laughed together.

The train journey from Kyoto to Tokyo took several hours. We saw the heartland of Japan at close quarters and passed Mt Fuji, a most majestic and imposing sight. Sherlock Holmes looked carefully through his notes, while I busied myself again with my diary and accounts.

My first impression of Tokyo as the train entered the city at about five o'clock in the morning was of a crowded and congested city. We were received at the station by the Japanese lady that Sherlock Holmes had spoken of, Miss Masako Nohara. I was struck by her extraordinarily confident demeanour and the manner in which she carried herself. She was attractive but not overly so. There was no question of being deferential; she spoke to us as equals. Her English was fluent, without the slightest trace of an accent. It was evident that she was very well travelled and knowledgeable.

'I am delighted to see you again, Mr. Holmes,' she said, as we settled into our carriage. 'I was never in doubt that you would arrive here unharmed, but I gather it has been quite an adventure.'

'Yes, a long and interesting journey, Miss Nohara. Dr. Watson and I have certainly had some interesting experiences. And how is Mr. Oshima now?'

'He has recovered. He sends you his regards and hopes to receive a complete report soon. Tell me, though, why did you come through Kyoto?'

'We thought we had been compromised. It made sense to seek a different access point. We sheltered at Kyoto for a time.'

'I am sure you were involved, somehow, in the recent incident at the Kinkaku-ji temple. I heard from my sources that two Englishmen had helped the police there deal with a rather delicate problem, concerning the suicide of a senior priest.'

'An opportunity to glean another insight into the workings of the human brain.'

'Well, we could do with you here, Mr. Holmes. The police are not—shall we say—adequately progressive and scientific in their methods.'

We reached the guest house to be greeted warmly by Jiro Hamada, the former sumo wrestler and bodyguard who had helped Holmes earlier by introducing him to Japan and its language and culture. While I refreshed myself, Holmes and Miss Nohara spoke on many matters for a couple of hours and she then excused herself, promising to be back by noon. Holmes then turned his attentions to his preparations, playing a few snatches on his violin while referring to the sheet music he had brought with him. In the midst of a singularly serious situation, it is remarkable that he could turn to music and keep his mind occupied.

Miss Nohara then escorted us to the Office of Intelligence Research. Sherlock Holmes took with him several sheets of paper on which he had made copious notes.

We reached Oshima-san's office and were escorted inside by his aide, Mr. Suzuki. Hamada-san sat outside, on guard, on Miss Nohara's instruction.

Oshima-san bowed.

'It has been too long, Holmes-san, too long, *ne*! Two years! I am delighted to see you well and back again in Japan.'

He turned toward me. 'This is a great honour, Dr. Watson. I have heard so much about you. I am hopeful that we shall have time to discuss some of the many cases that you have chronicled so admirably. Perhaps one day the story of the services rendered to our nation by Holmes-san and you will be made known.'

'Miss Nohara mentioned that you had been ill but I did not expect to see you this pale and weak. You seem to have lost weight as well,' remarked Holmes thoughtfully.

'Yes, an unexpected illness. I had a delicacy, a fish called *fugu*, which requires great care in preparation because it is very poisonous. Perhaps the cook erred. Nevertheless, I am quite well now.

'You did well not to communicate till you actually reached the shores of Japan, Holmes-san. We are unsure of so many things now. Professor Moriarty's reach is deep inside Japan as well. I cannot imagine your struggles in reaching Japan. We received news of you last from Bangkok. Then you seemed to have given everyone the slip. Most commendable.'

Holmes sat back in a large chair with half-closed eyes. Oshima-san's attendant opened the door to enquire if he could bring in some tea, but Miss Nohara waved him away impatiently and asked him to return in fifteen minutes. The door was shut. Oshima-san, Miss Nohara, and I waited, expectantly, for Holmes to speak.

Holmes stood abruptly and shook his head.

'No, Mr. Oshima. What I have to say must be presented to the entire group that is familiar with the objectives of Operation Kobe55. The ramifications are so extreme that we simply cannot afford to keep this information with us any longer. Japan will be at war with every European power. Diplomacy will be stood on its head—no one will trust the other. A rot has set in that needs to be savagely excised, without delay.'

Oshima-san was silent for a moment. 'I can certainly bring in the ministers and the chief of police. Sugiyama-san reached Tokyo from Switzerland yesterday to attend to some matters. Of course, you may perhaps not be aware that the list of eleven has been reduced to eight over the past three months, with the unfortunate deaths of Nishikawa-san, the minister of Finance, Takenaka-san, our ambassador to France, and Kasama-san, our consul in Shanghai.'

Sherlock Holmes spun around. 'Really? I was not aware of this. A singular coincidence—three deaths in the past three months! What were the circumstances?'

'Nishikawa-san had a heart attack at a cabinet meeting. Takenaka-san died in his sleep in Paris and Kasama-san slipped in his study in Shanghai and suffered a fatal concussion when his head hit the edge of a table.'

'Did you not find that unusual?'

Miss Nohara spoke. 'Certainly, when you look at it in totality, it does seem peculiar. I personally looked into the deaths of the ambassadors, but the police and medical reports appear to be above reproach. There was no poison detected in the first case and the injuries in the second were consistent with the shape of the object that caused the concussion. Nishikawa-san's death was not unexpected as he had long suffered from a weak heart. And—'

'No!' Holmes shook his head, disagreeing vehemently. 'No! I am afraid I must insist—*insist*!—on a meeting this evening at five o'clock—three hours from now—of the remaining members. There is absolutely no time to lose. These deaths are not mere accidents or isolated events. The matter is converging by the second. Anarchy is mere days away. Our lives are in serious danger. I must insist further that Dr. Watson be present at the meeting. The time for action is *now*. The Kobe55 Committee must meet immediately and that must include the emperor!'

Oshima-san shifted uneasily in his seat. 'An immediate audience with the emperor? I am afraid that is impossible. There is protocol and it would take days for his palace officials to grant us an audience. I can convey your message to the emperor's private secretary in a sealed envelope if you insist on secrecy, but I—.'

Holmes slammed his fist down on Oshima-san's table. 'The entire committee! I want the entire committee! Not one member less. I insist! The emperor must hear me. Japan's very existence is in grave danger. We have no time for protocol. Do you understand, Mr. Oshima?'

Oshima-san demurred. 'It would be very, very difficult, Holmes-san, please understand. Everyone is preparing for the *Obon* vacation…'

Sherlock Holmes stood up, his eyes flashing angrily. 'In that case, Mr. Oshima, we must let events play out their course. There cannot possibly be anything more critical to the future of Japan, yet I find you strangely bound by absurd protocol and crippling procedure and thinking about the *Obon* vacation. I appear to have wasted months of my life in a pointless pursuit. I have also endangered the life of my closest associate and dear friend. We shall leave Japan at once! I wish you a good day. Watson, let us—'

Miss Nohara intervened. 'Holmes-san, we are very grateful for your work and sincerely apologize for the inconvenience you have experienced. Doubtless you appreciate that this is not a very normal situation. Please give us a moment to collect our thoughts.'

She spoke in Japanese to Oshima-san for about five minutes. The conversation was animated, but it seemed clear that Miss Nohara was making a very persuasive argument.

Oshima-san finally held up his right hand and stopped Miss Nohara. He looked weary. 'Holmes-san, I shall call Otawa-san and Sasaki-san and seek their immediate intervention. They may help. If they refuse, or if the information you present to the committee proves of little value, my career is obviously over. Nevertheless, in deference to the sincere efforts you have made on our country's behalf, I shall try.'

Holmes bowed. 'I would not ask this of you unless I had every reason to believe it necessary. You have trusted me thus far. Please trust me one more time.'

Oshima-san placed calls to the minister of Internal Affairs and the chief of Secret Police and spoke to both at length. After what seemed an interminable wait, a call came through. It seemed that Holmes' request had been granted. The emperor would see us at five o'clock and the remaining members of the committee would also be there.

'Never in living memory, Holmes-san, has the emperor granted an audience at such short notice, without his secretaries already having an idea of the nature of the information to be presented. I congratulate you.' Oshima-san smiled. 'Let us proceed immediately. We may have time for some tea. Suzuki-san always keeps some ready for us.'

We stepped outside and saw a gruesome spectacle.

Hamada-san was sprawled in a chair, a few feet from the threshold of Oshima-san's room, frothing at the mouth. A cup of tea was on its side on the floor beside him, its contents spilt.

On a small table near him was a tray filled with empty cups and a kettle of tea.

Holmes sprang to Hamada-san's side and grabbed his wrist to feel his pulse, while I examined the jugular vein for signs of life.

'There is still a slight pulse. Summon a doctor. A stomach pump may help him!'

Oshima-san's and Miss Nohara's faces blanched.

'Dr. Watson…?' asked Miss Nohara, in an unsteady voice.

I nodded. 'He appears to have been poisoned, but is still alive.' Miss Nohara rushed out to fetch a doctor.

Holmes bent down and lifted the tea cup from the floor and sniffed at the residue. 'Yes, he has been poisoned. I cannot say with what, but I certainly sense the faint odour of an unfamiliar chemical.'

'Perhaps you can call your security forces immediately, Mr. Oshima.'

'They have penetrated to the very heart of my office!' Oshima-san was leaning against the wall, completely shaken.

'No one in this building is above suspicion, Mr. Oshima! Please detain your aide, Mr. Suzuki, as a start. That tea in the kettle was intended for us. Mr. Hamada helped himself to some and unfortunately came in the way of the assassin's plans.'

Three policemen rushed into the little room and took charge. Oshima-san spoke to them rapidly and one sped out.

'I have asked him to trace Suzuki-san,' Oshima-san explained.

In a minute, the policeman was back.

'Suzuki-san left the building some ten minutes ago; he was apparently in a hurry. Obviously, no one asked him where he was going and why.'

'Now the only place that can give us safety is the emperor's palace, Mr. Oshima. If the Yakuza has penetrated this far, you can be sure we will be watched as we leave this building. Mr. Suzuki may well have heard of our plans and may have set up another incident enroute to the palace—'

Miss Nohara interrupted, 'There is more than one way to the Imperial Palace. Let us leave this minute!' She gave each of us a small snub-nosed revolver. The meaning was clear.

We rushed outside after locking Oshima-san's office, leaving the doctor and the police to supervise matters pertaining to Jiro Hamada's poisoning.

For safety, we decided to take a public coach to the palace rather than Oshima-san's personal carriage. Miss Nohara gave instructions to the coachman and we seemed to move in a direction logically opposite to the Tokyo Imperial Palace. At a suitable point far from the office, Miss Nohara gave fresh instructions and the coach meandered in various directions, finally turning again toward the palace.

The roads were clear, and while we kept our revolvers cocked for any eventuality, no fresh incident occurred as we approached the palace gates.

At the gates, we alighted and Oshima-san approached the guards. They had already been notified to expect us and we were rushed through without hindrance.

The Imperial Palace was everything one might imagine it to be—large, lush, with beautifully maintained lawns, buildings with the most delicate and exquisite façades. I was not oblivious to the fact that I was soon to meet Emperor Meiji, who was already being given critical acclaim, Holmes said, for the ongoing Meiji Restoration. Japan was asserting itself as a world power and this emperor was the architect. History was soon to be made. Though I had, even then, no hint of what Sherlock Holmes was planning to share, I could guess that it was to be of extraordinary import.

We were escorted to an ornate meeting room with a very long, oval-shaped mahogany table in the centre. The Savonarola chairs with elaborate *zabuton* cushions, the *noren* silk curtains on the windows, the breathtakingly beautiful *bonsai* arrangements around the room, the large gold and silver foil paintings from the Azuchi-Momoyama era on the wall—everything spoke of the utmost elegance and refinement in taste. At one corner, a gentle fire had been lit to keep the room warm; it was unseasonably chilly in August. Except for the emperor, who had not yet arrived, all the others were already seated. Holmes knew them from his previous sojourn in Japan. Sugiyama-san was of course present and a smile of acknowledgment passed between them. They shook hands first, their pleasure at seeing each other evident. We went around the room, bowing and shaking hands.

'Mr. Otawa, a great pleasure meeting you again. This is my colleague and trusted friend, Dr. Watson.'

'Of course, of course! You are very well known here in Japan, Dr. Watson. I am most honoured to make your acquaintance,' said the minister of Internal Affairs, bowing. He was a small, stout man with quite a presence, accentuated by a large head and piercing, intelligent eyes.

'Mr. Yoshida. We meet again. Thank you for assisting me in Berlin, Stockholm, and Madrid.'

'Holmes-san, I am so grateful to you. The citizens of Japan will never know how much they owe you. But I know and so does the emperor. Thank you. Though I must ask how you know about my intervention,' the slim, elderly minister of Foreign Affairs said, with a twinkle in his eyes.

'Let that be a diplomatic secret, Mr. Yoshida. And here is my esteemed colleague, Dr. Watson. Without him, I would not have been able to reach Japan again.'

'His fame precedes him, Holmes-san. We are honoured to have you here,' Yoshida-san said, in his suave and cultured voice.

Sasaki-san, the chief of the Secret Police, came forward and bowed to Sherlock Holmes. His English was poor, but nothing could diminish his obviously charismatic and powerful presence. He was short and stocky, and carried himself with great confidence and authority.

'I thank you, Holmes-san,' said Sasaki-san, simply. 'Very difficult journey, very difficult problem, *ne. Arigato gozaimashita*.'

'Mr. Sasaki, thank you.'

We seated ourselves. Holmes sat, by default, at the end of the table, opposite where the emperor was to sit. I sat on his immediate left and further along were Miss Nohara and Oshima-san. To Holmes' right were Sasaki-san, Sugiyama-san, Yoshida-san, and Otawa-san.

It was 4:55 p.m.

The Imperial Palace

You say, my friend, that Majesty stems not from the accidents of heredity, but dedication to the truth. When the truth flows from the heart, he is the Emperor for those few minutes. A palace is simply the home of he who is always the Emperor.

In perusing my notes, I find that Holmes surpassed himself in every possible way during that definitive meeting with Emperor Meiji and the other members of the team who knew of Operation Kobe55. From the time I had known him, Holmes had approached each assignment with a clinical mind; matters of the state or matters touching upon crime or others of significant import to his clients were handled with utmost precision and professionalism. Even today, I am unable to make public certain cases of great sensitivity. Those that the reader has learned about are no longer likely to make a difference to the lives and careers of men or women who were involved. In a few instances, Holmes suggested that I make changes in describing events or locations. I always obliged because I knew what that great mind was capable of calculating.

With so many years having elapsed after the event, perhaps the reader might wonder at the dilemma confronting me. Does the reader not deserve to know the facts? Or does the sensitivity of the matter warrant secrecy for at least another hundred years? Sherlock Holmes recommended the former, for, in his view, the lessons derived from our experience touched upon so many aspects of diplomacy and crime that it could even serve as a kind of elaborate monograph on aspects of diplomatic convention and crime detection. I do believe an aspect of his ego was involved in his coming to such a conclusion. This, in my view, was quite forgivable. Sherlock Holmes did not believe in unnecessary modesty and, in his view, this particular case represented the apex of his career.

The emperor was announced and we all stood as he walked in swiftly, accompanied by two guards. He was not in his formal robes, yet his elegant kimono and bearing made it clear that he was royalty; he glanced in our direction and nodded. We bowed low and waited for him to sit down and permit us to be seated as well. He did so with a wave of his hand.

Emperor Meiji was in his late thirties at that time and presented an impressive sight. Holmes had told me that he was a strong and far-sighted visionary. He was also an introspective poet of some standing and given to the study of the classics.

Standing behind him, at attention, were his guards.

He looked slowly across the assembly and then directly at Sherlock Holmes. A current of respect flowed between them and then the moment passed as Holmes bowed.

Otawa-san stood up and bowed again to the emperor, addressing him in Japanese. He told me later that he had sought permission from the emperor to have Sherlock Holmes present a report of immense significance and sought pardon for requesting an audience at such short notice.

The emperor addressed Holmes through Otawa-san since his command over the English language was poor.

'I am grateful to you for having taken so much trouble for the sake of Japan over the past three years. I am ready to listen to what you have to say.'

Holmes nodded.

'Thank you, Your Majesty. I have much to say and I ask for your patience and that of my colleagues here.

'I arrived in this wonderful country, escorted by your esteemed ambassador to Switzerland Mr. Sugiyama, and was briefed on Operation Kobe55 by Mr. Oshima. Thereafter, I met all the members of the group, one by one. I regret the recent passing of Mr. Nishikawa, Mr. Takenaka, and Mr. Kasama. I believe that they fell in the line of duty, assassinated by forces inimical to Japan, perhaps bent on creating a crisis for the country and lowering its standing in the eyes of the international community. I must compliment the members of this group for having recognized the cancer as it developed and taking a courageous decision to deal with it.

'You may be aware that I spent a few months in Japan in the company of Jiro Hamada, primarily in Tokyo and Osaka, to become acquainted with the many aspects of Japanese culture. He taught me the basics of your fine language, introduced me to the sport of sumo, took me to the *kabuki* theatre and to music performances. All this was to let me immerse myself in the culture and pick up the nuances of Japanese customs. The other reason was, of course, to learn about the Yakuza from experts in Mr. Sasaki's organization. Why did I do this? Quite simple—I had to prepare for my assignment in Europe and had to plan my course of action. What was the assignment? To independently gauge the extent of the Yakuza's infiltration into the Japanese Diplomatic Services and understand how the nexus with Professor Moriarty's organization and the Shanghai Opium Triad was operating. Let me make myself clear once again—that is what I understood the assignment to be. However, I was quite unprepared for what I discovered—but I shall come to that later.

'Working closely with Mr. Oshima, Miss Nohara, Mr. Otawa, Mr. Sasaki, Mr. Nishikawa, and Mr. Yoshida, I first prepared for myself the infrastructure I would need in order to operate undercover in Europe. Since the world at large was convinced that I had been killed at Reichenbach Falls, I needed time to allow the matter to die down and to prepare a separate identity. This I did with the assistance of Mr. Yoshida, who created an elaborate set of identities for me, sometimes as an American businessman, other times as an English banker, elsewhere as a Spanish violinist, and more. My financial needs were to be taken care of by Mr. Nishikawa's arrangements; I needed clear assurance that I would have access to money when necessary. Mr. Sasaki's undercover network was to help me with weapons and access to police information when needed. Mr. Oshima arranged for my activities in Europe to be seen as legitimate—I was set up to import *sake* from a bona fide manufacturer in Sapporo and other liquors from other countries. All this was very important; we believed that it might take over a year to fully assess the extent of the problem and develop a plan. Mr. Takenaka in France and Mr. Sugiyama in Switzerland were judged to be best placed to help me with diplomatic couriers when I needed to communicate with Mr. Oshima or Miss Nohara or provide me with a safe haven if necessary.

'I visited Shanghai on my way to Europe and met Mr. Kasama, your dynamic consul there. I was thoroughly impressed by him. A perceptive and dilligent man, he was very knowledgeable about the activities of the Shanghai Opium Triad. In fact, he had independently developed his own intelligence network and was aware of the expansion plans of the Triad to a far greater extent than anyone else. This was not surprising given his location. He was also a gregarious person, who had developed good relations with members of the Diplomatic Services of other countries who were stationed in China. Indeed, I recall that my first appreciation of the enormity of the problem came from Mr. Kasama's insights.

'I spent two weeks in Shanghai with Mr. Kasama. We visited a couple of opium dens together, incognito, since he wanted me to understand firsthand the extent of the opium business and how it affected people. It was there that I noticed a few Europeans walking about—some were customers, while some seemed to actually be involved in running dens. That is when Mr. Kasama broke the news to me at a small restaurant.

'Holmes-san, you will find Europeans of every nationality involved in the opium den business.'

'Not surprising,' I said. 'People are driven by the same desires everywhere.'

'But what may be surprising to you is that there are some European diplomats who are involved—not just as consumers of opium but as active business partners.'

'What?'

'That is correct. Certain diplomats are in the employ of the Triad. They have business interests and are often used as couriers—not necessarily of opium, but to guarantee the movement of funds.

'It is possible that it is not just the Japanese Diplomatic Service that has been compromised at many levels—the rot has spread to the other consuls based in Shanghai as well. From there it will move elsewhere.'

Holmes turned to me. 'Watson, do you recall the mysterious affair of Miss Bryant, who said she was the tutor to the children of the Japanese consul in Shanghai? That was an obvious lie as I knew Mr. Kasama, the consul-general, and he did not have children. She turned out to be an expert in Chinese martial arts in the pay of the Shanghai Triad, assigned to assassinate anyone who took too active an interest in the affairs of the Triad. It was she who slipped a sleeping potion in your tea, entered your cabin via the porthole and killed Mr. Hashimoto, your friend. And do you recall hearing some sounds earlier that you were wondering about? That was her practising for the kill. She had the slim build needed to enter the narrow porthole and the high intelligence to stage such a daring murder. I believe she had discovered that Mr. Hashimoto was in fact a member of the Japanese Secret Police returning to Japan after a meeting with Scotland Yard.'

'That…that…is astounding, Holmes!' I stammered, recalling the pleasant lady who had travelled with us. She was actually a cold-blooded trained assassin!

'You would also recall that the ship's doctor commented that he was puzzled by the nature of the wound. You did not have a specific response at that time, but I noticed that the wound was particularly narrow and deep and that the knife had been plunged in under the ribs at the diaphragm and then up cleanly into the heart. Death must have been very quick. I conjecture that Miss Bryant hung down from the side of the bridge, broke open the porthole, quickly entered the cabin and surprised Mr. Hashimoto. She struck him under the ribs, the long knife directly hitting his heart, precisely as planned. This was the work of a professional assassin, gifted with ruthlessness, knowledgeable about the human anatomy, using the right instrument and fully aware of the advantage of the element of surprise.'

I shuddered, thinking of that morning of discovery.

'That should also explain to you too, Watson, why the two Japanese men who boarded at Marseilles were surprised to see Miss Bryant. They knew she was an operative of the Triad and did not expect her on the ship. I would not be surprised if it was Miss Bryant who subsequently killed Mr. Kasama in Shanghai. Who could ever imagine a small, slim Englishwoman of uncertain years as a professional assassin? I believe she was Professor Moriarty's "ambassador," if you will, to the Triad. Their calculation was perfect. I would suggest, Mr. Sasaki, that you ask your Chinese counterpart to detain this lady, who, I think, would not be difficult to trace in Shanghai.

'David Joyce, who I knew personally, was from Scotland Yard and had been deputed by Lestrade to keep an eye on me and Colonel Sebastian Moran, masquerading as Colonel James Burrowe. Joyce joined us at Marseilles to allay any suspicions. I am sure that it was Miss Bryant and the two Japanese who murdered David Joyce under the direction of Colonel Moran, who was equally shrewd and must have guessed who Joyce was and that he was watching him. But the matter was executed with such professional finesse that we shall never have conclusive proof on the matter. Who induced him to open the cabin door, who killed him, who threw him overboard? The body will never be found and we shall have to declare him "Lost at Sea, Presumed Dead." Miss Nohara can easily trace these two Japanese and that should not concern us further.

'But to return to my story: Sometime after I met Mr. Kasama, I left for Marseilles and then Paris, taking on the identity of an American businessman, Jim Hodges, supposedly running a business importing wines into the United States. I took up rooms in the Le Marais neighbourhood and changed my appearance, for obvious reasons, and was seen as a stooping, balding middle-aged businessman. Of course, I had connections in the Paris underworld but I avoided using them, as it was risky. I created my own network, using the good offices of Kazuo Takenaka, your ambassador to France.

'This was by no means easy—but by setting up a legitimate business that involved importing beverages from various countries, including *sake* from Japan, I was able to visit the Japanese Embassy from time to time and meet the ambassador. We communicated, when necessary, by meeting each other accidentally at the Louvre or the Catacombs.

'You will recall Mr. Takenaka, an extremely gifted man with a great facility for languages, history, and economics. A man of utmost integrity and circumspection—a credit to your Diplomatic Services, Your Majesty. He will be missed.

'Then began the very difficult process of investigating the matter. I was soon able to befriend the Japanese commercial attaché at Paris, who Mr. Takenaka believed was involved in the matter. His intuition was correct, and the attaché, Mr. Takada, proved to be my primary source of information for a long time, before he returned to Tokyo earlier this year. You can perhaps have him detained shortly after this meeting.

'I remember meeting him at the Café Le Petit Château d'Eau near the Eiffel Tower once we had become very friendly.

'*Hodges-san, how your business is doing?' he asked me, over a meal of escargots and veal and some excellent Bordeaux wine.*

'*Very well, Takada-san, but I occasionally worry that supply from Hokkaido is not regular and predictable.'*

'*Why you import only wine? Why you not try something new, Hodges-san?'*

'*Well, you know, I've been in the spirits business forever, Takada-san. My father built his whiskey business in Kentucky and that's the only thing I've ever done. Would I be able to understand a new business?' I demurred.*

'*New things happening in the world today, Hodges-san! Can I give you idea?'*

'*Of course!'*

'*You good man, Hodges-san. Many business enquiries today about opium importing. People in Japan need reliable agent in Paris to distribute. Very easy business. Much demand. You make the money. You import wine. You import opium.'*

'*But isn't it illegal?'*

'*All business have problems, Hodges-san,*' *he shrugged, rolling his eyes.*

'*What you mean by illegal? Everything legal, everything illegal. You take risk and you make the money. Why you worry? Why you not try? I introduce you to my* tomodachi—*I mean friends—who distribute opium.*'

'*Why not? Let's play ball!*' *I said. We proposed a toast to a new business possibility.*

'And so I entered the world of opium smuggling. The front was perfect—an American businessman involved in a legitimate wine import and export trade in Paris, secretly acting as a conduit for opium distribution.

'Now I visited the Embassy more frequently. I kept Mr. Takenaka informed in our usual way, but the meetings were with Mr. Takada. Within days, he introduced me to other Japanese individuals who were clearly not always diplomats; I met Mr. Murakami, who Miss Nohara had told me about. There was no doubt about it—this man was from the Yakuza. Junior diplomats were also affiliated.

'Murakami and I became friendly. I behaved as a naïve oafish American, easy to manipulate. Later, I was to learn that he had my references checked in Sapporo, but Mr. Oshima had made precise arrangements and they passed. I was completely legitimate.

'Let us understand the matter again. The Japanese Embassy in Paris was used to facilitate commerce by issuing permits and identities to the Yakuza and also by identifying channels such as my business for the import of opium in various ways. The Yakuza liaised with Professor Moriarty's network for two reasons—for the actual distribution of the opium in Europe and to ensure that physical protection was provided against any investigation by the police—the Sûreté in this instance. The Chinese Triad used the channels created to push opium into Europe through the protection of the Yakuza and Professor Moriarty's network, which was finally involved in creating opium dens and creating and fulfilling the demand. They also knew the right persons in the Customs Department and in the Police Department. Everywhere—whether in England, France, India, Japan—corruption exists and is endemic. Everyone needed each other. I hope this is clear.'

We all nodded, leaning forward, fascinated by Sherlock Holmes' narrative.

'My company now started importing opium, though smuggling might be a better word. Please remember that I was not the only importer. There were quite a few, and I have the list. The imports were in very small quantities. It was decided that the market and system would be tested for a couple of years before a full-scale operation. This kind of layered strategic thinking could only have come from Professor Moriarty himself.

'Soon I spoke to Mr. Takada, expressing happiness that the new business was showing signs of promise. He was pleased and asked me to meet his other friends if I wanted to expand my business in Europe. I readily agreed and we travelled together to Madrid, Lisbon, Zurich, Rome, Warsaw, Berlin, Stockholm, Copenhagen, Moscow, and London—yes, Watson, I visited London at least five times during the period you thought I was dead! I assiduously built my image of a corpulent, malleable American businessman for whom only profits were important and the law existed to be ignored or used to his advantage.

'The sophistication of their planning was truly remarkable, Your Majesty. At each Embassy, I met diplomats who would otherwise have passed for upstanding representatives of the Japanese Diplomatic Services, but who were completely in the pay of the Yakuza. They identified importers and cleared the way. The Yakuza took over and liaised with Professor Moriarty's men and kept accounts of the transactions. I thus slowly but surely created a directory of all members of the Diplomatic Services who were—are—involved. This took me almost two years. Remember, I had to develop relationships one at a time and gain the trust of everyone. In return for *sake* and whiskey, the diplomats would slowly yield and take me into confidence.

'I actually met Professor Moriarty himself in Paris. It so happened that Mr. Takada, getting bolder and bolder with every success and transaction, told me about his connections with the underworld. We were at the same Paris café, meeting for an early Sunday lunch and had this conversation.'

'Thank you, Takada-san, this business is very interesting and not so difficult. My Sapporo source receives his shipments of opium from Shanghai—he does not know what it contains, but is kind enough to add the package to the exports he sends to me. No problem at Customs.'

'You are very reliable man, Hodges-san, we are happy, very happy! We soon expand the business many times and you and I become very rich.'

'Your network is very strong. I admire you,' said I, raising my wine glass in his direction.'

'You want to meet the man who does the distribution? He is great man, Professor Moriarty—very smart, very smart. Not so easy to meet him but we can try.'

'Certainly! It would be an honour. If it weren't for him, I can't imagine how this would have worked right under everyone's nose!'

'And so, two weeks after that meeting, Mr. Takada and I, accompanied by Mr. Murakami, set out to meet Professor Moriarty. Our coach went to various places and finally reached…the Louvre!'

'I could not imagine Professor Moriarty being willing to meet anyone in public. The most shadowy figure in Europe, the greatest criminal mind I had ever encountered—why would he seek sunshine? Then again, I could see why that locale was perfect because who could imagine that the most feared and dangerous man in Europe would meet people in one of the world's greatest museums? Remember, there was not a single case ever registered against him anywhere in the world. Suspicion, merely suspicion, yes—but never anything definitive.

'We purchased tickets and wandered about the magnificent museum. The delicacies of Japan, the treasures of China, the wonders of India, vignettes of Assyria, the mysteries of Arabia, the treasures of Rome, Etruscan vases, the paintings of

Leonardo—the distilled beauty of the world's culture were all present at the Louvre and I could have wandered about for days. But that day, my mission was different.

'"How will we find him?" I asked Mr. Takada.

'"He will find us," he responded, with a knowing nod.

'And sure enough, as we turned into the deserted Egyptian section and looked with some awe at the sarcophagi and other fascinating examples of the art of that culture, a voice spoke brusquely behind us.

'"You are late!"

'We turned around. Professor Moriarty was standing at the opposite wall, his back turned toward us, his hands clasped behind his back. I would have recognized him anywhere, so many months after our last encounter at Reichanbach Falls. He wore a long overcoat and had a walking stick. As he turned, I saw that he had changed little; the same glowering deep-set eyes, the huge frontal lobe of his cranium suggesting extreme intelligence, thin-set lips, a pale face, a balding head with hair straggling behind and to the side, the slight stoop in his posture.

'He glanced at us and I was pleased that my disguise had been effective.

'He did not offer his hand to shake.

'Mr. Takada and Mr. Murakami bowed to him, while I doffed my hat. He did not respond.

'"Is everything going well?" he asked Mr. Takada. "The last shipments were delayed. I cannot accept that. This is too small a business for me to worry about such matters. I am more interested in ensuring the system is in place."

'"I apologize, Moriarty-san," responded Mr. Murakami, practically grovelling. "There were some delays in the arrival of ships and it seems that shipments out of Shanghai were delayed too. Very sorry."

'"I am not interested in excuses," snapped Moriarty, his choleric temperament on display. "If there is a delay again and I am diverted from my other businesses, I will consider shutting down this activity. I am in any case not very happy with the blunders of your people in Berlin and Copenhagen. They seem utterly inept!"

"'May I have pleasure of introducing you to Mr. Hodges, Moriarty-san," said Mr. Takada obsequiously, eager to change the topic. "He import our material from Shanghai through *sake* manufacturer in Sapporo. We very pleased to work with him."

"'At this moment, I am still not satisfied that we can expand to the scale I need," Professor Moriarty said, ignoring me completely. "If your men with the missing digits don't show more urgency and intelligence in dealing with my men, I will reconsider. Why you use such people who will be noticed easily is something I cannot understand.

"'And talk less!" he snapped, this time at Mr. Takada. "The more you talk, the more you are in danger of exposure. You are expanding too fast—and carelessly. I do not believe in short-term profits at all. This is not just a matter of money. My goal is beyond—to control Europe and its economy.

"'Good day, gentlemen," he said abruptly, and turned and departed. We looked after him in silence.

"'So that was Professor Moriarty?" I remarked.

"'Yes. Very ambitious. He have big plans. Very good business-man. Very good methods. But very dangerous. Very dangerous. Maybe you never see him again."

'And indeed, I did not have a chance to do so.

'In the meantime, Mr. Kasama's prediction had started prov-ing to be accurate. One day at Mr. Takada's office in the Japa-nese Embassy, we had a couple of visitors. They were from the commercial section of the Portuguese Embassy and knew Mr. Takada well. D'Silva and Sequeira came straight to the point. They were already involved in small-time smuggling and were quite interested in the opium angle.

"'We do test for one year in Portugal, D'Silva-san. Murakami-san visit Lisbon with you to see how it work."

'It was agreed and Mr. Takada asked them to meet a certain contact of his at the Japanese Embassy in Lisbon. It was made clear that the network was in place and that diplomats from other

European countries were also interested in sharing the expected profits. We had De Groot from Holland, Herr Schmidt from Germany, Senor Cruz from Spain, Markevich from Russia—and even Cosgrove from the British Embassy, to my personal agony, a man from Cambridge, no less! Yes, Murakami helped me connect with the Japanese Yakuza network in all the European capitals. It was an extraordinary situation.

'In effect, Your Majesty, I am telling you that the Diplomatic Services of most European countries have been compromised and, far from being standards for probity and dignity, are involved in smuggling. This is extremely painful for all concerned.'

'What must be done?' the emperor asked, clearly shaken. 'If I understand you correctly, our Embassies have been responsible for legitimizing smuggling and laying the foundation of a vast network for opium trafficking and consumption in Europe. And they have induced several European diplomats to become part of their plans.'

'That is correct. And to answer your question, it seems clear, Your Majesty, that you will have to personally do something. I have with me the complete list of all diplomats from all countries who have been involved in a small or big way. I obviously have the list of Japanese diplomats as well, which no doubt will be most embarrassing for all of you, because they have operated under the watch of the Foreign Ministry and Japanese Secret Police. It has taken me a long time to gather these names; I regret to say that every second person in every Japanese Embassy in Europe is suspect, including some ambassadors—'

'Where is that list?' interrupted Sugiyama-san. 'Our ambassador at Moscow—'

Holmes shook his head. 'No, he is clean, but I would not like to speak for or against any diplomat here. That is not the point. It is for you,' he nodded at Sasaki-san, 'to quickly verify the case. You can take care of that quite easily, by calling them to Japan on some kind of apparently legitimate briefing mission and then arresting them. But the bigger fallout will be the exposure of the European diplomats, who can quite easily claim that their Japanese friends entrapped them. This can be very embarrassing.

'I believe, Your Majesty, that the only way for you to handle this is to preempt the matter—before you are confronted by other countries with evidence of the involvement of Japanese diplomats. I suggest you write a letter directly to the head of state of each country, carried by a personal representative. Give a compressed version of the facts and provide the names of their diplomats along with circumstantial or direct proof of their involvement. I possess such proof against each name.'

There was silence.

'There are 138 Japanese diplomats involved and about seventy-nine European diplomats.'

'Why did you not send us details along the way?' asked Oshima-san, sounding a little angry.

'For a simple reason that you will appreciate immediately. I had no guarantee that my correspondence would not be intercepted. The only things that I could write to you about were my financial needs and general information that was not really a secret—for example, the recent cases of the investigation of the murder of Admiral Santiago or the case of the abduction of the heir to the throne of Schleswig-Holstein. As events have proven only a few hours ago, my suspicions were perhaps well-founded; the Yakuza has penetrated your offices. And your own case of *fugu* fish poisoning was anything but accidental.'

Yoshida-san spoke. 'At what point did you decide that Operation Kobe55 had reached a logical conclusion? Why did you return?'

'I came back because Professor Moriarty had become suspicious. Mr. Takada had taken me to many cities to introduce me to his counterparts in the Embassies as a legitimate importer of Japanese *sake* who could additionally import opium. Then he returned to Japan. His successor is clean and not involved—yet. In the meanwhile, rumours spread that an American businessman had started expanding his business quite well in Europe. That would not have been a problem, except for the fact that

Professor Moriarty investigated my American background and was not satisfied with the results, or so I believe. He became suspicious. When my requests for appointments at the Japanese Embassy in Copenhagen and then in Berlin were turned down by the very same persons who had met me at least three times before, I understood that something had changed. Your attaché in Berlin, Mr. Uchiyama, met me in a park and confessed that he had been given instructions by the Yakuza—who in turn must have received instructions from Professor Moriarty—to keep an eye on me. I then went to London to find a means to convey my accumulated information to you and to consult Lestrade and Mycroft. I believe I was followed across the English Channel.

'Mycroft, as you are possibly aware, holds a sensitive position at the Home Office, where his sagacity is much valued. While I have always had the inclination to action, he prefers to address challenges of great import from his chair. He wields enormous influence and it would be no exaggeration to say that he occasionally *is* the government. He could not be bothered if you agreed with him on any matter or disagreed. He prefers spending time at the exclusive Diogenes Club, where speaking is strictly forbidden—such is the loathing of its strange members for social intercourse. But I digress.

'I had, of course, kept him generally informed of my whereabouts in Europe. He often told me to immediately cease what he called a juvenile adventure, most likely to end in an unfortunate way. He had already concluded that these were deeper waters than was apparent and had even deduced who the persons involved were. But he did not think it necessary to intervene, feeling that my tiresome ways were perhaps more suitable to the handling of the situation.

'He is the person who advised me to leave forthwith for Japan and seek an audience with you directly, Your Majesty. He further hypothesized that it was very possible for the Yakuza, given his knowledge of the psychology of successful criminal groups, to precipitate matters in a clouded political environment by taking extreme and very bold action. Specifically, he felt that the possibility of an assassination attempt on your person by insiders could not be ruled out, and he wanted me to warn you. I believe that the two Yakuza gentlemen on board the *North Star* were the appointed assassins, having been specially trained by Colonel Moran himself in the handling of air rifles that use revolver bullets, which is why I needed to reach Japan before the arrival of the ship into Yokohama. They can doubtless now be detained on arrival.'

While the group struggled to find expression, Holmes continued. 'Lestrade was, of course, absolutely delighted to see me. He too believed I had been killed at Reichenbach Falls. I explained the situation and he, after some initial incredulity, understood the gravity of the matter. He agreed that I should make good my escape to Japan soon and try to speak to you directly. We hit upon the idea of having Dr. Watson carry the information to Tokyo without his knowledge.'

'Holmes!' I exclaimed, outraged.

'It was all quite simple, Watson. We arranged for your ticket on the *North Star* and created the blind—it was quite easy to fake a letter from Japan supposedly stamped in Yokohama.'

'How did you have him carry the information?' asked Oshima-san. 'Would that not have been equally dangerous?'

'If a person does not know he has information, that information is safe with him.' Holmes' face was flushed with triumph. 'And this is what I did—I had the entire list of names and proof against each person codified into musical notation and transcribed. In short, I used a cipher that only the trained eye could have made sense of. The sheaves of "music" that emerged could not possibly have been recognized as a list of any kind. Lestrade arranged for one of his agents to enter Dr. Watson's house and place it with my violin, which was in his possession, and which he had very graciously not opened even once after my "death." And so Dr. Watson carried my violin with him throughout. Along the way, on the few occasions I opened the case and played my violin, I told him the sheaves were the compositions of a young composer in Prague. Here they are!'

Sherlock Holmes waved the sheaves of sheet music triumphantly in the air. This was his moment of glory, without a doubt.

'That paper, Holmes-san, contains the complete list of diplomats, Japanese and others, who have been part of this operation. And specific proof of their activities. Is that correct?' asked Emperor Meiji.

'That is correct, Your Majesty.'

'Was it wise to have travelled in such a manner with such sensitive information?' asked Miss Nohara.

'Naturally I had taken precautions. But I could not do it any other way. A letter would have taken too long and might have been lost or stolen.'

'What is the cipher?' asked Otawa-san.

'An ancient but effective system devised by the Italian composer Porta. In his system, the first half of the alphabet would be matched to a sequence of thirteen half notes going up the notes on a musical stave and the second half of the alphabet to a descending sequence of thirteen quarter notes. However, a musician would find any such score unusual and potentially unmusical. The system was altered later by another composer, Thomas Thicknesse, so that it made musical sense. Perhaps it sounds complicated. But that does not matter at this stage; the deciphering is easy and will not take long. I can do it myself within two hours.'

'Innovative and admirable, Holmes-san,' nodded the emperor.

Holmes bowed. 'This, Your Majesty, is your property now for you to act on in the manner you deem fit. I request that my suggestions be taken into consideration. I have been witness to many diplomatic challenges and have discovered the great value of being candid as a means of diffusing tension. Taking immediate steps is important. If you do not, it is likely that Professor Moriarty will communicate with foreign governments in a manner different from ours. Japan will be accused of misusing its diplomatic channels to encourage criminal activity aimed at undermining the sovereignty of independent nations. Unfortunately, the personal actions of diplomats cannot be distinguished from those of the nations they represent and then you will not be able to convincingly deny that this was part of an official strategy. Retribution will be swift and may include the arrest of Japanese diplomats, the suspension of treaties, and confiscation of Japanese assets. It may include war, if the objective of deliberately subverting European governments and cultures by distributing opium through diplomatic channels is accepted by various governments. It is not a price you can afford to pay, especially given your recent initiatives to modernize Japan.'

The emperor nodded, his face pale.

Holmes stood up, his expression grim and solemn.

'At the same time, it is also my painful duty, Your Majesty, to say that this group has been compromised. The Yakuza has infiltrated the core committee overseeing Operation Kobe55. I regret to say that you have a traitor in this very room.'

Closure

 Let the sea, the wind, the fire, time and us come together, my friend. There is such beauty in the melding of our essences. You have such fine sensibilities. I yearn to be like you. That is my dearest wish.

There have been times when, as a chronicler of the brilliant career of my good friend Sherlock Holmes, I have found myself struggling for the right words to describe an event, especially the electric atmosphere caused by the revelation of one or more astonishing and completely unexpected facts at a delicate point in an investigation. Shock results—as does humour, surprisingly—when the new information overturns one's knowledge or assumptions. What seems obvious and not even worth remembering may contain layers of information. In several cases in the past—especially those related to diplomacy—Sherlock Holmes thought it best not to bring to anyone's attention certain crucial facts that could exacerbate tensions and would serve no useful purpose. That was not the case here. The time to reveal an unpleasant truth had come.

Holmes' solemn and dramatic pronouncement had the desired effect. Everyone, including the emperor, shrank back in consternation. Miss Nohara, however, did not and I could see the hint of a smile on her face as she looked down at her hands.

'That is a very serious allegation, Holmes-san,' said Otawa-san, finally, his voice not quite steady. 'All those who conceived and executed Operation Kobe55 are in this very room, except for the three who have regrettably passed away. The emperor himself approved this list. What you have presented was precisely what the committee anticipated for the most part and we are completely aware of the consequences these people face. How is it possible that anyone in this group could prove to be a traitor?'

'Ah! An extremely good question. And yet the facts are so startlingly clear. My conclusion is based on certain points.

'First, I pondered for quite some time why I had been selected so easily for this role without everyone first meeting me. I could understand Mr. Sugiyama's earnest efforts to bring me to the notice of the Kobe55 committee and escorting me all the way from Switzerland in the hope that someone with my reputation and experience could help in some small way. But I could not understand why I should become so singularly critical to the execution of the strategy. It seemed extremely convenient and a little too swift. Why would you trust a man you had never met, going purely by reputation, especially if he was not Japanese and knew little about the country, its history, and its language? Nonetheless, it was not the first time this has happened. I recall at least two assignments in which I was given full authority to operate on behalf of the governments of Brazil and Liechtenstein, based purely on internal government recommendations and without anyone from either government actually meeting me.[14]

'Let us then look at the extreme ease with which I was granted access to various functionaries. True, there was a secret government order from you, Mr. Yoshida, giving me access to Japanese Embassies anywhere, but I was still surprised that my cover as an American businessman was never challenged even once. Further, the meeting with Professor Moriarty was just a little too easily arranged. Why would the commercial attaché be so ready to introduce me to him? Was it perhaps to help the professor check on who I really was? Remember that I was just *one* of the businesses acting as willing conduits for opium imports masked as something else.

---

[14] One was the case of the lost treaty between Brazil and Ecuador that would have plunged South America into its gravest crisis if not found. The second was the case of the treaty between Liechtenstein and Spain that would have resulted in questions being raised about the neutrality of the former state in the tensions prevailing at that time in the Mediterranean. In both cases, Sherlock Holmes had demanded and received *carte blanche* to operate on behalf of the states, and both matters were closed to everyone's satisfaction, with the public entirely oblivious of the matter.

'At Lisbon, at Berlin, at Prague—the gates opened as though by magic. Information was shared very easily—*too* easily. Money was made available for my expenses without question. It struck me that perhaps the network was allowing me to investigate it, to help it to identify its own weak links, rather than the other way around. The shipments that I was importing were notional—I was never a major player and I could hardly have been expected to make a difference to their business. No, I had been selected because I would not stand out in Europe and because of my knowledge of Professor Moriarty's network. I was a mere pawn, though an important one. Professor Moriarty was a thorough professional—he wanted to be sure that the network was perfect and what better strategy than to have it tested by his greatest adversary, me?

'And though the meeting with Professor Moriarty at the Louvre was brief and he gave no sign of recognizing me, I reflected that the conversation he had had with the commercial attaché, Mr. Takada, and the Yakuza representative, Mr. Murakami, did not warrant his exposure in public. He reprimanded Takada for delayed shipments and certain operational errors that he had observed. It is not the job of a general to check whether the rifles of his soldiers are in working condition. He could easily have conveyed the same message in a more discreet way. No, his primary objective was to personally satisfy himself that Hodges was Holmes. He was, obviously, too clever to allow recognition to flash on his face. The meeting was clearly initiated by *him* and not by us. He had been tipped off.

'Someone in this room—yes, *this* room—was working with the Yakuza and keeping Professor Moriarty informed. Let us look at the possibilities.'

There was a breathless silence in the room.

'I was never comfortable with Miss Nohara, since I have always had a particular view on the ability of women to keep secrets. I suspected that she was a possibility because she had access to Mr. Oshima's correspondence. Further, she had been the person to give us the initial information about the arrangements of the *saiko-komon* of the Sumiyoshi-kai and Inagawa-kai with the Shanghai Triad and of the commencement of the Europe project. It seemed probable that she was the weak link. But I had nothing definitive.'

Miss Nohara did not respond, continuing to look down demurely.

'Then I considered Mr. Yoshida—how could this deterioration of the Diplomatic Services have happened without the knowledge of its head? Was it possible that he had deliberately looked the other way?'

Yoshida-san's face was red with embarrassment and shame. He too did not respond.

'However, I had no proof. Further, I also discovered that except for a couple of them, most ambassadors were not involved. He had spoken to me once with great feeling about the damage that could be done to Japan's image if the suspicions were brought to light. This seemed to rule out Mr. Yoshida, though more evidence was needed to establish his lack of involvement.'

Sherlock Holmes turned to Oshima-san and smiled grimly. The tension in the room was acute.

'Mr. Oshima. What a delicate position to be in! To be aware of your nation's greatest secrets and often being unable to act. To watch events, to conjecture, and to consider how events a world away might impact your nation. I do not envy you.'

The emperor gasped. 'Oshima-san! Impossible!'

Oshima-san's face was ashen. 'You have made a mistake. I must protest! I am a loyal servant of the emperor!' he said in a hoarse voice.

'Of course you are, Mr. Oshima,' responded Holmes in a soothing voice. 'I never accused you of anything. I merely said that your position was delicate. In my considered opinion, you are one of Japan's greatest patriots.'

Holmes sat down. 'One of you, Mr. Otawa, Mr. Sugiyama, and Mr. Sasaki—one of you is in the pay of the Yakuza. And I know who it is. I can review the case for and against each of you, but I do not see the point. Let us not waste time. We have none. A confession may be best.'

Sugiyama-san shot out of his chair and, before any of us could act, swiftly positioned himself behind Miss Nohara. He took out a revolver, and pressed it to her head, while pulling her hair back violently.

'Hand over the papers to Masako, or I shall kill her without hesitation!' he barked at Holmes, completely transformed from the mild-mannered, urbane diplomat he had been seconds ago.

'What is the meaning of this outrage? How dare you enter this room with a gun?' shouted the emperor.

His guards leapt forward, standing in front of him with their swords out. The others in the room sank back in their chairs, shocked. Holmes was quite unperturbed, as was Miss Nohara. I was considerably dismayed by the unexpected turn of events.

'I will shoot her if anyone moves! Believe me!' shouted Sugiyama-san, holding Miss Nohara's neck firmly.

Holmes handed over the sheaf of sheet music to Miss Nohara.

'Stand up!' cried Sugiyama-san.

Dragging Miss Nohara roughly, Sugiyama-san took her to the fireplace.

'Throw them in! Now!'

Miss Nohara threw the sheaf of papers into the fire. They crackled and sputtered and were burned to ashes in less than a minute. With them went the complete list of diplomats and the proofs of their complicity. We watched in silence and horror as the product of years of painstaking intelligence was destroyed.

'Your work is gone, Holmes-san. I am sorry.'

'You will not be able to escape, Sugiyama-san,' said Oshima-san, quietly. 'It is best you surrender. There is no escape. None.'

'That we shall see. We are now everywhere, including this very palace!'

'I knew it was you, Mr. Sugiyama,' said Sherlock Holmes in an even voice. 'I was suspicious of you when we met for the first time, then as we travelled by train to Vladivostok, though I knew nothing at that point. It was all too easy and perfect.'

Sugiyama-san laughed. 'It really does not matter, Holmes-san. Our plans are in place. You will not be able to interfere.

The Yakuza will soon take over Japan. The world will bow in acknowledgment of our superiority and be guided by our glorious nation. We are opposed to the Restoration! The purity of the Japanese race must be preserved at all costs, and foreigners with their corrupting ideas cannot be allowed to roam about unchecked! As we speak, my colleagues are entering the Imperial Palace and will be here in precisely two minutes.'

'This from a distinguished ambassador to Switzerland,' remarked Holmes, amused. 'I would have expected you to have developed a liberal perspective on many matters.'

'My long sojourns in Europe taught me one thing, Holmes-san—Japan is superior! In all ways. Europe is decadent and their people impressionable and easy to control. But their pretentions are corrupting. The Restoration will corrode the glory of Japan and that cannot be permitted to happen. Do you think Japanese diplomats acting in concert with the Yakuza are driven solely by money? No! Many strongly oppose the Restoration and are prepared to do whatever is necessary to subvert it and restore Japan to its pure state. I, like many other diplomats, belong to an ancient Samurai family and cannot tolerate the slow erosion of Japan's position of preeminence!'

'Tell me, was it you who informed Professor Moriarty about me?'

'Of course. He knew about you having escaped death by the time we reached Moscow.'

'And the assassination of the guard on the Trans-Siberian?'

'It was I, of course.'

'The murder of the agent at Vladivostok?'

'The work of my agent.'

'The accident at Gare du Nord, Paris?'

'Of course!'

'The runaway carriage in Madrid? The boat incident at Rotterdam?'

'Really, Holmes-san! You already know the answers. Why do you ask such questions?'

'What can you tell me about the meeting with Professor Moriarty at the Louvre?'

'Precisely as you guessed. The professor wanted to verify your identity with his own eyes. You tried your best with a good disguise, but he knew immediately.'

'But why all this?'

'To lure you into our trap and to keep you close. Professor Moriarty was clear that the only man who could come in the way of his plans for the domination of Europe was you. It was better for us to have you under constant observation, feed you incorrect information, and get an idea from you about how the Japanese government was responding. We were successful to a very large extent.'

'The demise of the Japanese ambassador to France, Mr. Takenaka?'

'A simple matter of the introduction of shellfish poison in his soup, Mr. Holmes. A painful attack of respiratory paralysis preceded his regrettable death. He was altogether a nuisance and we did not appreciate his sending back Takada-san to Tokyo.'

'The accidental death of Mr. Kasama in Shanghai?'

'You correctly deduced the hand of Miss Bryant, our singularly efficient Shanghai operative. And, of course, we followed you from the moment you embarked on the *North Star*—you were attacked in Angkor Wat. Of course, I am aware that our agents mistook some other gentleman for you till Bombay and you therefore missed death in Alexandria. You are a very lucky man, Mr. Holmes. But not anymore. And now, enough talk. My friends from the Yakuza should be here any moment.'

'They will not be coming, Sugiyama-san,' Miss Nohara spoke for the first time. She was smiling.

'You are not the only person with deep contacts in the Yakuza. You have been under observation for a very long time now and your views against the emperor and his vision of the Restoration are well known in the leadership ranks of the Yakuza. I may not belong to the Yakuza, but Honda-san and I did whatever was necessary to convince those who you thought were your friends that a militant Yakuza operation in the Imperial Palace of the

Emperor, with the possible objective of capturing or assassinating him, would turn public opinion very strongly against them.

This afternoon, when you were informed of this emergency meeting, you visited them and asked them to take positions, since you guessed Holmes-san would inform the emperor and you needed to seize the opportunity, rather than wait for the two Yakuza assassins to arrive on the *North Star*. They assured you they would and promptly informed Honda-san. None are in position. You have made a very bad miscalculation. Please surrender. There are three revolvers pointed at you now. And, oh yes, the bullets in *your* revolver are harmless. We replaced them in the afternoon while you were at lunch.'

Sugiyama-san's face lost colour and his hand faltered. 'A lie!' he snarled. He pointed his revolver at Miss Nohara and fired. Nothing happened. He fired again and again.

The revolver fell from his trembling hand and clattered on the floor.

Within seconds, Sherlock Holmes, Sasaki-san, and I had overpowered Sugiyama-san, held him down, and tied him up.

'And Mr. Sugiyama, the papers that you burnt were useless. They were a copy of a genuine musical score *Lieder Ohne Worte, Songs without Words*, by one of my favourite composers, Mendelssohn. The original papers with the musical scores had already reached the emperor's office this morning through the good offices of Miss Nohara. They are being decrypted as we speak. You don't think I would be so foolish as to have only one copy? I made two more copies—one for my personal records and the other to be kept with my brother Mycroft, with specific instructions on what to do if he did not hear from me within a specified time.'

The emperor's bodyguards quickly escorted Sugiyama-san out of the room, while Oshima-san and the others watched, paralyzed with shock.

◇◇◇

In the days that followed, Sherlock Holmes and I were treated with great honour and accorded the most gracious hospitality by the emperor. One lavish banquet was followed by another and a fascinating *kabuki* performance, *Yoshitsune Senbon Zakura* (Yoshitsune and the Thousand Cherry Trees) was succeeded by another splendid performance on the huge *kodo* drums.

Emperor Meiji showed us his bonsai collection and also took us inside rooms that contained the greatest treasures of ancient Japan, not accessible to the general public. He was clearly a connoisseur of the arts; paintings, calligraphy, sculpture, music—he was interested in everything and had an opinion on it all.

He showed us his private collection of the paintings of the great artist Hokusai, noted for the use of Prussian Blue. In another room were fascinating examples of the *ukiyo-e* art from the Edo era.

The emperor regretted his lack of knowledge of the English language, but knew a great deal of English history. He asked us many questions about the attitudes, work habits, food habits, and languages of Europe. He spoke of transforming Japan and making it a world economic power one day. 'Sometimes too much history is not so good, Holmes-san,' he mused. 'When we are too proud of our past, we do not think of our future.' His sagacity shone through in those simple words.

At one banquet, the emperor invited Japan's finest writers, poets, and artists to meet us. He took me aside at one point.

'Watson-san, I have request for you.'

'Certainly, Your Majesty.'

'I know you are famous writer. You will write about this matter one day, *ne?*'

'With your permission, Your Majesty.'

'We have many great writers in my country. Please help them become known outside Japan.'

'Certainly, Your Majesty. Do you have any suggestion?'

The emperor beckoned and a tall distinguished gentleman came forward. He had the most gentle but confident eyes and a pleasant warm manner.

'This is our writer Akira Yamashita, very famous, very wonderful. We call him Living Treasure of Japan.'

I shook hands with the writer, who smiled but said nothing. And yet, I had the feeling that he had much to say. There was instant mutual liking.

'Please read some of his stories. And please include one of his stories when you write about this adventure. I will be grateful.'

'The privilege is mine, Your Majesty.'

The emperor spoke to Yamashita-san in Japanese and then excused himself. The two of us then stepped away from the banquet and exchanged thoughts about our literary interests. Ideas transcended the barriers of language.

Akira Yamashita showed me his magnificent stories, a few of which we translated over the course of a couple of days together. Here was a man with a complex mind, seeking beauty and shunning the conventional in unusual ways. His work was remarkable and stunning, and my lack of knowledge of Japanese nuances did not make the impact any less. His writing spanned music and the arts and addressed every weakness of the human psyche in a manner I had not witnessed before. I am pleased to say that Holmes entirely agreed with me and applauded the unorthodox idea of including a story in the chronicles.

After much deliberation, I selected his powerful story "The Ghosts of Music"[15] to be included in this chronicle. It will not detract from enjoying this book; rather, its beauty will give my story an additional hue of charm.

The emperor had earlier composed a much-admired *Waka* poem on friendship, which he wrote out in his own hand and presented to Sherlock Holmes on the occasion of our last meeting. The palace-authorized official translation (not a very good one) runs thus:

> *To be friends*
> *To show each another*
> *Your faults*
> *Is the true spirit*
> *Of friendship*

---

[15] See page 267.

'What next, Holmes, or should I say Holmes-san?' I asked, resting at our lodgings a few days later, waiting for confirmation of our return journey on the *North Star*, which had docked in Yokohama. The two arriving Yakuza members had been immediately arrested to their surprise and discomfiture.

Holmes spent several minutes playing an extremely mournful Indian score on his violin. The wailing assailed my eardrums and I saw visions of Mr. Binayak Sen, the chortling Indian guru in Calcutta.

'The detention of Mr. Sugiyama does not necessarily solve the issue. After his debriefing, I am certain he will be asked to commit suicide as an honourable means of closure. I fully expect that the emperor will follow my advice and send special envoys to seek out audiences with the heads of state of all European nations, with a personal letter from him expressing his deep mortification that elements in his kingdom actively conspired in illegal activities carried out in their territories. He will present the names of their officials as well, with the relevant proof needed to effect arrests.

'But, as usual, we shall have to live with the spectre of Professor Moriarty's presence in Europe. Yes, the Shanghai Triad's European operations will be rooted out and many criminals will be arrested. I am quite sure that there will be no evidence linking Professor Moriarty to any of this. He is ahead of us in these matters, Watson, and we should respect him for that. He will view it as just another temporary inconvenience that I have created for him and will already be working out his next stratagem with renewed vigour.'

The large and cheerful Jiro Hamada entered with an excellent selection of *sashimi* and hot *sake*. He had recovered from the attempted poisoning and was his usual hearty self. He left the room and returned in a few minutes with a *koto*.

'I present you with this, Holmes-san. You take back to England as memory of Japan and of me, your *tomodachi*—your friend.'

Sherlock Holmes was never a man to display emotion, but he held Hamada's hand warmly. He accepted the *koto* with gratitude, holding the instrument respectfully and with care. He made an attempt to play it and produced a tune tolerably well. Then he bade good-bye to Hamada-san and shut the door.

'Watson, before I forget…though news of these events will certainly trickle back in due course, let us remember that I am still considered missing by many in England. I wish to use that impression to my advantage for several months more. When the time comes and I reveal myself, please exert your histrionic abilities and pretend to be extremely shocked.'

'By all means, Holmes.'

'And now, Watson, my dear fellow, please do me a favour and write out an urgent wire to be dispatched in the morning.'

'Yes, Holmes, what shall I say?'

'Say this: Safe in Japan with Sherlock Holmes. Will return together on the next available voyage of the North Star.

'Address it to Mrs. Mary Watson. You know where the telegram is to be delivered.'

Home

識 The Sensei in our village school said I was a fool because my
head was filled with useless facts. I know yours is filled
with the desire to know more. You wish to live
forever and be an eternal student. How wonderful!
I pray that your wish is granted.

Clara Bryant was detained in Shanghai. She was tried for multiple murders, found guilty, and sentenced to death. She was subsequently executed.

Hiroshi Sugiyama, the suave ambassador of Japan to Switzerland, identified as part of the nexus between the Diplomatic Services and the Yakuza, was persuaded to commit suicide by jumping off a bridge near Sagami Bay near the Buddha of Kamakura. This was found to be a better solution than subjecting him to a trial, which would have caused other sensitive matters to come to light.

Shamsher Singh, the fascinating aide to the maharajah of Patiala, kept up a lively correspondence with us. He was in touch with Holmes when the scandal pertaining to the proposed marriage of the maharajah with the daughter of his Irish horsemaster broke out.

Sherlock Holmes was accorded the highest civilian award of Japan, the Red Ribbon, and I too was given an award, the Green Ribbon, which I believe I did not deserve at all. We were also made honorary citizens of Japan.

Yoshida-san resigned, accepting moral responsibility for having allowed the rot in the Diplomatic Services to reach such depths.

Sasaki-san became a votary for the increased use of science in intelligence-gathering. He convened a meeting of the Intelligence chiefs of several countries to exchange ideas and planted the seed for the establishment of an International Police Bureau. On Holmes' suggestion, he sent an invitation to the Indian scientist Jagdish Chandra Bose to visit Tokyo; we have no idea whether he accepted.

Oshima-san retired three months after we left Japan. He was replaced by Masako Nohara. No one could find reason to object to the appointment of a woman of such sterling merit to the position of the director of Intelligence Research. I understand that she commissioned a portrait of Sherlock Holmes and had it hung in a prominent spot in the office to serve as a permanent reminder of the man.

Kasama-san and Takenaka-san were posthumously honoured for their service to Japan.

In the expected purge, all 138 Japanese diplomats who had become pawns of the Yakuza were withdrawn from Diplomatic Services and arrested for various crimes, including sedition. While some committed suicide through the complex ritual of disembowelment called *seppuku*, others were sentenced to life in prison and a very small number were executed (Takada-san, for example).

The Yakuza withdrew its personnel from Europe and terminated the arrangement with the Shanghai Green Gang Triad. I would imagine that the individuals involved were forced to undergo yet another *ubitsume* ceremony—or two.

Sherlock Holmes wrote a monograph called *The Classical Music of India* and thereafter another, *The Japanese Koto—pentatonic musical possibilities for the Western string ensemble*, both of which received critical acclaim from scholars across the world. He is applying finishing touches to another monograph, *The Flora of the Malay Peninsula*, and is spending time at the Reading Room of the British Museum researching some aspects of the rule of the Khmer King Jayavarman VII, who was the force behind Angkor Wat, the grand symbol of Cambodia. He has hinted at many more monographs to come, but I have chosen to ignore his threat.

Holmes has considered discontinuing the use of cocaine after the heartfelt pleas of Oshima-san. Holmes and the Indian scientist, Jagdish Chandra Bose, have maintained a vigorous personal correspondence. He has, to my consternation, also become a passionate votary of a vegetarian diet and spoken—persuasively, I understand—at the Royal Society.

Emperor Meiji took the advice of Sherlock Holmes and sent personal emissaries to all the heads of state in Europe where Japanese diplomats had operated in an offensive manner equivalent to subversion. He took full moral responsibility for the actions of his representatives, and explained in detail the various steps he had taken to prevent the recurrence of such incidents as well as to reverse the damages that prior actions might have caused. As Holmes had guessed, after the initial outrage, the gesture was warmly appreciated. Various European governments embarked on a purge of their own Diplomatic Services, guided by the proof supplied by the Japanese government; all seventy-nine identified diplomats were dismissed from service and arrested. Some were released because the proof was not conclusive. Some were hanged, others guillotined, and the rest sentenced to various terms in prison. Two of these diplomats were in Her Majesty's Service, a matter that caused great embarrassment to us. In sum, a cathartic event played out in the diplomatic world, leading to stricter considerations in the selection of career diplomats and the creation of a stern and uncompromising code of diplomatic conduct, unofficially referred to as the Holmes Convention. The reader may possibly be familiar with this.

Akira Fujimoto, the former Yakuza member who visited Bodh Gaya, returned to the Kinkaku-ji temple in Kyoto to resume a life of spiritual enquiry. He took up the role of the late Hayashi-san and served as an able administrator at the temple.

Professor Moriarty vowed to continue his campaign against the majesty of the law. You may perhaps read about his subsequent battle of wits with Sherlock Holmes in the Case of the New York Counterfeiters, which I am presently documenting; much depends on the eccentricities of modern publishers, driven by lucre rather than good taste and outstanding writing such as this, but time will tell.

Our voyage back to Liverpool on the *North Star* was uneventful. We did not feel the need to disembark at Shanghai, Singapore, Bombay, Aden, Alexandria, or Marseilles. Holmes busied himself with drafting the many monographs I have referred to earlier, while I put together my notes on our experiences. Of course, he also spent time alternately playing the violin or the *koto* and became reasonably adept at the latter. I could not easily understand the mournful snatches of Indian music he would lapse into. The Japanese music seemed more meditative and pleasing when he played the *koto* correctly.

Captain Samuel Groves retired soon after our voyage. He informed the owners of the *North Star* that he had decided to become a beekeeper in Sussex South Downs, a prospect that Sherlock Holmes found intriguing and fascinating. Holmes himself became a beekeeper after his reluctant retirement several years later; they were to become neighbours and animatedly discussed the many fascinating traits of queen bees.[16] Privately, Captain Groves told us that he had become a nervous wreck after that harrowing voyage, since he was unused to being a witness to heinous crimes and was attracted to a lifestyle that was entirely more predictable and soothing, where contact with fellow men would be significantly reduced.

My wife was pleased to see me again, but I noticed that she was even more pleased to see Sherlock Holmes, a matter that rather perplexed me.

---

[16] Readers are reminded of Holmes' seminal monograph on the matter, *On the care of the Queen Bee and observations on its reaction to Brahms' Violin Sonata No. 1 in G major, Opus 78*, which was received with great acclaim at the Royal Society.

Epilogue

O Stranger
Let the first red rays of the rising sun caress your eyelids
while you meditate
Let the Buddha of Kamakura speak to you in silence

The early hours of the morning at Sagami Bay are like those on any other day: the Pacific lapping at the beach, the sound of crashing waves, the hiss of the mist, the salty tang in the air. From beneath the sea, the fish look up as the first rays of light diffuse into the restless water. The terns and gulls squawk unpleasantly but with happiness. In the death of others is the guarantee of their own life.

Many men have left the shores of Yokohama and returned as tormented ghosts held in an embrace by the spray of the surging waves. Time continues to paint everything gently. Love evaporates and kisses the restless gull; ambition disintegrates into the sand and slides down, down, several feet below. No man shall be spared death. The Amitabha Buddha of Kamakura will watch over acts of passion and hate, of evil and tenderness.

The fishing boats will take an hour to return from their overnight journeys. Hideo, the vagrant philosopher-poet, sits quietly on his haunches on the beach, letting the water touch him from time to time. Yes, there is a hint of red in the clouds and slowly, with a vicious intent, the red spreads over the bay. Hideo now sees a sea of blood in which even the ghosts have been drenched.

He walks along the beach wondering what the sea may have decided to reject today. It is the usual—dead fish, a couple of writhing eels approaching the inevitable, many shells and pieces of wood from ships that rest in the sea several fathoms below.

In the swampy area far from the harbour, he sees a larger shadow. Ah, perhaps a whale or a shark. He walks through the muck and the weeds, his feet making a sucking noise as he moves one leg and then the other. A few nesting birds squawk in alarm and anger and fly away, the sound of their flapping mixing with the dull thunder from below the sea.

A shark? An octopus? No. The light is not strong enough. He ventures closer and looks carefully.

A body hugs the swamp, face down. A man in a Western suit. Who is he? Why did he depart this way? Was he asked to? Who shall say?

Hideo looks back at Sagami Bay. The red is even more profound, but again, a sliver of sunlight edges up and meets a passing cloud.

The Buddha of Kamakura continues to meditate, his gentle smile frozen as it has been for so many years.

Two gulls fly upwards in joy, silently.

The Ghosts of Music

by Akira Yamashita

That which is music is divine. That which is not is merely transient, tinsel.

I say nothing new, yes. Through the decades of my career as a classical *koto* player in Kyoto, I had vaguely recognized the vibrations my music had provoked within spirits in other worlds. Of course, the potent realization came to me slowly while I explored the steel strings, touching and moving with changing speed and pressure over many years. Till the age of fifty, this (the issue of music extending its tendrils into a secret world) was known perfunctorily and explained in words to awed audiences to help create a halo around me and—I say this without shame, as I had to make a living, after all—to make money. The real truth needed maturity and solitude and there was no substitute for the passage of time.

And so it was that one night, as I sat in darkness in my hut on a small cliff overlooking Osaka Bay, exploring new sounds on my *koto* on the balcony, I chanced upon a note that I had not heard in all the years of relentless practice. That of course is nothing new, for music is an onion, and unpeeling it never ends. Sound is a continuum and the intensity, juxtaposition, and context makes a note different each time it is invoked. Alas, the weak and music mad live only in these haunted spaces, restlessly seeking more and more gratification and the rest of their lives erode, in the company of impatient men and women, with more pressing material and chimerical needs; a writer I know once said .. "There was music elsewhere. In the soft whispers of the leaves deep inside jungles. Lovely notes and sounds that only we heard. In the black airless spaces between planets where lost souls roamed restlessly crying out for their partners." I felt that way too and became more and more interested in it as, curiously, I felt my virtuosity decline while my intellect was stimulated further and further. But I digress.

This sound was different. I had applied the right pressure at the right place and a sound came out that seemed, in its glorious vibration, a summary of the Universe.

As it floated away into the night air, and I tried to enjoy my ecstatic immobilization, I became conscious of a presence. Against the night sky, I saw a nebulous white silhouette. My fanciful mind imagined that it was the ghost of a woman. And indeed it became so—a woman of astonishing beauty, her hair waving gently and her feminine form undulating and shimmering. Her eyes seemed moist. I had an overwhelming inexplicable feeling—the image was the sound—the sound was the image. She looked at me with the deepest sorrow. I imagined that she said *Why did you release me? How this hurts—I now must float forever, searching for love, for him whom I lost, from him whom I escaped, caught in the whorls of a hidden note. And now, now you have released me. Why, oh why? Why?* Her tears spread like pearl necklaces across the night sky.

I was overwhelmed by the deepest guilt and my own tears burst out. But my fingers were stuck to the same point on the string and I kept repeating the note like a man possessed, bent on drowning in quicksand. I could not stop—she wept and she wept and the sky seemed to break up into a million pieces.

The night passed, though time had stood still. The morning sun touched Osaka and the spell was broken. But I was too devastated to function, and for the first time ever, I canceled my classes. My students inquired if I was unwell and needed help.

The next evening, I tried again. But even though I had marked the spot with a piece of chalk, I failed to find the note. I tried everything but the note was elusive and declined to reveal itself.

But, as though by instinct, but probably more by accident, I touched a completely different string at a different spot. And this time, the note was low and threatening, echoing ominously in a room that had been designed specifically to ensure no echoes.

I felt the rush of evil spirits about me, roughly caressing my hands and arms in a gesture of thanks, applying cruel pressure on my fingers to ensure that I would keep playing, releasing more and more of their friends. I tried to close my eyes, but to no avail. Bright evil danced in front of my eyes, as each sound morphed into a key to release evil trapped in the ether about my *koto* string. Ah, the feeling of reeling horror, of utterly hopeless tragedy and cruel depravity, of decay and ruin, of gruesome putrefication…. Much, much beyond what men could even imagine….an eternal reality far beyond our shallow temporal one. My body shook but my fingers stayed firm, as a thunderstorm broke out spontaneously and rain poured down outside. On the clouds above, the released spirits of evil painted their plans, while the puzzled citizens of Osaka merely looked up and unfolded their umbrellas, shutting out the final warning.

I awoke the next morning, and stared at my *koto*. That which had nourished my body for so many years now threatened to savage my soul, with messages of love and evil that could never be reconciled. Now, when I tried to find the night's note, I again failed to find it and was grateful for it. I sat back, trembling. I knew not what I had accidentally unleashed. I called my students and cancelled my classes again. They were astonished. I slept the whole day; it was a restless and tormented sleep.

Now my eyesight and sense of touch had become acute. I actually felt that the string had developed kinks and was no longer the smooth metallic continuous piece I had known. I understood now that other emotions were seeking to come alive again and were craving my attention. But I had aged twenty years in a couple of nights and feared to touch my instrument.

My human trappings were too weak to comprehend and decipher the complex notions finding release one by one from the world of sound into the world of you and me.

The *koto* moved and shifted in my living room, threatening me physically. I, Shohei Yamada, once hailed as the greatest *koto* player of all time—I, I was powerless to act against my own music. For a while, I tried to satisfy the *koto* and released vapors of emotions bound by sounds I had never heard. Whether the most caressing tenderness or the roughest projection of power, an unfathomable meditative ocean or an acute nervousness—I experienced them all. But soon my physical limitations came to my defense and my complete lack of strength forced me to stop. The *koto* moved and shook, and the strings hummed together in anger. My arms were cut cruelly by the strings as they lacerated me, forcing me to play, but I could do nothing. I prayed for release.

And one night, while I was asleep and while I was awake, I suddenly found strength and grasped the *koto* and lifted it up. I went to the open window and hurled it out into the air.

As it fell, the strings came apart, and then came together, distinct from the body of the instrument, which fell on the seashore and shattered into a million pieces.

The strings formed a noose and rose slowly into the air and toward me. I retreated into my apartment, shaking with fear, closing the balcony's windows behind me, wanting to shut out what I simply did not want anymore. The metallic noose entered as well, passing through the windows as though they did not exist.

My time has come. I write this farewell note as the noose fastens itself to a hook on the ceiling, knowing the inevitability of my forthcoming action. It has waited for the past half hour, patiently, for what is time to it?

In the room, sitting on the sofa to witness the deed, are the ghosts of music that I helped release.

To receive a free catalog of Poisoned Pen Press titles, please provide your name and address through one of the following ways:

Phone: 1-800-421-3976
Facsimile: 1-480-949-1707
Email: info@poisonedpenpress.com
Website: www.poisonedpenpress.com

Poisoned Pen Press
6962 E. First Ave. Ste 103
Scottsdale, AZ 85251